Ben Arogundade

GW00587132

The Sexual Language Of Strangers

WHITE LABELS BOOKS

LONDON TOWN

Published in 2016 by White Labels Books
www.whitelabelsbooks.com
Copyright ©Ben Arogundade, 2016

ISBN 978-0-9569394-6-3

Email: enquiries@whitelabelsbooks.com
Twitter: @WhiteLabelsBook
@BArogundade

Designed by Ben Arogundade
Typeset in Times New Roman

Printed by CreateSpace
Available from Amazon.com, Createspeace.com and other retail outlets.

Thanks to:
Ade Arogundade, Anna Murphy, Jeanette Baartman, Hugh Barnes,
Karen Bishko, Liberty Blackburn, Deborah Brand, Thomas Carty,
Anthony Ebelle-Ebanda, Fish, Jim Fuerst, Claudia Fumo, Eugenie
Furniss, Zak and Madeleine Gaterud, Sarah Hirigoyen, Emilie
(Babyeyes) Irvin, Sarah Keen, Martin Kelly, Nicole Nodland,
Adrian Palengat, Nicole Portieri, Peter Robinson, Curtis St
Clements.

ALSO BY BEN AROGUNDADE
Obama: 101 Best Covers - A Commemorative Collection

Black Beauty:
The Story Of Black Hair & Beauty Through The Ages

Sex, Drugs & Civil Rights:
The Story Of Donyale Luna, Fashion's First Black Supermodel

Faster Than Jesse Owens:
The Story Of Sprinter Eulace Peacock & The Battle For The 1936
Olympics

1

Time is precious, but also worthless, thought Dennison Carr as he glanced at his watch. He gazed at it for longer than necessary, as if he'd momentarily forgotten how to read its face. He was alone again, this time in a basement bar in Soho, London. He'd selected the venue randomly, although his purpose that night was anything but that. As he sat watching and waiting under the low light, the profile of his black hat formed an eerie silhouette that protruded menacingly, like the beak of an unknown creature.

He shifted slightly in his seat, and as he did so the fabric of his suit between his inner arm and his torso rubbed together with a certain secret friction, yielding a tiny noise — a *swaasssh-swaassh*, like the sound of a feint cabasa. It was a moment of little consequence, and yet Dennison looked down at his garment as he heard it, as if to acknowledge its place in the world.

The bar was crafted around a series of curved banquette-style booths set into alcoves around the perimeter, all facing into the centre of the space, where an oval-shaped free-standing bar was located. The crowd consisted of a boisterous, eclectic consortium of locals — media executives, market traders and sex workers from the area around Brewer Street.

The briefcase was on the floor by his feet. It possessed a distinctive design, with gold-coloured locks and a floral pattern etched into leather veneers on both its sides. Inside was a mini-video recorder. Not the digital kind, but the old-fashioned model that used micro-cassettes. The money was in the inside pocket of the jacket of his bespoke suit. Four thousand in cash, in crisp fifty pound notes, and divided into two envelopes of one thousand pounds and three thousand pounds respectively.

Dennison had selected his man. He was in his early thirties, with cropped black hair, narrow brown eyes and a mole on his left cheek. His clothes were baggy and shapeless — a T-shirt, black flight-jacket, cargo pants and trainers. Dennison studied him again as he prowled the space. He watched as he approached a woman, made a clumsy contact, then apologised as she arched away from him and moved on. As she departed the man looked around to see if anyone else had witnessed his rejection. He quickly shook off his embarrassment and scanned for another. The expression in his eyes was like that of a man looking for a lost suitcase on an airport carousel. Dennison was amused by his failures, by the embarrassment he'd tried to hide — but then as he looked more closely at the man he saw a certain melancholy invade his face. He knew then that he would be perfect for the proposition.

In that moment, the memory of a secret misery from Dennison's own past gusted into his consciousness. He quickly took control before the recollection could alter his mood, and the disruption lasted but a few seconds.

He permitted himself a moment of distraction as the song *Think*, by Lynn Collins (1964), seeped into the loudspeakers positioned overhead. Involuntarily almost, his head angled upwards in a sideways motion to meet the sound, as if hoisted by an invisible thread. Despite feeling the energy of the song, he resisted the temptation to move his body to its infectious beat.

He sat cross-legged, back straight, hands resting gently on his knees. He waited with the patience of an animal stalking its prey. His eyes diverted from the man momentarily and settled on another potential candidate. This one seemed better at the hunting, but Dennison's instinct reassured him that his original choice was correct. Underneath the rim of his hat, Dennison's eyes tracked the man as he worked his way across the bar. As he did so the man turned suddenly, as if he'd felt Dennison's gaze upon him, and he looked straight into the shadowy booth in which he sat. He could just make him out, staring motionlessly, his glistening eyes piercing forth from the low light. The man felt a slight chill as their eyes met, and perhaps he sensed the danger that was to come.

As the man continued to stare, the top of Dennison's hat suddenly began to extend and grow upwards in a circular column, as if it was made of liquefied plastic. As it neared the ceiling it suddenly divided into sections, like a stack of chequers, which then transformed into a cluster of black hats which whizzed in satellite around his head, like miniature orbiting spaceships. After hovering for a few moments they then flew off rapidly in every direction. The man blinked, looked again at Dennison but everything was back to normal.

Dennison scrutinised his mannerisms — particularly the way, when he was nervous, that he rubbed the top of his head in a circular motion, then checked his palm for sweat. He liked that particular detail. He liked it in the same way that he liked the gap between

Lauren Hutton's front teeth, his favourite sex symbol of the 1970s.

As he reflected upon this, Dennison felt privileged to be alive in this era of the Earth's evolution. He had witnessed many amazing things — events that would be recorded in the future annals of history. But he questioned the usefulness of all the knowledge he had acquired in his life, because one day he would be dead. The secret terror of his own mortality was something he had never shared with any of the women who had tried to love him. He showed them no vulnerability, ensuring therein that each relationship would fail.

Does God exist? Do humans have souls? If so, where do they go upon death? He was restless about such questions, despite the books he'd read, despite the spiritual journey of discovery he'd embarked upon during his two year sabbatical from his business. He partially believed in the idea of an afterlife, but was haunted by this perpetual question; *What if I am wrong?* His wealth and comfort had only increased his sense of discomfort about such things. He felt cursed by the luxury lifestyle he had worked so hard to procure for himself.

He focused again, examining the man in closer detail as he passed under the bright lights distributed around the bar. Dennison noticed the way he paid for his beer with loose change, and also the wear-and-tear on the sleeves of his jacket. He also detected something in his eyes. Dennison was curious to know what trauma had befallen him, and how it compared to the disappointments of his own life.

Inside Dennison's booth a vodka on the rocks sat gently fizzing on the table in front of him. Beneath the glass was a white paper napkin. Dennison's eyes diverted from his purpose and focused on it. He hated these cheap, limp slithers of paper. He much preferred a real coaster, a plinth with some thickness. As he reached forward and lifted his glass, the damp napkin clung to the bottom like a graft of wet skin. He sighed with disgust, peeled it away and dropped it on the table.

As he took a sip he noticed a woman's shoes as she walked by. They were black leather sandals with ribbon ties extending around her lower legs, by YSL Rive Gauche. The inspiration was Roman gladiator. As she passed she slowed her pace and glanced at Dennison as if she knew him. She lost control of herself momentarily, stumbled, then recovered and walked on. Dennison did not react. He was fully aware of his own charisma, and it bored him. Women interested him, but these days only in select moments, and seldom more than sexually.

The waitress, dressed in white, drifted between tables serving customers. Eventually she arrived at Dennison's booth and enquired if everything was OK. He looked up slowly from under the tilt of his hat and nodded. She smiled politely and moved on. As she departed, a boisterous couple, drinking champagne, stumbled into the booth looking for somewhere to sit, and they asked if they could join him. Dennison lied and told them the seats were taken, but they insisted, and so he told them again, but still they persisted, as if he was joking. Dennison angled his torso menacingly towards them, and a flicker of light from somewhere washed across his face, revealing nothing but his mouth beneath the cantilevered peak of his hat.

He spoke in a low growl, "I said no," and that was enough.

As he watched them go he glanced around again to find his man. Just as he thought he'd lost him, he walked right by his booth. As he did so Dennison stretched a hand out of the darkness toward him, but he missed the connection. He was amused by his own misstep, as if the action belonged to somebody else.

Dennison took one final look at his chosen target to make sure. He watched him as he returned to the bar to order another drink. This was the moment. He picked up his briefcase and swooped across the room with the stealth of an eerie predator, and settled behind him.

2

The man turned and saw Dennison's face up close. Immediately his head bolted back with surprise. Dennison studied the man intensely, as if he were staring into the back of his skull. The man's eyes drifted upwards and focused on his hat, which seemed to hover on his head like a miniature UFO.

Dennison spoke. "Three. For three. In four."

There was a silence. "What?" The man regarded Dennison strangely, as if they'd met before and he was trying to remember. Dennison just stared. Amidst the stillness a light from above strobed across his head, and the shadow from his hat intruded across the man's face like a stain.

"Excuse me?" Dennison began. His voice was deep and authoritative, like that of a king. "Do you mind if I ask, what do you do?"

"What?"

"Your vocation?"

The man looked him up and down. "Why do you want to know?"

"Forgive my rudeness," said Dennison. "You seem to me to be a creative person. I can tell. I also like to think of myself as such."

"Well, if it's any of your business, right now, I'm not doing much," the man conceded. "But, I used to be a graphic designer."

"Ah, graphics," said Dennison with a muted enthusiasm. "The construction of meaning through the utilisation of words, colour and images. A crucial endeavour."

The man smirked. "Allow me to introduce myself. I'm Dennison." He extended his hand. The man looked at it at first, then reluctantly shook it.

"Erskine," he replied.

"Erskine? Unusual. Is that your first or your last name?"

"That's what they call me."

Dennison nodded approvingly, as if that made complete sense. Then he stared for several seconds, until Erskine looked away uncomfortably. He wondered if Dennison was gay. He considered walking away, but something within him that he did not understand compelled him to stay.

"So, what do you do?" Erskine asked eventually, attempting to break the uncomfortable silence. "Apart from approach total strangers in bars?"

Dennison smiled. Erskine was not a stranger to him. He knew him, knew his character. "What I do is not important," Dennison replied. "What's important is my next sentence."

Erskine waited. "Which is what?"

Dennison smirked. "I've said it....Three. For three. In four." As he spoke he held up the corresponding fingers in front of Erskine's face, as if he was deaf.

Erskine frowned impatiently. "What are you talking about? What are those numbers?"

Dennison paused, rubbing his fingers together. "Did you ever hear that story about Steve McQueen?" he asked.

"What story?"

"He's driving along the motorway in England one afternoon, with his friend Cliff Coleman. He glances across and sees a pretty girl in a car in the adjacent lane. He waves to her. She waves back. Then both cars pull over. McQueen steps out, calmly gets into the girl's car without even exchanging words, and they drive off. He went missing for two days."

Erskine was looking at him quizzically. "What's that got to do with anything?"

Dennison glared back as if that was the world's most ridiculous question. "*Carpe Diem*, Erskine," he said.

"What?"

"Check your cranium on that," said Dennison. "Check your cranium." He tapped his temple three times.

"What are you on about?"

"I'll give you three thousand pounds if you can sleep with three women in four days."

Erskine erupted with laughter. "That's funny," he said. This confirmed in his mind that Dennison was a joker — mad, instead of sinister. He looked at him sympathetically, as if he was wearing a straitjacket instead of a bespoke suit.

The garment in question was by Ozwald Boateng, deep purple, double-breasted, single button closure. The black shirt and matching tie were by Gieves. The silver cufflinks were by Ian Flaherty. The watch was a Patek Philippe, in white gold. The shoes were by Gérard Sené of Paris. His black cotton cap, shaped like a chauffeurs hat and tilted slightly off axis in a Frank Sinatra-style, was the cheapest thing on his body — £3.92 from Laurence Corner, the former army surplus store, once on Hampstead Road, Euston.

"Do you accept the proposition, or not?" asked Dennison. "Yes... or no?"

Erskine wiped his mouth with his forearm, shook his head. "But it's been nice meeting you."

Dennison pulled an envelope from his top pocket, placed a thumb into the leaf and showed Erskine three thousand pounds in fifty-pound notes. He held them up to his face and flicked through them. Erskine's attention locked. He looked at Dennison afresh, and adjusted his body to face him more directly. Dennison saw this and smirked. He put the envelope away and rubbed his fingers together.

Erskine looked again at the stranger — his face, his clothes, his shoes. He rubbed his head, checked his palm for sweat. "So let me get this straight," he began. "You're going to give me three grand to sleep with three women in four days. That's what you said, right?"

"Correct."

"Why?"

"For fun, that's why. Just to see if you can."

"What's the real reason?"

"What reason do you need to have casual sex? You're a man aren't you?"

Erskine huffed, mumbled something to himself.

"Tell me something," said Dennison. "If you had to choose, would you rather be mad, or in constant pain."

Erskine thought for a moment, then gave up. "I don't know."

"The choice is meaningless, because they are both the same," replied Dennison. "You hesitate in making this choice, when all choices are neutral. One choice is not better or worse than another — just different."

Erskine fell silent as he pondered Dennison's words. He took another gulp of beer. Then another. "So, what is this, some kind of game?"

"Exactly," said Dennison. "Think of it like that. A game — one that you must win."

"Where'd you get the money to burn on something like this?" he enquired.

"That's my business," replied Dennison. "I don't ask you where you get your haircut, so don't ask me where I get my money."

Erskine laughed again. Now he was thinking about the money. In his mind he had already spent it. He had paid off enough of his back rent not to turned out of his flat at the end of the week. He had made some preliminary repayments on the numerous credit cards he was living on. He had replenished his supply of skunk. Erskine was aware that he had made too many mistakes in his young life, and that this was going to be another one. "So, who are these women I'm supposed to fuck?" he asked tentatively.

Dennison's eyes sparkled. "I'll select three at random," he replied, holding up the fingers again. "In here, right now."

Erskine looked across the bar at faces. "Why do you get to choose them?"

"Those are my terms. I'll give you a thousand now, plus the rest on completion. But only if you get three."

"And what if I don't?"

"I'll kill you."

Erskine fell silent again. He leaned away from Dennison nervously, unable to fathom whether he was serious or not. "What do you mean....you'll kill me?" he asked.

Dennison did not answer. He simply stared. Erskine, hoping he was joking, waited for him to smile. He did not. "And if you accept, there are conditions," Dennison continued.

"What conditions?"

"The women must not know about the challenge, the sex must be consenting and safe, and you must never see them again afterwards. The classic one night stand."

Erskine looked down at the floor, shaking his head. "This is crazy."

"Crazy? This is not crazy," said Dennison. "Sunbathing. That's crazy."

Dennison glanced away to the floor, distracted by a woman's legs as she passed. She was wearing kitten-heeled slip-ons with a pointed hologrammed toe, by Miu Miu. He nodded a silent approval to himself.

"You ever wonder why people meet people?" he asked, re-focusing on Erskine. "What the forces are in the Universe that bring people together?"

"Don't tell me this is destiny?" Erskine replied sarcastically.

Dennison shrugged. Erskine glanced across the room at the women in the bar and his heart started beating faster. "OK, well if you want me to fuck three women, you've got to select me at least me six of them," he said. "That way I've got at least a fifty per cent chance."

Dennison chuckled patronisingly. "You get three targets and you convert all three," he said, holding up three fingers. "A hundred per cent. That's the deal."

9

"What? No one scores a hundred per cent," said Erskine.

"Yes they do," Dennison insisted. "One hundred per cent — the world's most aspirational proportion."

What if he picks three fat, ugly trolls? What am I going to do then? How's my dick going to rise for three beasts from The Lord of the Rings?

Dennison looked Erskine up and down. "You afraid?" he asked.

Erskine threw him a dirty look. "No," he said. "It's just that....I'm used to being in control of who I sleep with, that's all."

"Control?" scoffed Dennison. "What do you mean, control? You live on a planet that orbits the sun at 18.5 miles per second. What exactly do you think you're in control of?"

Erskine rubbed his head, checked his palm for sweat, gulped his beer. Dennison's proposition intrigued him like nothing he had ever heard. In the emptiness of his life, in the nothingness of the passing of his days, here was a purpose.

"OK," he said finally. "Who are the three?"

3

Earlier that same day, outside a school in west London, a sea of teenage schoolgirls all dressed in identical black and red uniforms, spilled out through the front gates and onto the street, dispersing rapidly in all directions. Richard sat in his car, his head weaving from side to side as he scanned for her, a seemingly impossible task amongst the camouflage of identical outfits.

He didn't notice her walk right past the car with two of her friends. At the last second he saw her out of the corner of his eye, leaned his head out of the window and called to her.

She turned. "Oh, shit, it's that guy I was telling you about," said the girl to her friends.

"Where?" said one of them, looking around.

"There. In the car...don't look, don't fucking look, shit!"

Richard smiled and beckoned her to him.

"Don't go," said the other, grabbing onto her arm.

"I'm not afraid," she said with her chin up. "What's he going to do, eat me?"

She pulled her arm free and walked confidently over to his car, peering in through the window. Richard was in his early thirties, but looked younger. He had thick lips, blonde hair and blue eyes. He introduced himself. Her name was Andrea.

"Andrea?" he said it as if he'd never heard such a word. "That's nice. Where are you going.....Andrea?"

"I'm going home."

Richard nodded. "Shame." He looked left and right. "You want to come for a ride with me instead?"

She shook her head. "I don't think so."

"Oh, come on," he smiled. "Don't be like that."

She looked toward her friends, who were standing at a distance waiting, gesturing anxiously for her to return.

"How old are you?" he asked.

"Sixteen...And a half." She clamped a strand of her hair between her lips.

"Sweeeeeeet sixteeeeen!" Richard proclaimed.

She laughed, at once feeling more at ease. "You're mad," she said.

"Tell you what," said Richard. "I think we should have a little drink. Just you and me. Get to know each other better. You know the Starbucks on the High Street there, opposite that pizza place?"

"Yes."

"OK. I'll be waiting for you in there. Tea or coffee?"

"Er...tea, but I'm not coming—"

"I'll see you in there."

"No, I don't thi—"

He hit the accelerator and sped away. She took a deep breath and held it. Her girlfriends rushed up to her in frenzied excitement."What did he say, what did he say?"

"He wanted me to go with him," said Andrea casually.

"Aaaaaaaiiiiii! Are you going to?" asked her friend.

"What, for sex?" asked the other one with a look of total disgust.

"Well, I don't think he wants to take me fishing," said Andrea.

"You can't," said her friend. "He could be a rapist or a murderer or something."

"I seriously doubt that," said Andrea.

"How do you know?"

"I think I'm a pretty good judge of character."

She was cocky now, feeling good that her life was suddenly more eventful than theirs. Her friends looked her up and down. Afraid for her, jealous of her. Andrea was popular in school — one of "the specials", as they were called — and now, outside of the school gates, she was still special. Her friends were not, and this uneasy barrier hung over their relationship, felt but never spoken.

Andrea didn't tell them that Richard was waiting for her. As they walked she thought about the stranger sitting in the café, and her heart pounded with excitement. She made an excuse to her friends, something about having to go to the library, and then she detoured away to the coffee shop, walking briskly, charged with excitement.

As she approached the café she covered her face and screamed quietly, in fear and delight. As she walked in, Richard was already sitting with two steaming cups in front of him. He smiled to himself, muffling his surprise. *She's shown!* He was relieved that he was still desirable to someone, even a sixteen year old. He had come to doubt it after Jane. "English breakfast?" he asked.

"Pardon?"

"The tea?"

"Oh, yeah, OK, fine. Fine."

"Sugar?" He spoke with a slow drawl, made it sound like

something.

"Yes, please. Two."

She watched as he ripped the sachet and poured into her cup. He took a wooden spatula and stirred it slowly. He stared at her, and stirred. "So. You got a boyfriend, Andrea?"

She shook her head.

"Come on. I don't believe that. A pretty girl like you? I bet you've got loads of boys after you."

"The boys I know are all idiots." She spoke with a mature tone, as if she was twice her actual age.

"I hear you. But you'll fall in love with one of them one day. Get married. Kids and all that. Isn't that what you want?"

"No."

"Why not?"

She shrugged one shoulder. "Because I'm young."

Richard looked down into the black swirl of his coffee and nodded thoughtfully. Then he flicked his eyes up and smiled. Their eyes locked, and Andrea suddenly felt a cold rush of regret. "Have you got a girlfriend?" she asked, trying to hide her nervousness.

"No."

"But your last girlfriend...Did she..."

"What?"

"Did she have a good body?"

"What?"

"I mean, that's important in a relationship, isn't it?"

He nodded.

"Do you...like my body?" she asked

He was startled by her question, but pretended not to be. He scanned the curved line of her breasts, leaned to the side and looked down at her legs extending from her perfectly pleated skirt, "Yes. It's very nice...very nice." His approval seemed to mean something to her, and she turned away, pretending she'd heard something behind her, just so she could hide her smile.

As they drove away he talked some more, about the music she liked, about fashion, trying to find a way to connect with her. He pulled over in a quiet street not far from her house. Slowly he moved his left hand from the handbrake across to her knee and slid it along the inside of her thigh. She inhaled sharply and retracted backwards against the seat. His confidence swelled when he saw this, and he leaned over, directed her head with his hand, pulled her hair away and kissed her gently. "You like that?"

She nodded, her head retracting nervously into her neck. He

needed her to say yes, to endorse his skills. In her nervousness she placed her left hand underneath her thigh, gripping her flesh tightly between her fingers, bruising herself. Richard kissed her again, harder this time. She half pulled away at first, then she moved clumsily toward his mouth. He put his hand on her knee and rubbed it up past her pleated skirt to her crotch and back. She breathed in and held it.

He whispered, "Your panties wet?"

She bit her lip and nodded.

"I bet they are. I bet they're properly wet." He put his hand into her skirt and pulled them down. She hoisted her pelvis as they cleared her backside. "Can I ask you another question?"

"What?"

"What kind of sex do you like?"

"I...I don't know." She thought about it, then she said, "I saw this porn film — on my mobile. Me and my friends."

A film conversation. Richard's favourite topic. Now he was officially having a great time. "You like porno, huh?"

He slid his hand into her crotch and slowly pressed his fingers into her. He smiled as he heard her quick, erratic breath.

And then she farted.

"Shit, I'm sorry, I'm so sorry, shit!"

"It's OK, it's OK. It's a natural thing, right?"

Her hands were up over her face. She was silent for a few seconds, and then there was a sudden flurry of panicked activity — she leaned down, grabbed her pants, yanked them up, rearranged her clothing, all the while proclaiming, "I'm sorry, I'm sorry, fuck, I'm sorry," and she opened the door of the car and got out and ran and ran and ran.

4

Dennison was unsurprised that Erskine had agreed to his proposition. He smirked, then turned away to scan the room. A few moments later he gestured with his chin. "Her."

Erskine turned and saw a well-built redhead exit the women's lavatory. He watched her return to her table and sit down with a girlfriend. "She's quite fit," he said encouragingly. "OK, who else?"

Dennison looked again. His eyes locked onto another. "Her."

Erskine looked in the direction. "Who?"

"This one. In white."

Erskine looked again. "You mean — the waitress?"

"Correct."

"No way."

"Yes, way."

"Nobody pulls waitresses," said Erskine with a frown. "They're unfuckable. They've heard every line. Choose someone else."

"No. The waitress is the one."

Dennison tilted his head so that Erskine could only see a single eye glistening under the slanted ridge of his hat. "You go over there, you introduce yourself, then you have sex with her. You fuck the unfuckable. If you want the money, you do it just as I say. Understand?"

Erskine shook his head in resignation. "OK, OK, who's number three?"

Dennison looked across the room once more, and after some moments he smiled and gestured again with his head. Erskine looked and saw a woman with a chiselled face, piercing brown eyes and long black hair, wild and unkempt.

"But she's with a guy, look," he groaned. "How am I supposed to get her? What if that's her boyfriend, or her husband?"

"So what? People with partners have affairs all the time."

"I'll need back-up," said Erskine. "Someone to distract him while I talk to her."

"There is no back-up," Dennison replied. "Just you, Erskine. Only you."

Erskine shook his head. "This is not going to be easy."

15

"Easy is for the weak." Dennison slipped his hand into his pocket and passed Erskine the envelope containing one thousand pounds. "There's one more thing," he said, as Erskine stared at the money.

Dennison put his hand into his briefcase, pulled out the mini video recorder and placed it on the bar before him.

"What's this?"

"I need evidence," said Dennison. "You and the women. In action."

"What?" Erskine craned his neck, as if that would help him understand. "You want me to film myself fucking them?"

"Correct. But they must not know."

"No fucking way."

"Yes fucking way."

"No."

"Yes."

"Why can't I just bring you their knickers or something?"

"A pair of panties?" said Dennison with feint disgust. "This is not proof. They could be your grandmother's for all I know — or your wife's."

Erskine's expression suddenly hardened. "I don't have a wife — anymore."

Dennison nodded thoughtfully as he realised the source of Erskine's secret pain. He fell silent, waiting for him to elaborate. Erskine looked away, looked at the money in the envelope. Dennison was amused by his attempt to conceal that which he could not.

"The only proof I will accept is video," said Dennison.

Erskine rubbed his head and stared at the machine.

Dennison ran his fingers slowly along the ridge of his hat, waiting.

Erskine thought about how thrilling it would be if he actually got away with it, like a secret agent. But then he thought about the women he would deceive. His face tightened as he imagined what Genevieve would say if she could see what he was about to do.

"Fuck it." He reached out and took the machine.

Dennison smiled with the satisfied expression of a chess player who'd just declared checkmate. "It's loaded and ready," he said. He looked at his watch. It was ten-thirty. "Now remember, in exactly ninety-six hours you bring me the homemade porno. Understand?"

Erskine nodded. "How do I find you?"

"In the envelope," Dennison replied.

As Erskine began to look inside it, Dennison picked up his briefcase, turned and walked out.

Erskine pulled out a black business card. It was blank, aside from Dennison's name and a telephone number printed in white. He smiled to himself as he watched Dennison leave. *What a fool.* He looked at the thousand pounds and the video recorder. He was pleased with his night's haul. He gulped down the last of his beer, waited a few minutes for Dennison to get clear, then headed for the exit.

When he got out into the street he took a few steps and then stopped abruptly as he thought about the money. The thousand pounds seemed inadequate now that he knew there was more. He had to have all of it.

As he stood reasoning with himself he glanced across the street and saw a parked car with its headlights on. There was someone behind the wheel. Erskine could not make out if it was Dennison. He could only see a black, motionless shape. He felt a chill as he remembered Dennison's words — that he would kill him if he did not carry out the proposition.

Seconds passed. Finally, Erskine turned slowly and returned to the bar. The car drove away.

5

At that moment, less than half-a-mile away, Hof and Nicky were at her flat in Seven Dials, Covent Garden. It was a small one-bedroomed apartment decorated Moroccan-style and lit with candles. Nicky, unable to stop fidgeting, stood pressed against the wall furthest from Hof, who sat calmly on the sofa looking at her. She was chain-smoking — so nervous was she in her own home.

"Why don't you come and sit down," said Hof, casually patting the space next to him. Hesitantly, she peeled herself from the wall and shuffled across the room in stop-start segments, as if she was walking by instalments. When she finally made it across the room she perched herself on the edge of the sofa, as if she was the guest and Hof owned the place.

He was thirty-one, of muscular build, with a shaven head and a gap between his teeth. He had piercing grey eyes and a whiplash smile. He smiled in that way that snakes smile in cartoons.

Nicky smoked using two hands — one to put the cigarette to her mouth, and the other to support the elbow of the hand holding the cigarette. She was a coy glancer who always addressed people with her head turned sideways, as if she only had one eye. She wore three-quarter length jeans with a navy blue suit jacket, plus a Seventies-style shirt with rounded lapels. A black handkerchief was tied around her neck and she wore white plimsolls. She had an androgynous face, with her hair shorn along one edge, with the rest swept to the other side. "The frozen tsunami" is what her hairdresser called it.

Hof studied her, working out his angle of approach. As he looked at her mouth he could see a feint moustache breaking through her pancake make-up. He moved his head slightly to get a better angle, but she saw him and turned away. Hof stroked his chin and laughed privately. "Why have you plucked your eyebrows like that?" he asked.

"Don't you like them?" she asked hopefully, stroking the spot where they used to be.

"You've fucking nuked 'em!"

She crumbled a little. "I think eyebrows are one of the most attractive features on a person." She swept her hand across her face in the shape of the letter S, extending it down her neck.

There was a silence in the room, and this unnerved her, and so she started a conversation about love. She did not know why, as she hardly knew him. She mentioned the last time she'd felt it — a cute boy in Thailand while there on a month's holiday. Then she asked him if he'd ever been in love.

"No," Hof replied.

"What? Never?"

"Never."

"Why?"

"I don't know," he shrugged. "Just never happened."

"How sad."

"No, not at all. I'm not crying about it. I've had a laugh fucking different babes."

She winced gently, his words like blades. *How did you get to be so — like concrete?* "You think I'm pretty?" she asked hesitantly.

"You're interesting, yeah."

"What does that mean?...Interesting?" She sprang off the sofa, feigning anger. Hof stood up, grabbed her by the wrists and threw her back down onto the sofa as if she weighed nothing.

"Oh my!"

She sat up slowly and adjusted herself. "Would you like me to change into something more comfortable?"

"If you like," Hof shrugged. "Doesn't really bother me."

She left the room and returned a few moments later in a blue silk Japanese kimono. She stopped to pose in the doorway, like a Fifties Hollywood starlet. Hof glanced down at her groin. A bulge. He walked over, put his hand there and squeezed. She squealed and jumped back. "I knew it," he proclaimed. "You're a geezer!" He let fly with a deep, mocking laugh.

She scurried away into a corner of the room, pretending to be frightened. Hof followed her and boxed her in. "Stop fucking mincing and come here," he said, grabbing her by the arm.

She slapped his face. "You brute!"

Hof laughed at her lame resistance, then he slapped her back, forcefully. She screamed, and her pancake make-up came off in a sudden puff that hung in the air under the candlelight. He grabbed her again, pressing against the flimsiness of her weak, narrow frame. He leaned in and kissed her. Her mouth tasted faintly of cucumber, and this surprised him, as he was sure he'd only taste tobacco. She attempted to struggle, a feeble, theatrical wiggle of the shoulders, the kimono beginning to unravel, but Hof kept pressing against her with his mouth until she succumbed.

Then she broke off. "Oh, my," she said, re-arranging herself and touching her mouth. "You do kiss beautifully." With a sideways glance she asked, "Do you mind if I fuck you...with a strap-on? It's just that...it's just that...well, my dick's not very...well...y'know."

"You want to fuck me in the arse with a strap on?" repeated Hof, pointing to her, then to himself, as if to confirm who was proposing what to whom.

She nodded. Hof shook his head. "No, no, no. The only thing my arse is used for is sitting and shitting."

She lowered her head in disappointment, then her eyes flashed up to him. "What are you going to do to me then?"

"Don't worry, sweet cheeks," he said. "I'll use the strap-on — on you."

Her expression brightened. "Alright."

"I got to warn you though," said Hof cautiously. "When I fuck someone, it's not just fucking — it's industrial fucking. It's heavy duty."

She rubbed her hand across her face in the shape of an S. "Oh my!"

6

Rossi had dressed smartly for dinner with Christina that night. He wore a black suit and a crisp white shirt with a high collar fastened to the neck, and his hair pulled loosely off his face. He walked into the hotel and made his way through the bar. Two women perched on stools saw him and froze, startled by his beauty. One whispered to the other and they followed him with their eyes until he disappeared from sight.

Rossi. Twenty-nine, with Latin features and a dark, broody sex appeal. He was square-jawed, with olive skin and brown eyes.

The restaurant was located at the far end of the bar. It was a light, ethereal space, draped in white curtains, with blonde wood floors and tasteful designer furniture. Christina was already seated at a table waiting for him. She was in her early forties, with a round face and a long nose. She wore a two-piece black trouser suit, sculpted tightly around her fleshy frame. Her hair was cut in a crisp 1920s-style bob. She was wearing glasses, going over some paperwork. When she saw Rossi she smiled as if they'd known each other for years, stood up, removed her spectacles, then pulled him to her and kissed him politely on the lips. He kissed her hand. She scrunched her nose, loving his old school manners. He watched as she gathered her papers and packed them away into a briefcase on the floor by her feet. He took out his mini notepad and scribbled:

r u high power biznizz woman

She laughed, her perfectly straight hair swishing back and forth like a cluster of pendulums. Her eyes sparkled as she thought about how funny and gorgeous he was. She felt lucky to be in his company. A woman like her, who had only ever attracted plain-looking men with bellies and baldheads, men who complained, who snored, who aged badly. Rossi was a jewel compared to them, and even though their relationship was not real, their limited time together would be real enough for her.

tell me about u

21

"Oh, that's pretty boring, Rossi."

I got all night + some morning

She smiled. "You're very sweet." Rossi raised his eyebrows twice, as if it was a secret code for something.

"I really, really like it when you write messages down," she said. "Maybe we could pretend you were away in the war and you could write me love letters."

love letters r lovly

It was her last night in London. She was heading back to New York in the morning. Midway through dinner she asked, "I'm not boring you, am I?"

Rossi smiled and rubbed her hand.

"I take it that means no then, does it?"

He pumped his eyebrows up and down twice. Then he picked up his notepad and sketched a picture of her face, prettier than she actually was. When it was finished he ripped it out and presented it to her. She smiled, flattered by the exaggerated portrait. He felt protective of her, despite the fact that they had only met once. This was how he was with women. There was an incident just over a year ago, when he got into a street fight — his only skirmish in years. He saw a woman being attacked by her boyfriend. Instantly, a rage took hold of him and he ran over, pulled the man away and hit him once. His face exploded with blood.

"Have you slept with a lot of girls?" she asked.

He shrugged innocently.

"I bet you have."

He made a gesture, Why?

"I don't know. You're incredibly attractive, obviously — and you seem very confident."

Just then, one of the girls from the bar who'd spotted Rossi earlier, walked by the tables pretending to go to the lavatory. She scanned the room looking for him, saw that he was with someone, and sighed with disappointment.

r u married

Christina shook her head. "It just hasn't happened," she said disappointingly. "I haven't had many relationships." She felt the texture of her wine glass, then took a large gulp. "I find that a lot of the men I meet are intimidated by the fact that I'm a successful businesswoman," she said.

Rossi nodded sympathetically, as if he knew all about such things.

"I think most men don't want really women to be their equals. They say they do but really they don't."

men r pigs I ~~lick~~ like women

She laughed suddenly, her mouth cracking so widely that Rossi could see her back teeth.

After dinner they went up to her hotel room. As she walked along the corridor ahead of him he tilted his head and smiled at the wiggle in her walk. A half-Marilyn-Monroe-half-Sophia-Loren-style of motion. He took a finger and stroked the groove at the back of her neck, and her shoulders hunched on contact. Without turning to look at him she extended her arm behind her, took his hand and led him to the door.

"How do you like my room?" she asked as they stepped inside. Rossi bobbed his head in a funny motion, like a puppet on a string. "I just had an idea," she said. "We could arrange to meet here every year. On your birthday, or mine. This could be our special room. I could wait for you here, naked on the bed." She made a theatrical gesture and fell backwards onto it with her arms up. Rossi smiled at her playfulness, flopping down beside her.

"We could do it every year until we die, Rossi. Regardless of our other relationships. It could be our one constant in life."

He kissed her, and she coiled into his body and made a noise like she'd just tasted fresh ice cream. As he undid her buttons and pulled open her blouse he came across a scar, which ran from the base of her neck to the middle of her breasts. He gently ran his finger along it.

"I had heart surgery when I was a younger," she said. "I had a hole in my heart." Rossi placed his hands over her heart as if to seal that hole. She made a sad face, then quickly changed the subject. "How about my suntan," she said with a sudden smile. "Isn't it cool? I just got back from a business trip to Ghana." She adjusted the angle of her body so that Rossi could see. He nodded approvingly. She gripped his forearm and pulled him to her, but after a while she broke off and held his head in front of her between her hands. "Rossi. I've got something to tell you."

He raised his eyebrows and waited.

"It's just that...Well...I've never made love before."

Rossi's eyes widened. He made a sign, the flat of both his hands cutting the air. *Never?*

"I'm a virgin," she said. "I grew up in a convent. I was there until my early twenties."

u scared

She nodded. She knew everything about business but nothing about sex. She felt like half a woman. He nodded, smiled, made the OK sign and resumed kissing her. After a while she broke off again and looked at him earnestly. "Can you show me how to make love, Rossi? I want to know. I want to know everything."

He shrugged, made the upside down smile.

"Can you show me how to give a man oral?"

no teeth

She laughed, her hair jerking like dancing tassels.

u should meet my mother

"Why?"

she hooker. she teach u ever thing.

7

Genevieve. Twenty-eight. Long black hair, centre-parted. A matching headband holding it out of her face. Almond-shaped eyes of green, with black flecks. Fat lips, curving downwards at the tips. A child's face, with a fixed expression of slight surprise. Then the body of a dancer.

She met Erskine at a party in London six years previously. Amidst the noise and the carousel of guests, they noticed each other, but kept looking away, then back occasionally to check if the other was still curious. She whispered something to her friend, and then walked past him, hoping for contact. He noticed her walk, an effortless gait, like a dancer. As she passed he touched her gently on her shoulder, bare from her halter-neck dress, and said a polite "Excuse me?" She smiled to herself, but muffled it as she swivelled like an actress, as if she'd never seen him before that moment, and waited for him to speak. Immediately when he saw her up close he was dumbstruck by her beauty. She looked down and saw the nervous shake in his hands, and that melted her guard, although she pretended not to have seen it.

Immediately he noticed her laugh. It went straight from zero to maximum with nothing in between — like a sprinter exploding from the blocks. She had her laugh ready, as if it was hidden behind a screen. Her long mouth would expand like elastic, instantly exposing an immaculate crescent of the finest teeth. Erskine had never seen anybody laugh with such dedication, such love of life.

After one such moment, he waited for her rubber mouth to contract, then he said, "People with big mouths like you have got to have excellent teeth. It's compulsory. Can you imagine a smile as big as yours if you had teeth like Nosferatu?"

She ran a market stall selling vintage women's fashion, and so she was always dressed stylishly. Her trademark item was a large, black floppy felt hat with an undulating rim, which she wore when they met up for coffee a few days later. They sat in the window seat of a café, their eyes excited by each other. They spoke quickly, bouncing off themselves like a double act. "What do you think of women with moustaches?" she asked abruptly.

"I don't know. I've never really thought about it."

"I have this slight fuzz here, you see," she said, raising her head slightly and running her fingers under her nose. "When the sun hits it a certain way you can just about see it. Awful. I'm expecting to look like Groucho Marx any minute."

Erskine laughed. It pleased Genevieve that she was the cause. She was always funnier than the men she dated. She'd often wondered if there was something in her that drew her to men that were not as funny as she, so that she would retain the upper hand. "So, you're a graphic designer, Eskimo?" she continued.

"Erskine."

"I know what your name is, you doughnut. I like Eskimo. It's cute."

"OK then."

"Couples should have pet names for each other, don't you think? It makes things personal."

"Are we a couple then?"

"I don't think you'd be here if you intended otherwise," she said, staring at him defiantly.

"You're pretty sure of yourself aren't you?"

"No. It's just that life's too short to be anything other than direct."

They pondered the moment. Erskine nodded his head approvingly, then broke into a smile.

"MAC or PC?" asked Genevieve.

"What?"

"I don't date PC men, you see. Boring. MAC guys are more arty."

"Well, I'm a MAC guy," said Erskine proudly.

"Thank goodness."

"What about you?"

"I'm a MAC girl. There you go. A fit. Two big MAC's."

"With extra cheese."

They laughed together, as if they'd been friends for years. "I just realised something," said Erskine.

"What?"

"You're a total fruitcake."

"You mean I'm wholesome and I taste yummy?"

"Well, I don't know about the tasting yummy bit yet."

"Well, what are you waiting for, dummy?"

She closed her eyes tightly and pouted exaggeratedly. He kissed her, then leaned back, frowning thoughtfully.

"Fruitcake. Definitely."

8

Erskine looked across the room at the three women Dennison had chosen for him, not knowing where to start or what to do. What he did know was that he had to get to each of them quickly, before they left the bar. He studied each of them in turn, trying to formulate an approach. First, the redhead sitting with her friend. He took a deep breath and another mouthful of beer. As he put the bottle down he saw that his hands were shaking. Just like the time he first met Genevieve. He looked nervously at the woman. *What if she laughs at me? What if I go over there right now and she tells me to fuck off, out loud, in front of everyone? I'm going to die, that's what I'm going to do.*

He took two nervous steps toward her, stopped, and turned back. *Come on, you lame duck. She's a girl, not a bomb.* He psyched himself again, walked over and introduced himself.

"Sorry....sorry for the interruption," he began. "I've been standing over there looking at you ever....ever since you walked in here...er...yes."

"Oh, really?" said the girl, raising her eyebrows in surprise.

"Yes....You've got a beautiful face. Lovely face. Really lovely. It jumped out at me from across the room...like a punch...like a rabbit bursting from a hat, y'know? Rabbits?" He stretched out a hand. "My name's Erskine."

"Could you just leave us alone please? I'm trying to catch up with my friend."

She left Erskine's hand hanging in mid-air. He felt the sting of rejection as he slowly withdrew his fingers like a wounded claw. "Sorry," he mumbled feebly as he backed away, cussing himself for his clumsiness.

He quickly shook off his disappointment and focused on his second target — the waitress. He sat down in a booth and looked over at her. She was medium build, curvaceous, with a round face and a strong nose. He noticed that her shoes had a broken buckle, and that her hair had split ends. He took out the thousand pounds, divided it into two equal portions, put them into separate pockets and then called to her. He introduced himself. Her name was Jennifer.

"Do you mind me asking, how much do you make waitressing here?" he asked.

"Not enough. What would you like, Erskine?"

"Beer, please."

Before she could leave, Erskine said, "Can I ask you something?"

"What?"

"Will you sleep with me for five hundred quid?"

"Excuse me?"

"Er....I said, will you have sex with me....for five-hundred pounds?"

"Is that all you think I'm worth?" she sneered.

"What?....Well, no, I mean....I just—"

"I'll do it for ten grand, how's that?"

"Ten grand? I....I don't have that much."

"Then don't ask for what you can't afford." She glared at him contemptuously, then walked away.

"Fuck!" Erskine clasped his hands over his face. After a while he looked up and scanned the room, thinking perhaps that Dennison might be back, watching him from one of the booths. He got up and checked them all, then slumped down again at the bar.

Jennifer returned with his drink. "I like your hair like that," said Erskine enthusiastically, trying his best to sound complimentary. "Really do....Really."

She smiled politely and thanked him for nothing. Her hair was like this yesterday and the day before that and everyday. It was work hair.

"I'm serious, y'know," said Erskine.

"Sorry?"

"About fucking — I mean sleeping — with you. Shit! For five hundred pounds. Yes. I..." He clumsily pulled out the money and showed her.

She huffed at his ineptitude. "Why do you need to pay for sex anyway?" she asked.

"What?"

"Well, you're not bad looking, you're quite charming — why do you need to pay for it?"

"Er....I don't have a girlfriend right now."

"You could get a hooker for a hundred, or less. Why do you want to pay five hundred to fuck me?"

Erskine looked lost. "I don't want some scuzzy hooker," he said finally.

"Anyway, I'm married," she declared, and then walked away.

Erskine's mouth fell open. He fell back in his seat, shocked and deflated. He pondered the nonsense of what he was doing. He thought again about abandoning the whole exercise and quitting with the money he had. But he had come too far now. He glanced across the room at his third target, the woman with the wild hair who was sitting with a male companion. She was wearing a tight black sleeveless T-shirt with a large silver motif of a dancing woman on the front.

After a few moments the man rose from his seat and headed for the lavatory. Erskine saw his chance. As he approached her from behind he recalled that day in the street when he saw the back of a woman's head and thought she was his Genevieve — same hair, same walk — and he ran after this woman as if it was her, and called out Genevieve's name, and the woman turned, but when he saw that it was not her, he stopped suddenly and put a hand over his mouth, and for the rest of that day he was lost in sadness.

"Excuse me?" said Erskine. She turned and looked him up and down, her action loose and sleepy from alcohol.

"Do you know what time they close in here tonight?" he asked hesitantly.

"One-thirty." She spoke slowly and carefully, as if the words hurt.

"Thanks." Erskine nodded, then stared, trying to think of something. She looked away and smiled knowingly to herself.

"You know that if you want to fuck me you can't be my friend," she said casually.

"What?"

"There are friends I like and others that I fuck."

Erskine buried his hands in his pockets and nodded his head. "Does that mean you don't fuck the people you like?"

"Liking and fucking don't mix," she said, shaking a drunken finger. "People try to put them together. I think they call that a relationship."

Erskine was captivated. He took a step closer, wondering if this was her real personality, or if the alcohol was the cause. She was more attractive up close, now that he could see the detail of her face. Her unkempt hair could do nothing to disguise this. He wondered what shapes and contortions her face would make when he slept with her.

She tilted her head to one side and studied him, as if she was looking at a painting in a gallery. "So, what type are you?"

"Sorry?"

"There are only three types of guys."

"What?"

"Either you're lonely and you just want to talk, or you want to fuck me, or you want to love me. Which one are you?"

Erskine was speechless. "Well I...what makes you think...?"

"Well you're here aren't you?" she interrupted. "You've introduced yourself. It can only be one of the three."

A sheen of sweat began to bristle on Erskine's forehead. "No....I...I just, er...well, umm."

She was amused by his clumsiness. "What's your name? Let's start with that, shall we?"

"I'm Erskine."

"Bear skin?"

"No. Erskine."

"Foreskin?"

"Erskine...ERSKINE."

"Erskine?" She sounded surprised. "What is that, your stage name? Like Bono? You a rock star?"

"No."

"Well, my name's Natascha. But unlike you, I have a surname."

Erskine asked about her vocation, but before she could answer her friend returned to the table. He abruptly took his leave and backed away, promising to return later on.

Erskine's brow compressed with disappointment as he sat back at the bar. He'd now made contact with all three of Dennison's choices and got nowhere. He rubbed the top of his head, checked his palm for sweat, then ordered another beer. As he sat nursing his failure, he turned and saw the woman he had approached first, ordering drinks at the bar beside him. He perked up, stole a quick glance of her body.

"Sorry about that just now," he said, grinning hesitantly. "I didn't mean to intrude."

She turned to him and smiled. "Oh, hello. It's no problem. You just caught me in a conversation, that's all. I haven't seen my friend for ages."

Her name was Katarina. She was Czech, from Prague. Erskine suggested they meet for a drink sometime. She thought about it, then asked him why.

"Excuse me?"

"Why do you want to meet me?" she asked again.

Erskine looked around aimlessly. "Well, you look like a nice person, and I just thought it would be cool to have some company."

She studied him long and hard before agreeing. Erskine tapped her number into his mobile. As she turned to leave he asked, "Don't you want my number too?" She smiled, shook her head, then walked away.

"Yes!" Erskine shook both his fists and grimaced with relief. Then he glanced at the counter and noticed that Katarina had left her drinks behind. As he turned to call her, he saw her exit the bar. Her behaviour puzzled him, but he shook it off, picked up one of the drinks and sipped it. Then he turned and scanned the room. He looked over to where Natascha was sitting, but she was gone. Suddenly worried, he scanned the room again. Nothing. He dashed to the women's toilets and checked there. Again, nothing. Then, as he headed back to the bar he looked toward the door just in time to see her leaving. He rushed forward, dodging bodies, up the stairs, through the doors and out onto the street, only to see her wild hair through the rear window of a cab, moving away quickly. He scanned the street desperately for a taxi, but to no avail. Foolishly he began chasing the car, but it was soon out of sight.

In the back of the cab Natascha sat with her eyes closed and the side of her forehead pressed against the cold window, juddering intermittently as the car barrelled forward, drifting in and out of a delicate sleep. Then the car hit a bump and suddenly she snapped awake.

She looked at the driver. "Excuse me? Is this is a talking cab or a non-talking cab?" she asked.

"Talking isn't part of the service," replied the driver. "You're paying for the ride, not conversation. If you want noise I can turn on the radio."

"Frosty," Natascha replied. "It would be nice if you'd talk."

His name was Mohammed, but to the English he called himself Mo.

"Where are you from, Mo?" Natascha asked.

"I'm from Hackney."

"No, I mean originally?"

"Hackney."

Natascha laughed. "OK, your parents then. Where are they from?"

"Algeria."

"OK, cool." Natascha scanned the interior of the car. "Nice ride, Mo. Nice leather seats. Is it yours or Uber's?"

"It's mine. Uber don't supply cars."

"I see," said Natasha. "And a little digital speedometer there.

They're so cute."

"For sure."

"Exactly twenty-five pounds and seventy pence to get me home — bargain."

"Yeah, but for you it's going to cost extra," said Mo with a wry smile.

"What? Why?"

"Because you got me talking. Chat is extra tax."

"How much extra tax?"

"Ten pounds extra."

"Is that ten pounds exactly, or like, ten pounds and seventeen pence, in Uber-style funny pricing?"

"Just ten, straight."

"That's steep. What about a discount, Mo? Friends rates?"

"I make ten new friends a night in this gig," he huffed. "Then, when I get them home we aren't friends anymore."

"Yes we are."

"No. Friends see each other. They talk, they text, they go for beers. After tonight, I'm never going to see you again."

"Well, Mo, for an extra tenner you better deliver one stupendous line in chat. It'll have to be the conversation to end all conversations."

"That's your problem. You ask a brother whose skill is driving cars to entertain you. That's like getting a butcher to rewire your house."

Natascha laughed and nodded at the same time. "That's funny. I'll give you two pounds for that one. Eight to go."

"You coming from the bar?"

"Yep," Natascha sighed. "Another bar."

"Is it a cool place?"

"Bars are all the same."

"Yeah? Maybe you shouldn't go then?"

"Maybe, maybe, maybe." Natascha yawned, her mouth forming a perfect oval. "You married, Mo?" she asked.

"Yes."

"You like your wife?"

"What kind of question is that?"

"It's not so silly. Lots of men don't like their wives....after a while."

"The other way around too." He asked if she was married. When she said no he replied, "You got a man?"

"I don't do...men."

Mo looked at her in the rear-view mirror. "You lesbianic?"

32

"No, I'm not...lesbianic, as you call it. I mean, I do do men, but I don't do men in terms of relationships, y'know."

"Why?"

"Long story. If I tell you, you'll end up giving me money, then maybe I get home for free."

"I seriously doubt that."

9

Erskine returned to the bar and sat alone drinking. He had lost Natascha, and with it the other two thousand pounds. He was angry with himself that he had not got her number earlier — that he'd backed away at the key moment. He looked about the room aimlessly, up at the lights in the ceiling, and then he fell into sadness, losing himself in the melancholy of Genevieve, as he had done so many times, on so many nights.

He remembered the first time he came to see her on her market stall. He stood back and watched her unseen as she busied herself with customers. He remembered how stylish she looked in her floppy felt hat, poncho, jeans, trainers and fingerless gloves.

Cautiously he approached, staying out of sight, and began browsing through the racks of clothes. He picked out a floral dress and then dashed behind a curtain at the back of the stall to try it on. When he was ready he called to her in a mock female voice, as if he was a customer needing assistance. When she came to him he sprang from behind the curtain wearing the dress. Genevieve jumped with fright, then stepped back creasing with laughter.

"How do you like me?" Erskine asked, striking a pose.

"You scared the shit out of me, you freaky freakster!" She looked him up and down approvingly. "You look cute though. Have you ever considered a sex change?"

"I'm not sure I'm into you enough to cut my dick off."

"Coward."

"Would you still sleep with me if I did?"

"If your tits were bigger than mine, no way."

As Erskine sat drinking he glanced down and noticed a flyer lying on the counter. He reached for it. There was a picture of Natascha on the front, singing, wearing a full-length, black sequinned dress. The text read;

THE NATASCHA MASON JAZZ REVUE
LIVE ABOARD THE BARRACUDA

Erskine smiled to himself. "She's a singer," he mumbled.

He didn't see Jennifer looking over his shoulder. "She's very pretty, isn't she?"

Erskine hurriedly stuffed the flyer into his pocket. "In an obvious way, I suppose," he shrugged. "If you like that whole, er...beauty thing, y'know."

Jennifer was off duty and out of uniform. She had let her hair down, and was wearing make-up. She wore orange lipstick over her lip-line to make them appear fuller.

"Jennifer, listen, I'm sorry," Erskine began.

"For what?"

"I was rude, I was stupid, I know....I shouldn't have offered you money. That was an insult. That was stupid. I'm sorry."

She stared at him, biting her bottom lip. His confession seemed to satisfy her. She smiled, then took his arm. "Let's go."

He felt the weight of her arm interlocking with his. It was the first such contact he'd had with a woman since his Genevieve. As they walked he pretended he'd left something at the bar, and he doubled back to look, just so he could release himself from the connection.

They walked along Brewer Street toward Bar Italia on Frith Street. Erskine noticed that her clothes were stylish and expensive. Not what he'd expected from a girl waiting tables. The café was busy, with late night revellers spilling into the street with their coffees. They ordered cappuccinos and drank them as they strolled. Jennifer scooped out the froth with a plastic teaspoon, skimming the rim then working her way inwards, eating it like a dessert. She saw Erskine watching her, and suddenly she was self-conscious.

"Can I ask you a question?" she began.

"What?"

"You....you don't feel sorry for me? Do you?"

"What?"

"I mean....That's not why you're here."

"What do you mean?"

"Nothing."

Jennifer finished scooping the froth from her coffee, then took a big gulp. "So, why haven't you got a girlfriend then?" she asked.

"There was somebody. There isn't anymore."

She asked what had happened but Erskine pretended not to hear. She was curious now. "Did you love her?"

Erskine hesitated — the language was painful to say. "Yes."

"Have you loved anyone else since her?"

35

Erskine stared silently at his shoes. "What about your husband?" he asked, desperate to switch the attention.

"We're separated. He's...." she waved her hand, making a gesture like a bird flying away.

They hailed a taxi on Shaftesbury Avenue and headed to her flat. Erskine glanced out of the window behind him, wondering if Dennison might be out there following them. There was something about being in a taxi at night disturbed him. It was Genevieve. The hollow memory of returning home night after night during those times after she was gone. He recalled the sense of loss and loneliness he'd felt during those journeys — the cavernous emptiness he felt as he sped through the big dead streets of the sleeping city. He wondered what it was about the cloak of night that so consistently opened the portal to his pain.

A memory came to him — the first time he and Genevieve went to the cinema together. He remembered nothing about the film, so distracted was he by his new love. What he did remember was the way she would grab clusters of popcorn between all five of her fingers, and then press her loose fist to her closed mouth and hold it there, picking off the pieces one by one with her lips. He never spoke to her about such things — the little habits he loved about her — as he did not want to taint their innocence.

In the back of the taxi Jennifer finger-combed her hair and adjusted her seating position to face him better. She looked at him and wondered if he was a good kisser. She wanted him to take her right there, to push her back against the seat of the cab and kiss her hard and put his hands on her. Erskine noticed the shift in her body language. Her knee was now touching his, despite the abundance of room on the seat. He was nervous, and so he kept talking, trying to avoid any silences.

When Erskine failed to make a move Jennifer turned to the window and looked out at the city flashing by. She liked the way the speed of the taxi made the lights in the street stretch and deform against the night. There was a lull in the conversation as Erskine ran out of things to fill the silence. Jennifer seemed more distant suddenly as she stared out of the window. "I had this boyfriend once, about seven years ago," she began. "On our second date he kissed me outside my house — and he did it with such force that I felt myself actually tipping backwards. Then he put his hand between my breasts and pushed me back against the door, and kissed me again, even harder. It was such....such a strong thing to do. I never told anybody that."

Erskine nodded and mumbled something. He looked at the taxi driver, the back of his head, wondering if he had been listening. He turned back to Jennifer as she stared out of the window, and she sensed it and turned to him. She smiled gently, then looked back out into the night.

Soon they arrived at her flat. Erskine watched her put her key into her door, open it and switch on the hallway light. He took a deep breath, pulled her from behind by her arm and pushed her back against the wall. She glared at him in stunned silence. He pressed his mouth into hers. She released herself to him, gripping him around his shoulders and waist, kissing him harder.

Suddenly she stopped, as if she wanted to say something important. "Erskine?"

"Yes."

"Would you....like some tea? I've got peppermint? Or builder's, if you prefer."

Erskine shook his head, kissed her again, and they stumbled into the living room and collapsed onto the sofa. After a while she broke off to go to the bathroom. Erskine, hearing the low sound of teeth brushing, seized his chance, found the bedroom and went to work setting up the video recorder. He took off his jacket and put the machine through one of its arms until the aperture poked slightly through the hole. Then he placed it carefully on a chair aimed at the bed and pressed the record button. He sat on the bed looking at it as it recorded him. He glanced away in shame, as if Dennison was actually present in the room, watching him through the aperture. He got up to turn it off, but then Jennifer stepped into the room.

She drew the curtains, undressed hurriedly and slid under the sheets before Erskine could see her thick hips, her cellulite, and at that moment he changed his mind about wanting to sleep with her and glanced toward the door.

Minutes later he was lying beneath her and they were connected. She pushed cautiously against his body, trying to guide her suspended weight, afraid to bear down on him fully. In the rhythm of Erskine's stroke, in the silent ergonomics of his sexing, she felt sad that he felt nothing for her, that his regard for her was nothing but mechanical.

As he pressed himself upwards against her, her skin felt waxed, as if she'd just bathed. She felt looser inside than his Genevieve, and this surprised him, as if somehow all women were designed the same way. Her mouth opened and she looked afraid, and Erskine wondered if that was just her style, or if she really was fearful.

The kinetics felt stupid to him — the loveless, indifferent rhythm. He wanted it to be over. He wished he was at home, away from her.

Suddenly she spoke. "Stop," she said. "Stop it, stop it!"

He froze. "You alright?"

She was breathless, writhing uncomfortably. "Sorry...I...just got freaked out for a second."

"Everything OK?"

"Yeah, fine, I just haven't done this for a while that's all." She turned away from him, blinking rapidly.

"You sure you're alright?"

She nodded, then swivelled and lay under him. "Come on."

Erskine started moving his hips again and then she vomited in his face.

He jolted backwards, landing at the edge of the bed.

"FUCK!"

They both froze with shock, the vomit dripping down his body — a fizzing soup of undigested rice and orange pith. He held his breath as the stench hit his nostrils.

"Fuck, Erskine I'm so sorry, shit, shit!"

He rose carefully, stepped into the bathroom and towelled himself down. He could hear Jennifer's voice apologising in the distance. She was too embarrassed to come any closer. As he wiped himself he caught his own reflection in the mirror. He stopped and stared at himself disdainfully. "What the fuck are you doing?" he whispered.

He returned to the bedroom, trying to look sympathetic. He was desperate to get away. He looked at his clothes on the floor. She saw him, but pretended she hadn't. Erskine stood naked at the edge of the bed, feeling awkward, his erection still proud. Seconds of emptiness passed. A car flashed by in the street outside, and the light from its headlights gauzed through the curtains covering the bedroom window, and Erskine was thankful for its brief distraction. "You OK?" he asked again. "Would you like me to get you something?" He didn't know what.

She couldn't look at him now. "Erskine, I don't know what came over me," she said, staring down at the bed. "I suddenly felt sick. It came up so fast, I just didn't—"

"It's cool," said Erskine, holding up his hands reassuringly. "No harm done." He perched on the bed next to her and touched her hand. "Fresh vomit is good for the skin, I hear."

They both laughed, a contrived chuckle, and this eased her shame, although not enough for her to tell him about her stepfather

— the one who molested her back then. She'd kept the secret — that ever since, whenever she orgasms, she wets herself. The boyfriends never stayed when they found out.

The last time it happened she was so ashamed that she stole the wet sheets from her boyfriend's bed, then bought him a brand new set, better quality than the ones she'd soiled. But she could not face him anymore, so she posted them to him. She never saw him again after that. She told her friends that she'd dumped him.

Nowadays she'd learned to tune out her orgasms, like turning down the sound on a television. But every now and again one would slip through, in an unauthorised breach. On this occasion she stopped herself just in time, but she was so nervous that her stomach emptied.

As Jennifer glanced down at Erskine's still erect penis, she grew worried that he'd try to have sex with her again, and that he'd discover her secret. She had to take the erection away, to protect herself. Over the years she had become particularly skilled at fellatio, out of necessity. She took Erskine's penis and lowered her mouth to it, but after just a few expert strokes he gently pulled her up and lay her down next to him with his arms around her. At first she was insulted. *What the fuck, doesn't he know that my blow jobs are quality?* She was surprised he had stopped her — men never did — and she couldn't help but think that maybe he was different from the others. Maybe he was the one who wouldn't run if he discovered her secret. She squeezed his arm in gratitude, and they held each other and looked silently upwards, like two lovers in a field staring at the sky.

After a while she turned to him and announced that she was going to divorce her husband. "Being with you has helped me decide that," she said.

Erskine hoped that she wasn't trying to like him. "Listen, I didn't mean to..."

"No, no, I was already over him anyway. This just confirms that I don't want to be with him."

Erskine remembered the video recorder. He glanced discreetly over at it, feeling the guilt rise within him. He turned away from it, ashamed of himself. As ashamed of his secret as she was of hers.

10

It was late the following morning when Natascha reached her mother's house in Harrow, Middlesex. She let herself in and went through to the kitchen. Her mother was still in her dressing gown, busy watering the plants on the window ledge. As she turned and smiled to greet her daughter the light from behind her sieved through the strands and S-bends of her unkempt hair, illuminating her head like an angel.

They embraced and looked each other over. Her father's affairs had prematurely aged her mother's skin, stretched and marked it, but her eyes were still bright and alert. Natascha smiled when she saw them, as their sparkle gave her hope that one day her life might be better.

She asked her how she was feeling. Her mother shrugged. "Well, you know....I'm functioning," she said with a weak smile.

Natascha nodded sympathetically. "Good. That's good."

They stood for a silent moment, then her mother said, "I've got the tea on."

There were two mugs on the kitchen table. Her mother looked disdainfully at them. "Shame about these damn things," she said, picking one of them up. "Nobody uses teapots anymore. Now the tea all comes in these neat little one-person bags. How anti-social. I think the move away from teapots to mugs heralded the break-up of the family."

Natascha opened a jar on the table, took out two circular tea bags and dropped them into the mugs, the symbols of the modern-day broken family. Circular bags into circular cups. The perfect invulnerable, self-contained shape. Natascha understood the emotional geometry of the circle. She empathised with its ruthless sense of containment. That was how she protected herself from the male species. "Species" was the term she often used to describe men. To her they seemed more like aliens than humans. She was careful only to take only pieces of men, never the whole. She was content with a swatch of a married man, a tourist or a toxic bachelor. She would stop them if they tried to confide or confess aspects of their lives to her. This was considered a breach of their arrangement.

40

She would end it with the lovers who could not control their verbal incontinence, who deviated too far from the kinetic business of sex.

Natascha and her mother took their cups and settled in the lounge. Her mother sat on the sofa, while Natascha went over to a cluster of framed family photographs on a side table. There were shots of her parents during happier times together; a photo of the three of them, heads together, smiling; another of her and her father in the den amongst his jazz records; a picture of her, aged four or five, trying to play his trumpet, red face, bloated cheeks, looking as if she was about to burst, him standing by nervously with his arms at the ready just in case she dropped it.

Natascha remembered how, toward the end of the marriage, her father tried to involve her in his adultery. He put his arm around her when he tried to explain what he'd done. Natascha glanced at that arm with veiled disgust, as if the limb was diseased. When he looked at her with his puppy dog eyes, she hardened. There would be no more jazz sessions in the den, now that she knew.

Afterwards she questioned how God, the Father, could be a man. How could Christ refer to him as 'Father', when fathers did such bad things?

She recalled the incident when her mother slapped her over her father's adultery. She was a teenager, and she let her congealed anger escape. "Where is your self-respect, mummy?" she snapped. "For God's sake, why don't you just leave him?"

Then came the slap. "DON'T YOU DARE TALK TO ME LIKE THAT."

"You're slapping me?" Natascha replied as she nursed the sting. "Daddy's sleeping with other women and you won't raise a hand to him, but you're slapping me?"

"I was reading the paper the other day," said her mother curiously. "There's something called 'booty calls' now, isn't there?"

"What?" Natascha turned in surprise.

"When a man calls you up in the middle of the night for a bit of sex. Do you know about it?"

"Are you alright, mummy?"

"Yes, yes, yes," she said, waving a dismissive hand. "I hope no one's doing that to you, dear."

"What?

"Bootying you, or whatever you call it."

Natascha chuckled to herself.

"What do they call it if footballers do it?" she asked. "Football booty, no doubt."

She watched as she got another laugh out of her daughter. Two in a row. She was surprised at herself.

"Have you taken your meds today, mummy?" asked Natascha.

"Bloody tablets," she scowled.

"You've got to take them if you want to get well."

"Get well? What have I got to get well for?"

Natascha was irritated by her words, because as long as her mother continued to be stubbornly depressed it meant that she would have to keep diverting her life to look after her. She'd nursed her all the way through the period after her father had left, and she didn't want to do it anymore. She felt she'd done her time. She cursed the fact that she was an only child, because now there were no siblings to take a turn at this duty.

"He's marrying her, y'know," said her mother abruptly.

"What?"

"Your father. He's going to marry her. That bitch."

"Is that what he said?"

"No, of course not. I just know."

Natascha sighed and glanced over at the pictures on the side table. "I need some sugar," she said. She got up and went to the kitchen. When she came back her mother studied her face and body as if she didn't know her, and then asked, "Have you got a boyfriend yet, dear?"

"Mummy, please."

"Well?"

"It doesn't make sense anymore for women to fall in love with men," said Natascha. "They never sustain it. Love between women is much more solid. If I wasn't so into penises I'd be a lesbian tomorrow."

"You don't mean that."

"I bloody do."

"But what about babies?"

"What about them?"

"Well, call me old-fashioned, dear but the last time I looked, two women couldn't make a child," she said. "Besides, it would be nice to have some grandchildren before I die. Life can get lonely. I could do with a little noise around the place."

So, I should have children just because you want to increase the noise level around the house, mummy? Why don't you just buy a radio?

Natascha didn't want to get into another of these conversations, but nevertheless she asked, "Is that what it's all about, mummy? A man and some babies?"

Her mother looked at her as if she was insane. "Of course. Why? You think you've invented something else?"

Natascha wanted to tell her to mind her own business, that she had better things to do than to wait for a man to propose in order for her life to have purpose. In her mind she heard herself say, *Marriage is crap, mummy — look what happened to you and dad —* but she suppressed the thought.

"You should call your father."

Natascha frowned. "Why?"

"Because he's your father. What he did to me has got nothing to do with it. You should still make an effort."

"You're too forgiving mummy," said Natascha coldly.

"Don't be silly dear," she replied. "How can anyone have too much forgiveness?"

"You have. People forgive everything these days. Infidelity is brushed aside as if nothing matters, nothing is sacred."

"Good things can't be done to excess," her mother replied. "That's not the way the Universe works."

Natascha shook her head, sipped her tea. "Well, dad never calls me," she said defensively. "Why should I always be the one who makes the effort?"

"Just keep in touch, that's all I'm saying."

Natascha admired her mother's sense of rightness, of compassion. She wished she had a little more of it. There were questions she wanted to ask her, things she had harboured for some time. *Mummy, do you still feel sexual desire? Do you masturbate? How do you cope with the loneliness, with dad not here anymore?* She did not ask because she knew the answers would make her cry.

"He never talks to me now you know," said her mother, staring blankly at the floor. "He's got another life. After all those years."

Natascha saw the sorrow slowly leak into her mother's expression, and watched her shoulders wither yet another increment. She tried to resist having sympathy for her, as she didn't want to be her nurse again. She wanted her old mother back. The one she remembered when she was growing up. The strong, happy, positive soul — the nurturing powerhouse who nurtured her from a baby. But now Natascha realised that it was her turn to be strong for the mother who now needed it from her. As she looked at her broken state she softened, then got up and sat beside her on the sofa. She held her gently, her hands caressing her face and neck, and she pulled her gently down to lay with her like the fragile child she had become.

11

Erskine called Katarina the following evening, and she invited him to her flat for drinks. She lived alone in a first floor one-bedroom maisonette on Redchurch Street, Shoreditch. When he arrived she was still in her work clothes — a grey wool-blend business suit with a figure-hugging skirt that wrapped snugly around the curve of her backside. Erskine noticed it as she walked ahead of him after opening the front door. He wondered what her flesh was like beneath the fabric. Was it firm, or was the garment holding back a mass of loose flesh? Erskine watched her as she poured a beer into a glass and handed it to him, then refilled her glass of red wine from an open bottle on the lounge table. She remained standing while he sat on a chair by the window. They made small talk, the usual things, but Katarina was soon bored. She found most men boring, apart from when they were having sex with her. She lit a cigarette, took a long drag, looked thoughtfully up at the ceiling and said, "You know the weirdest thing about my ex?"

"Excuse me?"

"His head."

"What?"

"It was actually square — like Frankenstein. I mean, it actually had corners. Freaky. A bit like that judge from TV. What's his name? From Factor X? Simon Cows."

"You mean Cowell?"

"Yes, him. Mr X."

Erskine laughed silently. She waited for him to settle, then casually asked, "So, what is it you want, Erskine? You want to sleep with me? Is that it? You want to....fuck me?"

Erskine choked. "What?"

"Tell me so I can hear it. Tell me you want to fuck me." She was looking down at him, her chin high and proud.

"Well, I...."

"Well, do you or don't you?"

Erskine squirmed in his seat. A shine began to form on his forehead. "Well, I...I do....I do find you attractive, yes," he said, rubbing his head then checking it for sweat.

"What is that?" she sneered. "Is that yes or no?"

"Er...."

"British men. So weak. Not like Italians or Puerto Ricans." She sipped her wine, rinsed it around her mouth and swallowed it slowly. "British men are not as interested in sex as the continentals," she said. "It's a fact. The Brits, on average, work a forty-eight hour week — far more than the rest of Europe. That means they are too tired for fucking. They come home, eat, then fall asleep in front of TV."

She paused, sipped more wine. "Me? I can't have that," she said with a stern shake of her head. "I need sex twice a day, minimum. The men I meet these days just can't keep up with that. They all try at first, like it's a macho challenge, right? At the beginning it's twice a day and everything's great and la, la, la, blah, blah, blah — then it slips to once a day, then once every other day, then once a week and blah, blah, blah," she said, waving her hand nonchalantly.

She studied Erskine's reaction, trying to figure if he agreed with her synopsis, half wanting him to challenge her. "Women always want sex more than men," she continued.

"You think?"

"Absolutely. Because men have to get their equipment ready."

Erskine wondered about her weirdness, wondered if she was a therapy case. He shifted nervously in his seat, rubbed the ball of his shoulder, then fixed her with a stare. "Yes, I do want to," he said.

"You do want to what?"

"To fuck you....I mean, sleep with you," he said finally. "I do."

"That's better," she smiled. "Some Latin courage at last. Good. Ha! Now we can relax. You want a cigarette?"

"I don't smoke."

"Good for you."

She paused, looked around her place. "You like my plants?" she asked, pointing to the windowsill. I just bought them from Columbia Road market. Such a great place."

Erskine turned and took a polite look. "They're lovely," he said. "Really nice."

She looked away from the window and back at him. "And when you fuck me I want you to take it slow, you understand? None of that ram-ram stuff."

"What?"

"I've had men, y'know. They all fuck like they're in a hurry, rush, rush, rush, like they're trying to catch a train from Victoria or something. Like they got epilepsy. You want a cigarette?"

45

"You already asked me that."

"I did? What did you say?"

"I don't smoke."

"Good for you."

Erskine nodded, then rubbed his head again and checked it for sweat. Katarina had told him how she was better at sex these days than she'd been in the past — that she'd learned fresh things. Erskine wondered what these were. He grew excited about getting a sample, but was worried about his ability to reciprocate. His moves hadn't changed in years. Tentatively he asked, "Do you....do you want to do it now?"

"Shut up," she said with an annoyed expression. "Passion killer! You don't decide when we fuck, OK? I tell you when. You wait until I give you the light."

Erskine held up his hands in mock surrender. "OK."

"And don't fondle my breasts when you do it. I don't like it. It irritates me."

"Fair enough."

"I honestly don't know why men think we like that."

She looked him up and down, took her time, then she stubbed out her cigarette and said, "Take off your clothes and wait for me in the bedroom."

She walked out. Erskine sat staring at the floor, shocked at her abrasiveness. Then he sprang to his feet, went to the front door, opened it, stepped out, changed his mind, stepped back in, closed it quietly, then went into the bedroom and began casing the room, looking for somewhere to put the video recorder.

In the bathroom Katarina had her hand over her mouth, not knowing whether she wanted to laugh or vomit. Her face shape-shifted from one emotion to the other. She felt sick, but elated.

In the bedroom Erskine was frantically trying to prepare the video recorder.

In the bathroom Katarina was silently talking to herself in the mirror, telling herself to be cool.

Erskine put the machine into the arm of his jacket and began to position it carefully on top of a small television set which faced the bed.

Katarina was changing into a special outfit.

Erskine pressed the record button, stepped away and started undressing.

Katarina had finished changing and was heading for the bedroom.

Erskine was naked, looking for a condom in his trouser pocket.

Katarina entered the room wearing a white wedding dress and veil.

Erskine's mouth fell open.

She looked at him as if nothing was the matter. "I'm ready," she said. Erskine was speechless.

"Get on the bed," she said.

As she passed, her dress brushed against Erskine's jacket on top of the TV set. It fell to the floor and the video recorder rolled out.

She turned, saw it, her face changed. "What's that?" she pointed. "Are you filming us fucking?"

Erskine froze, his heart pounding. "No...yes...I mean, listen, let me—"

She picked it up and looked into it. "How exciting!"

"Really? You mean, you don't mind?"

"No. What a great idea."

She studied the instrument. "Is it recording?"

Erskine breathed a sigh of relief. "Er...yes."

"Hold it." She handed it to him, then straightened herself while he filmed her, like a macabre wedding video.

She took it from him and positioned it carefully on top of the television set facing the bed. "Perfect," she said. "Now, get on the bed."

Erskine obeyed. "No, not like that," she said. "On your back."

He tore the wrapper from the condom, rolled it down his penis then lay down. Katarina carefully hitched up her wedding dress, no underwear, straddled him, her body cranked and taut. She grabbed his penis carelessly in her fist, as if she were swiping a set of keys from a table, then lowered herself slowly onto him. She locked both arms in front of her, pushing against his shoulders. Erskine felt the friction of the scratchy fabric of her dress against his body.

"Don't come until I say," she demanded. "Don't be weak."

That's enough, you bitch, why can't you be nice.

She looked at him beneath her, her chin high and proud. He looked back at her blankly and it was then that she slapped him. "Turn your face!" she commanded.

Erskine's head jolted back into the pillow, but on the edge of losing his temper he controlled himself and went with the moment, then laughed in a way that wasn't funny.

"I want you to say my name as you fuck me," she said. "Over and over."

"What?"

"Say it!"

He said her name, slowly, over and over, like a chant.

"Yes, that's it, that's it."

The feeling of sickness and elation consumed her again, and suddenly she was tender, her eyes closed, lost within herself. In that same moment Erskine drifted away to a memory of his Genevieve. She came out of the shower and walked past him, a small towel wrapped tightly around her, her legs and chest exposed and glistening, her breasts pushed up as if she was wearing a bustier. Consumed with a sudden lust, he pulled at the towel like a cord and she twirled into his arms like a startled ballerina, and he kissed her neck and body, fresh and shiny from the soap and water. He listened to her laugh and giggle as she pretended to struggle, then he said his favourite thing, which was, "I need a kiss to sweeten my mouth."

In the midst of it, Katarina looked at him and whispered, "Do you love me?"

Erskine opened his eyes suddenly. "What?"

"Tell me you love me. Say it."

"I...I can't."

"Be in love with me tonight, my sweet. Like it was."

Erskine frowned. "But I don't love you. How can I?"

She threw herself off him. "Oh, fuck you! Why do you always have to spoil everything? You always do this."

He sat up. "I'm sorry."

They looked at each other in silence. Then Erskine broke off, looked nervously into the eye of the video recorder.

"Maybe I should go," he said.

He got off the bed and started dressing. Katarina looked startled. "What do you think you're doing?" she said angrily. "You're not finished until I say. Take off your clothes and finish the fucking. I demand it!"

Erskine ignored her, continued dressing. "Oh, that's the solution, right?" said Katarina, throwing her arms in the air with exasperation. "Whenever a woman challenges you, you run away, yes? So immature. So typical. English pig!"

Erskine, still not responding, dressed silently. She glared at him, arms folded, imploding with rage. "Well, aren't you going to say anything? You bastard. You idiot. You total, absolute fuckwit!"

He looked at her on the bed, the crumpled wedding dress strewn around her in a flattened bubble, like a deflated hot air balloon. Her face twisted and she began to cry. He froze, wondering what to do. He opened his fingers to embrace her, then closed them again. He switched off the video recorder, then lifted her veil and put his hand gently on her cheek. She covered it with both hers and held it there tightly, as if her face might fall apart if she let it go.

She couldn't tell him about her life, and so instead she just said, "Hold me. Please, just hold me."

He put his arms around her. Her body was different now — trembling and brittle. It had lost the taut, sinewy toughness of just a few moments ago.

She pulled him tighter. In her mind she said, *Tell me everything's going to be OK.*

She said it. "Tell me everything's going to be OK."

"Everything's going to be OK," he whispered.

"Liar."

Time fell, seconds of sorrow passed, and still she cried, and Erskine wondered how to soothe her. He pulled away gently, went to the bathroom, turned on the taps and ran the bath, and when he came back in, she asked what he was doing. He put his finger over her lips, then silently slipped off her dress, but left her veil on. He hoisted her carefully into his arms, as if her body, her heart, were made of glass. He carried her to the bathroom as she sobbed and lowered her gently into the water. But the soothing warmth only released more tears, and she cried with even greater intensity. With both her trembling hands she pulled her veil tightly around her face, as if she wanted to suffocate herself, her tears soaking through its gauze. Erskine watched her silently. There were no words he could think of to say. He knelt at her side, waiting for the right moment to go.

12

Addison Road, Holland Park, six-thirty a.m. The life of the morning was bright. The first daylight had tipped the trees, fed the leaves, and they swayed appreciatively in the hush of the street of millionaires. Then lower, capping the fronts of the houses, rows of neat hedges, all clipped to attention like box-cut Afros. No sound around here, no engines yet, but the shrill whistle of birdsong dusting the air.

For three years Dennison Carr had lived in this exclusive stretch between Holland Park Avenue and Kensington High Street. The procession of dream houses along the west side of the street were large and detached, with crisp white stucco facades and huge rectangular windows that yielded views from the street right through to the gardens at the back. The driveways were generously plotted, allowing each house to float comfortably in its own space.

Inside one of these houses Dennison was preparing for work. He was listening to a tune by Steely Dan called *The Fez*, from the album *Royal Scam* (1976). As much as he loved this song, it was not in his Top 10. These were the ones that were (in no particular order):

Stone To The Bone, James Brown (1973)
Ride The Groove, The Players Association (1979)
Glide, Pleasure (1979)
One Nation Under A Groove, Funkadelic (1978)
In The Jungle Groove (the album), James Brown (1986)
Rock Steady, Aretha Franklin (1971)
Brick House, The Commodores (1977)
Jungle Boogie, Kool & The Gang (1973)
On The Serious Side, Tower of Power (1975)
Across The Tracks, Maceo & The Macs (1974)

Dennison slid open the door of his large dressing room and stepped inside. There were the suits — Boateng, Gieves, Gucci, Tom Ford — in black, navy, purple and gunmetal grey. The shirts followed a similar colour palate, but with white added. Down below were the shoes, all the same cut — long, narrow, elegant, by Gérard

Sené, Berluti, Prada, Gucci, Sergio Rossi and Kenzo. For Dennison, looking good was as compulsory as food. He made a quick selection of garments and began to dress.

As he put on his suit jacket, the sliding action gave off a certain sound, a quiet sizzle, like a single rush of ocean water as it licks the shore.

At the bottom of the wardrobe was a drawer. He opened it and there inside was a beautifully arranged row of identical black hats. He pulled one out, kicked the drawer closed, stepped to the mirror, placed it on his head and adjusted the tilt to the precise angle. Now he was ready.

He stepped out of the front door and bound down the stairs, cranking at the elbows and knees. His feet crunched on the gravel drive as he surveyed his cars — a 1956 silver Mercedes-Benz 300 SL Gullwing Coupé, a 1970 olive green Citroen SM, and a 2002 black Bristol Blenheim III.

He settled on the silver Mercedes coupé. He opened both doors, pulled them high and stood back briefly to admire the drama of its preying mantis shape. When he climbed inside, the interior smelled like a vintage leather jacket. Slowly he inhaled the aroma, savoured it, then he started the engine, pulled the doors shut and he was away.

As he turned out of the drive and onto Addison Road, heading toward Holland Park Avenue, he touched the CD player and the track *Ride The Groove* by the Players Association (1979) blasted through the car.

He parked in a car park two blocks from his office and made the short walk on foot. He walked with a rangy stride and a slight forward rocking motion in his neck that appeared to imbue him with extra propulsion.

Parked by the roadside he noticed a 1963 series 1 black Jaguar E-Type. He halted momentarily to admire its design. His concentration was intense and thorough, as if he was reading a passage from an incredible novel. He finished his sweep, nodded approvingly to himself and walked on.

As he stopped at the kerb to cross the road he saw a woman approaching ahead of him. He ignored her face and body and instead looked down at her footwear — a pair of black leather high-heeled boots by Bottega Veneta. He glanced up to see the body inside them — a Japanese woman in an exquisite red felt hat, pulled low across her forehead, in similar style to the way he wore his. Her narrow eyes, a perfect accessory for such a headpiece, sat in exact parallel beneath the rim. As she walked by she turned and caught his eye and flirted with him in that second. He smiled admiringly, then turned and walked away.

Dennison was first into the office, as usual. It was a large, tastefully designed space, rendered in black and white, and with a magnificent view across London, which extended the entire length of one wall. He had a long elegant desk by Zaha Hadid, placed in front of the window so that when he sat in his chair his body was framed by the dramatic backdrop. Hanging on the opposite wall was a large framed photograph of the Bilbao Guggenheim. In one corner of the room was a television running an Italian Serie A football match with the sound turned down. On his desk there was a framed photo of Dennison together with a certain woman, Alice, a beautiful ex-model in her late thirties.

Dennison had built up a successful venture capital firm from scratch, with offices in London and New York. Aside from his investments he had thirty million in cash in the bank. He'd achieved it all, both professionally and socially. At forty-five the challenge was over.

The phone rang. Dennison checked the caller ID before he answered. "Have you completed?" he asked.

"I have," said the voice.

"Excellent. Any problems?"

"No."

"Good."

"So, when do I come in, chief?"

"Call me tonight. On the other number."

"OK."

"By the way, I think we have a new member," said Dennison.

The line went silent. "Is he good?"

"We'll see," said Dennison.

"Is he better than me?"

"Just call me tonight."

At nine forty-five a.m. Dennison appeared from his office. His staff were busy working. They half bolted to attention and greeted him as he bowled purposefully through the open plan space. The suit that he wore that particular morning possessed a certain stiffness within the fabric, and as he walked it yielded a discreet sound, like the muffled crunch of chocolate box plastic.

In the kitchen two secretaries were busy preparing a round of tea and coffee. Dennison walked in and immediately looked at their shoes. One of them was wearing a pair of silver chain-mail mules by Christian Louboutin, the other, a pair of thin pointy heels with a tendon-plate and fine ankle straps, by Sergio Rossi. He looked up again, reached for the coffee percolator.

"I've been eight months now," said one of the secretaries.

"Sounds serious," said the other.

Dennison was stirring his coffee, listening, but pretending not to be.

"We're going away next week, skiing."

"Fantastic."

"Yeah. He's really lovely, actually," she gushed. "Really special."

Dennison stopped stirring his coffee, turned to them and said, "You think your boyfriend's special?"

"Yes, I do, Dennison," she said.

"When's his birthday?"

"What?"

"When's his birthday?"

"Er...June seventeenth. Why?"

"June seventeenth? Do you know that there are at least nine million people in this world who each have the same birthday? That's eight-million-nine-hundred-and-ninety-nine-thousand-nine-hundred-and-ninety-nine people born on exactly the same day as your sweetie. Is that what you call special?"

The secretaries erupted with laughter. Dennison raised his eyebrows and walked out. On the way back to his desk, his personal assistant Maggie, a short woman in her late forties, caught up with him. He kept walking while she shuffled alongside him, a forearm full of papers, annoyed at his pace but not daring to say so.

"I've received your ticket for the fashion show," she said.

This got his attention. He stopped in his tracks. "Front row?"

"Of course."

"Excellent." He resumed walking. Just then, one of his junior executives walked by. He called to him. The man stopped, gulped, turned to his boss. "Yes?"

"Have you set up the Frankfurt meeting with Helmut yet?"

"Er...no, I haven't."

Dennison's neck lurched forward slightly.

"I was going to do it tomorrow, when—"

"No, now," Dennison growled in a low voice that had the force of a scream.

"Yes, Dennison, right away." Dennison watched him as he scurried away.

"They're waiting for you in the boardroom," said Maggie.

"I'll be right there." She peeled off and he stepped into his office.

There were only two things Dennison liked more than music, fashion and beautiful women — they were architecture and football. He didn't support a team. He regarded the very concept as outdated. He considered himself above the base tribalism and bias of supporting one club when there were so many excellent players to admire throughout all the big European teams. He would often attend live games in England, Italy, Spain or Germany.

The morning mail was on his desk. He swept the letters aside and went straight for a magazine wrapped in plastic — his subscription to *Architectural Review*. He smiled as he ripped it open and quickly scanned the pages. His favourite architects were;

Le Corbusier
Antoni Gaudi
Oscar Niemeyer
Eero Saarinen
Erich Mendelsohn
Frank Gehry
Daniel Libeskind
Santiago Calatrava
Zaha Hadid

When Gehry's Bilbao Guggenheim opened in October 1997 he flew there specially. He spent a day circling it, going through it section-by-section, marvelling at every curve and detail of its silver titanium surface.

As he flicked through the pages of the magazine he picked up his cup, took a sip of coffee and put it back down. And the cup made contact with the table he slid it along the surface slightly, in a kind of L-shape, before it came to rest. Then he glanced at his watch, picked up his coffee again, plus the pile of business plans, and headed for the boardroom.

Ten minutes into the meeting and he was already looking out of the window, bored with what his executives were telling him. Managing director Trevor Johnson, in his fifties, conservatively dressed and wearing thick-framed black spectacles, was leading the discussion.

"We've been through this month's business plans and identified four possible ventures that look attractive and that meet our criteria," he began. "Two of them have come through Richard Freeton over at Parallax, and the other two are independents. I've been through them myself and the numbers look good. Dennison, I left the details on your desk for you to review..."

Dennison was distracted. He glanced down at his cup of coffee on the table in front of him. He stared hard at it, as if he was in a trance. Then he picked it up and slowly began pouring its entire contents onto the table. Everybody froze as the hot coffee formed a steaming lake in front of him.

Trevor balked with shock, then looked at the others in the room, as if to check that they were seeing what he was seeing. "Dennison, what are you doing?" he asked.

Dennison took his time to say nothing, keeping his eyes on the puddle. "I've been through the business plans, Trevor," he said. "They look excellent."

"Well....Good."

"But I don't think we should back them," said Dennison.

A curious silence filled the room. "Why not?" asked Trevor.

"They're boring," replied Dennison.

"Boring?" Trevor glared at him as if he did not understand what the word meant.

"I want us to back projects that are exciting."

"What?" said one of the junior execs.

"That's right. The four start-ups we've selected are all good bets and they'll probably make us a lot of money — but so what?" Dennison sneered and shrugged at the same time.

"But Dennison," said Trevor, removing his glasses and pinching the bridge of his nose. "Isn't that why we are in business?"

Dennison flashed his eyes at Trevor in a manner that made him feel like a child. "I know why we are in business, Trevor. I started this company, remember?"

Trevor could only meet his gaze for three seconds before looking away. He put down his pen, sat back in his chair and sighed deeply. "So, what do you want to do, Dennison?"

"I want us to back the losers."

"Sorry?"

"That's right. I want us to pick the most exciting, most innovative ideas, make them work, turn them into winners. Get involved with the entrepreneurs, revise their plans if necessary, then take a bigger cut for the privilege. We have to think differently to the other venture firms."

The room fell into a hush. Trevor rubbed his temple with exasperation.

"But that'll take a lot more management time, Dennison," said another junior exec.

"So what," replied Dennison. "We've made money. You all earn generous salaries. The question we need to ask ourselves is, what do we do now? Just make more? Why? That's dumb. We must look at content. You need to check your craniums on this — all of you." Dennison tapped his skull three times, as if to remind everyone where their brains were located.

Just then, the phone rang next to him. He answered. "Sorry to interrupt, Dennison, but John Carver's here to see you," said Maggie.

"I'll be right there." Dennison hung up and rose to his feet. "Let's work on a new list of possibles, OK?"

John Carver was waiting in Dennison's office. He was thirty-eight, with a round, fleshy face, studious looking in silver wire-rimmed spectacles. He was watching the football on the television in the corner of the room, totally immersed in the action. In his hand was a packet of cheap biscuits, Custard Creams. He munched on them ravenously, eating each one whole, as if they were crisps.

Dennison entered. John broke off, stuffed the biscuits into the inside pocket of his jacket, then grinned sheepishly at his client. "Italian football, huh? You can't beat it."

Dennison stared at him blankly. It was only because he needed his services that he tolerated him. John knew this, and it amused him no end. He was good at his job, arguably the best in London, and so Dennison was forced to deal with him.

"Well?" Dennison asked coldly.

John was irritated by Dennison's lack of engagement. He'd just asked him about football — a subject he knew he loved — but Dennison had ignored him. He was insulted. He pretended not to know what Dennison was talking about. "Huh?"

"What did you find out?"

"A little."

Dennison stared impatiently. John took his time, relishing the temporary power he had over his client.

"Spain," said John eventually.

"What?"

"That's where she is."

Dennison glanced at the photograph of him and Alice on his desk. "Living there?"

"Don't know yet. Working on it."

"That all?"

"So far."

"Come back when you've got news," said Dennison, muffling

his irritation. "Real news."

Dennison was annoyed. John could have relayed what he had on the telephone, but he liked to see his client in person, so he could watch him squirm. Dennison produced an envelope of money from his desk and threw it towards his head. John just about caught it.

What — you can't even hand it to me? Wanker.

John reached into his pocket, took out a biscuit and crunched it, deliberately letting the crumbs fall onto the carpet.

13

That evening Erskine ventured along the Embankment until he came to a large single-decker passenger cruiser with a glass roof. He checked the name, *The Barracuda*, with the flyer he took from the bar promoting Natascha's gig. He stepped onto the gantry, paid the entrance fee and boarded. He concealed himself by mingling amongst groups of other passengers. He sat at a corner table at the back, farthest from the stage. He scanned the audience. They were smartly dressed, over thirties. Erskine could tell by the way certain groups clustered eagerly around the stage that many were fans that had come specially to see the band.

Soon the boat's engine gurgled into life and its huge frame lumbered away from the pier, bobbing gently from side to side. It moved away slowly and began its careful journey along the Thames, low in the water beside the procession of towering buildings that lined the route, each with their contours stitched in light.

Inside there was a hush as the band appeared, followed by polite applause. Three men. Double bass, piano, drums. A pared down combo, specially designed for a sparse, haunting sound. They started to play. First, the double bass with a low menacing loop, then the piano and drums.

When the rhythm was in full swing, Natascha strolled out under the lights. She was wearing a black sequinned dress with a plunging neckline. A roar went up. An middle-aged man sprang to his feet and began clapping wildly above his head. Erskine was the only one in the audience who wasn't clapping. He was shocked at the crowd's enthusiastic greeting. He looked around at them in their excited rapture, then he leaned forward and squinted at this diva, to see if it really was the same woman he'd met in the bar previously. She was changed in her guise of glamour — the dress, the hair, the confidence, the attitude. His mouth fell open at the totality of her metamorphosis.

Natascha ignored the eruption of noise, stepped up to the microphone and began to sing. Her voice soared in the air, a twisting, soulful, melancholic sound. Erskine tuned into the lyrics:

I'm not sure about loving you
The hard thing to figure is what to do
A part of me's afraid of being two

Erskine took out the camcorder and began filming her singing, zooming in on her face. He found himself being drawn into her pathos, and he felt his mood changing, as if his emotions were wired to hers via some invisible umbilical. She unclipped the microphone from the stand and wandered out amongst the crowd, engaging with faces. The spotlight tracked her, amplifying the sheen of her dress and the sparkle in her eyes.

After the encore the crowd erupted. Erskine watched as men got up from their seats, slamming their hands together in appreciation, half respect, half lust.

Amongst those showing their appreciation was her best friend, Megan. She was in her mid-thirties, tall and elegantly beautiful, her facial features subtly caved and boned. There were times when she hated the skullishness of her appearance, and others when she liked its uniqueness. She was married with two children, living the opposite life to her best friend. They were drawn together by their differences, their sense of humour, and by their appreciation of each other's beauty. These simple connections had sustained them for years. Natascha envied the fact that Megan was married with two children, and had sustainable love in her life. She looked upon her with a certain curiosity, because she was a working example of something Natascha did not think was possible.

Natascha took her bow, gestured to the band, and they stepped forward and took theirs, and then it was over. The boat docked back at the Embankment and the guests began to shuffle out.

As the band started to pack up, Charlie, the bass player, sneaked secret looks at Natascha's body, her black figure curving like a panther in her skin-tight dress. Megan rushed over to her, gushing with enthusiasm. "You were great," she said. "So great. Every time I come to see you it just seems to get better."

"Thanks, Megan," said Natascha, squeezing her hand. She felt euphoric, but also hollow in her chest as she came off stage to no one — as she came away loveless.

"And where'd you get that amazing dress?" asked Megan.

"Oh, it's just one of my secondhand things."

"It's great." Megan looked her up and down with admiration and envy. They kissed and hugged, and Megan departed with a loving wave. "I'll see you in art class," she said.

Charlie saw the gap and walked casually over. He slipped his arm around Natascha's waist. She smiled at him, her lips curving upwards out of politeness rather than affection.

"Nat, me and the boys are going for a drink after," he began. "Want to join us?"

"No thanks, Charlie."

He hesitated, then said "OK....Shall I come round later?"

"No. I'm tired." There was the smile again — the polite twist of her mouth. The kind of smile an airline stewardess gives to an annoying passenger. Charlie backed away, concealing his disappointment.

Erskine had been watching close by. He approached Natascha from behind. Charlie saw him and watched as he packed away his equipment, pretending not to see, or care. Natascha turned sharply as she heard Erskine's voice behind her, and for an instant they were silenced by the sight of one another. She remembered him from the bar. She asked him what he was doing there and how he'd managed to find her. When he told her, she was annoyed and impressed that he'd gone to all that trouble to track her down. She was attracted by his newness, by the fact that she knew nothing about him, and that sex with him only existed within her imagination, unlike her other lovers who had grown stale from familiarity.

Erskine asked her to walk with him, no particular destination, and she heard a voice reply, "Yes," but she would swear that it was not hers.

They strolled along the Embankment. The promenade was beautifully illuminated against the night. Erskine re-assessed her face against the street lights. No make-up — a raw, unprocessed beauty. She wore flared jeans, flat slip-ons and a simple white vest under a lightweight black jacket.

As Natascha looked at Erskine her eyes were animated but her facial expression remained blank. There was a hardness, a caution to her now, unlike the night they met, when she was drunk and loose. Now she was closed and coiled — her emotions locked in storage deep within her. Erskine realised now that this was how she was, that on the night they met it was the alcohol that had opened her, and now the lack of it that had closed her again.

He complimented her on her performance, and she shrugged modestly. Then he asked how she was. She nodded in a meaningless way. She spoke in short sentences, listening, but not saying what she really thought. She stared without looking at him. Like someone glancing at words without reading them. He asked her something else — some kind of question — and she looked at him as if the question was so inconsequential that she could not be bothered to respond.

They came to a late night café and stopped for drinks. They made a move for a vacant table, and Erskine ambled nervously, not knowing whether to sit down first or to wait for her to do so before him. Finally they sat down together. He ordered coffee and she asked for a tin of lemonade and a plain croissant. As the waitress left he got up and went to the toilet. On his way back she glanced quickly at his groin, wondering about his penis, and what it might feel like inside her compared to the others in her collection.

When their order arrived she slipped off her jacket and took an enthusiastic bite of her croissant. Erskine watched as the pastry flaked and settled delicately on her vest like a cascade of tiny broken wings. Instead of brushing them off she left them there, as if they were part of her clothing now. She opened her tin of lemonade. Erskine glanced at her as he heard the *psst* and *cluup* of the ring-pull. He watched as she parted her lips and put the can to her mouth. He was aroused by this, and by the sight of her body in the vest. The outline of her breasts was an obvious attraction, but it was her neck and shoulders that drew him the most — they had a ballet dancers poise and elegance.

"Don't you want to know if I'm single?" he asked randomly.

She shrugged her shoulders. "What difference does it make?"

Erskine wanted to know what was behind her statement, what had happened to make her this way. This was not his business, but he was intrigued by her secrecy, and desired her more as a result. He watched her mouth, as if he was waiting for some exposition to tumble out.

She stared out of the café window, suddenly thinking about her mother. She wondered how she was, all alone in her house. She'd wanted to phone her earlier that day, but she hadn't. It was a chore she didn't want to do, and it made her feel guilty. She wondered if the reason she didn't call was because she no longer loved her as she once did. Ten years ago she would not have hesitated to call, even for the slightest of reasons, just to chat, just to hear her voice — but not now. She felt ashamed that after everything her mother had done for her, she was slowly phasing her out, loving her less with each passing year.

Erskine registered a change in her face, a mask of melancholy. She saw him looking, maybe on the brink of asking her why, and so she turned away from him. This broke the moment, and they got up to leave. Erskine watched as Natascha slipped on her jacket. Its collar became twisted, and so he reached out and straightened it, simultaneously touching the skin on her neck. She turned and looked at him, wondering what that touch meant, or if it was an accident.

They went back to her flat by the River Thames at Hammersmith. She didn't want to at first. She preferred to have sex with him at his place, so she could leave whenever she pleased. But she was tired from the gig that night and she had a bag of clothes with her, and so she relented. When they arrived Erskine stepped into the lounge and scanned the room. He focused on the jacket covers of classic jazz LPs she had displayed along the floor, propped against the wall like art. On the table there was a framed picture of her as a child with her father.

CD's nestled in angular piles everywhere, some exposed, with others in their covers. On the floor lay a large mound of pistachio shells. Four full-length black dresses were draped around the room on doors and hooks, shimmering under the light. But dominating the centre of the space was a harp, ornately decorated in gold and silver. Erskine gasped as he saw it. "You play?"

She nodded. "Ever since I was twelve."

She could see that Erskine was impressed, and this embarrassed her. She did not want to give him cause to like her, or to stay longer than necessary. She fiddled with her hair, then buried her hands in the back pockets of her jeans.

There were things she thought she wanted to say to him. The words revolved in satellite in her head — a carousel of options waiting to be selected. When the silence became unbearable she walked over to the CD player. *A Love Supreme* by John Coltrane (1964) kicked in, the shrill sweetness of its saxophone intro filling the room.

She turned the volume down, then went off to the kitchen to get drinks. She came back and handed him a glass. As he reached for it he accidentally touched her fingers, and in a reflex she retracted them, almost like she would from a hot stove. Erskine pretended not to notice. He had touched her again. A second signal — another prelude to things.

"Where do you live?" she asked.

"I've got a one-bedroomed flat on the moon," he quipped, trying to lighten things. "That zero gravity thing's a bitch though. I keep hitting my head on the ceiling."

Natascha let out a controlled laugh. Short and reserved. He asked her if she lived alone. She said she did. "Don't you get lonely?" he enquired.

"There's nothing wrong with loneliness," she replied coldly. "There are worse things in life."

He toured her flat, complimenting her on its cultured decor. She moved in his wake, watching him like an animal wary of attack. When they reached the kitchen she stopped and busied herself, preparing a snack. A salad was still in the colander in the sink. She turned on the taps and flushed the leaves, even though she'd already washed them earlier.

As they ate he studied the form of her mouth. He picked a moment and tried to kiss her, but she turned her head sideways — a gesture like a baby being offered food it does not want. Erskine was embarrassed. *What did you get me round here for if you don't want to fuck?*

She got up and walked to the window. He followed and stood behind her and they both watched the flow of the river outside. She felt his face at her shoulder, like a kind of heat. She half-turned and they exchanged a transparent kiss — a hollow delight, full of space, like an Easter egg.

What are you doing here? she thought. *Intruder.*

Erskine turned her by her shoulders and kissed her again, testing her mouth. Her eyes were open, watching him, and he realised that his were too. As his mouth met hers once more he thought of all the women he'd ever kissed in his life, and all the emotions he'd left behind with them, like jettisoned cargo.

They pulled away from each other and tried to talk again, but things were corrupted now. Erskine kissed her again, harder this time, trying to arouse something, to press out a sign. She met his energy, as if it was a contest. He ran his hand audaciously across her breasts and then down into her underwear, his finger against the groove of her. He would steal a sample of her moistness, as a memento for when he walked away later, and also to see if she smelt like his Genevieve. She let him do it, challenging him to arouse her, ready to sneer secretly at any lack of skill in his eager fingers.

Erskine thought about Dennison's proposition — that he had to film her to get the money — but he felt that he could not stop for that now. It was too late — and he already felt too guilty.

As they undressed Natascha thought of her other lovers. She considered that she'd never promised to be faithful to them. *Them.* As if she was married to them all equally, and therefore owed them fidelity. She realised that she was becoming like her father, and this made her feel sick. She wanted to stop, but she felt she couldn't now.

His hands found the stations on her body, like stops on a railway —the curve of her back, the nobbled track of her spine, the imperfect circularity of her breasts, the concave pools in the sides of her hips, the pepper of freckles behind her left ear. He focused on her hair, the way it fell across her face like a nest of cables, each settlement a fresh configuration, a new art.

He entered her, the connection taut and smooth. Somehow he could not believe that he was actually inside her, after everything, after all her resistance. As she gripped his flesh the air eased out of her lungs in a mellow gust, and she blew it gently into his mouth, like a present.

And in the sexual language of the strangers their connection was silent, two noiseless engines, all their energy in the action.

Sound seemed inappropriate in their synchronised see-saw. He had not earned the right to enjoy the audible gestures she might make if she loved him — her whispers, her moans of pleasure. No man had.

Natascha recorded this new intruder. The feel of his muscles, the texture of his skin, the weight of his touch, the proportions of his penis. She extended her neck sideways from her body — an action like an Indian dancer — and watched Erskine as he moved against her, assessing his thrust and rhythm with a certain detachment, as if the body beneath the head was not hers; as if she was there to judge, not enjoy. She tabulated and compared him with her stable of other lovers, placing him within a secret top ten in her mind.

She had lost some of her sense of pleasure. She could not extricate herself from her own caution, her anxiety and her fear of losing control. She wondered what she was doing it for, sexing him, if she could not even surrender to it.

She turned and pressed her backside against him and let him enter her from there where he could not read her, where he could not see her eyes or sample her mouth.

She had decided that she would have an orgasm, that she would authorise it, but it would be an empty delight, like an ice-cream cone with nothing inside.

But then strangely, against her will, she began to feel an intensity in their connection. As if to verify it she turned to face him, and quickly he slid over her, pushing himself inside her again, unable to stop. His eyes met hers, the pace quickened and they both felt themselves losing their caution. She felt a maddening friction as he rubbed against her insides, and the contact sparked her pelvis, bucking to meet his.

Their orgasm burned with intensity, beyond what either of them had ever experienced. They stared at each other, madly, fearfully, as if they'd both been punched suddenly in the face. In the confused pleasure of the moment they wondered how they, strangers, could connect so perfectly, so without rehearsal. And in that moment it occurred to them that they were strangers to themselves, as well as each other.

The energy subsided, and the two spent, fleshy slabs lay heaving and glistening under the low light and the stillness of the night. As their bodies crackled in the electric air the strangers rolled away from each other, alone again, afraid of what had happened, unable to comprehend it.

She wanted Erskine to leave, but he lay there waiting for either of them to say something about what had just happened, to offer some adjective of explanation. She turned to him, suddenly impatient. "You have to leave now."

"What?"

"Please go."

Erskine was stunned by her coldness. He stumbled up, backed into a bedside lamp with a porcelain base. It hit the floor and smashed, plunging them into semi-darkness.

Natascha looked away painfully. "Leave it," she said. "Just leave it and go."

14

The ring road that surrounded the grassy island of Shepherd's Bush Green was log-jammed with traffic, as usual — spewing forth its mass of noise and dirty air. Through the closed window of his flat overlooking the scene, Erskine could hear a low earthquake of engines, a continuous *duuuuuuududddu*. He looked disdainfully at the cars crawling slowly forward like suffering beasts. He saw a TVR, a beauty in gunmetal grey, its sculpted chassis sunk low and tilted like some kind of italic, its bulbous curves suspended in the gridlock like a thoroughbred caught in a net.

The Green was a desolate tundra. Deep tyre marks gorged its surface like wounds — the residue of a travelling circus that had recently departed. Blades of grass lay flattened and mangled and patches of land were stripped bare. Shrubs, stunted by the dead earth, refused to grow, and naked tree branches contorted like cursed bones. There was no life out there on this day. Benches without people, the playground without children.

Erskine pressed his forehead gently against the windowpane, feeling its fresh sting, then he pulled back and studied the hazy residue left by his skin. A cloud-shaped gel. A Vaseline. He put his finger in it and improvised a squiggle, then rubbed it away.

He wanted to open the window but he did not dare. He had to wait until late when things were calmer. But things were seldom calm here. There was always some kind of turbulence. Even though he'd only been living there a short while, already he hated it — the litter, the traffic, the crowds. He wanted to be somewhere else, but he did not know where.

He gazed up into the sky. The weather was a loop of confusion. Today it was cold and bitter. Yesterday it was half cold, half sunny. He turned from the window and scanned the room. He hadn't cleaned for months. Shoes, clothes, newspapers and empty bottles lay everywhere in a mosaic of untidiness. Dust filmed every surface. In the kitchen, dirty plates, cups and cutlery lay slumped in uneasy piles. He began to tidy up, but then he was struck by the fact that he would only have to repeat the act tomorrow and the day after that. He felt the futility of it all, so he stopped, sat down and did nothing.

Pictures of Genevieve were still present — in a frame on the table, another in the draw next to his bed, close to hand. He'd also kept some of her clothes. His favourite things: a black trouser suit, a pair of her shoes, her floppy felt hat.

Erskine remembered how, when they first met, she did not love him straight away. She was cautious. She'd dated playboys and time-wasters in her past, and the hurt had made her cautious. He captured her gradually in a slow lasso.

He proposed while walking through Richmond Park one afternoon. "Marriage is such a cliché, though," she replied. "I thought we were cooler than that somehow."

"Don't you want to be Mrs Eskimo?"

"Sounds chilly."

"Ho, ho, ho. Tell you what. Let's toss a coin."

Genevieve looked horrified, then she suddenly became animated. "OK, do it, do it now, before I come to my senses," she insisted, waggling both hands in the air.

Erskine produced a coin. "OK. Heads, we get married, tails, we forget the whole thing."

Erskine cheated to get the result he wanted, and Genevieve knew, but she did not protest. They went home to celebrate with sex and champagne. Afterwards they lay together, with Genevieve wearing nothing but her black felt hat. Erskine took it from her and put it on his own head.

"I just had a thought, Eskimo," she began.

"What's that, Fruitcake?"

"If I jumped off the earth and into space right now, and hung there and waited for the planet to turn, eventually you would come back to me."

Erskine stared at her lovingly. "That's the most amazing thing I've ever heard." He turned and kissed her.

"Will we be married for ever, Eskimo?"

"Yes." She smiled, held him tighter.

"Say we'll be married forever. Say it as if it's a vow."

"We'll be married forever, Fruitcake. For all time."

The marriage would last three years.

*

Erskine went into the bathroom and took a shower. As he stood under the jet of water he discovered a single strand of Natascha's hair, intertwined in a deformed figure of eight within his own pubic hair. He pulled it carefully away, as if he was pulling the ribbon from a present, and laid it on the edge of the bath so he could see it against the white enamel surface.

He stepped out, dried himself and flopped onto the sofa in a t-shirt and track bottoms. Then he rolled a joint and smoked it slowly as he stared at the wall, feeling hollow, unable to move. He had burned many days and nights in this manner, unable to find function or will.

He placed his fingernails to his nose. Natascha's aroma still lingered slightly. Thoughts of her flooded his brain. The video recorder lay on the sofa next to him. He picked it up, opened the viewer and turned it on. He watched the footage of her singing that he'd recorded earlier. Instantly he became intoxicated by her melancholy vocal style, calling out as if she was wounded.

His sexual connection with her was more potent than it had been with Genevieve, and he was ashamed of it. This new woman, this stranger, had no right to be better than her in this way, no right to take up such space within his consciousness. In his mind he tried to compress the volume of his memory of her, like a tent folding into a bag.

He went back into the bathroom and picked up the strand of Natascha's hair that he had retrieved earlier. His held it up to the light, then dropped it into the bath and flushed it away.

He found himself in the bedroom, lying on his front on the unmade bed. He did not re-collect moving there, or how long ago it had happened. It was getting dark outside, and the room took on a sinister air, with jagged shadows falling across the walls and floor like black knives. He looked apprehensively at them, as if he expected to be stabbed by one of the shards.

Genevieve's hat lay on a chair in a corner. He looked at it, thinking again about her, when suddenly it lifted off the chair and hovered in the air like a flying saucer. Erskine gazed at it with mild surprise. His psychosis started soon after Genevieve was gone, and after he started smoking skunk to help him forget. The episodes came and went, and he had almost grown accustomed to them now.

Before long he fell asleep in his clothes. He dreamt that he was sitting astride a glistening black racehorse covered in fire, galloping across a field of white flowers. As he glanced across he saw Genevieve sprinting parallel to him, half a mile away, moving at the same speed as the horse. Suddenly she changed course, coming towards him, and then she jumped high into the air, an Olympic long jumper's leap, her legs bicycling, until she landed behind him on the galloping stallion, and with one breath she blew out the flames on the horse's body and tugged the reins and slowed it down, and the horse stopped peacefully in the field of white flowers.

15

As Erskine turned off Holland Park Avenue and onto Addison Road, he immediately felt out of place amongst the houses of the rich that lined the route. As got to Dennison Carr's house he stepped through the gate and stopped as he saw the cars in the drive. He circled all of them in turn, cupping his hands to the windows and peering inside, nodding to himself at Dennison's good taste.

When he rang the doorbell he was surprised when Dennison answered it himself. He'd somehow expected a butler, like the rich have in movies. Inside, the house was a picture of taste and style. For two years, *World of Interiors* had been pursuing Dennison to feature it, but he had no interest in publicity. The finishes were glass, dark timber, leather and stainless steel. The walls were plain white. There were big vases full of oversized wild flowers, deep-pile rugs, cut-crystal chandeliers, antique Chinese cabinets, Italian sofas, and classic designs by Eames, Corbusier and Jacobsen.

In the reception room there was an antique Swedish sofa, lemon yellow and black with curved ends, upholstered in Malmö. Sitting on it with an outstretched arm cradling the frame was Hof. Rossi Nante and Richard Rieff were also present.

Dennison showed Erskine into his study. As Erskine stepped inside he felt a strange excitement at seeing him again. Immediately Erskine scanned the room, marvelling at the interior. "So, what business are you in exactly?" he asked.

"I'm in the business of business," replied Dennison cryptically.

Erskine huffed. "Well, you've done well...from business. Clearly." He nodded to himself. "So you really do have the money to blow on this...this...game?"

As Erskine spoke he saw the peak of Dennison's black hat begin to stretch and expand plastically, swelling in size like a huge amorphous oil spill, until it formed a shadowy roof engulfing the whole room. He looked up apprehensively at the shifting mass, then he blinked and everything was normal.

"So you slept with all three, but you didn't film the last one," said Dennison. "That's what you said on the phone, correct?"

"Yes."

"So, why didn't you film the last one? What was so special about her?" Dennison stared at him intensely. Erskine squirmed.

"Nothing. I just missed my chance, that's all."

"But then you slept with her anyway," said Dennison. "Why? You knew at that point that you'd blown the other two thousand. What was the point?"

"I just wanted to, OK?"

Dennison looked into Erskine's eyes, trying to fathom why a man who needed money as badly as he would throw away such an opportunity. "OK," said Dennison. "I believe you."

"Whatever," said Erskine. "Are you going to kill me?"

"If I were, you'd be dead already," Dennison replied. He held out his hand. "The recordings?"

Erskine hesitated. "I can't give you them."

"Why?"

"It's not right."

Dennison was amused by Erskine's sudden morality. "We had a deal."

"I know."

Dennison leaned forward menacingly. "The recordings, Erskine." He stretched out his palm even further.

Erskine stared at him, deciding what to do. Slowly, he reached into his pocket and pulled out a micro-cassette. Dennison took it, snapped it in half and dropped it in the bin.

Erskine was aghast. "What the fuck are you doing?"

"I have no use for it."

"What? So what did you get me to do it for in the first place?"

Dennison smirked. "Just to see."

Erskine sighed in disbelief. But he was relieved also. In that moment he respected Dennison a little more. The rest of the money was already on the table in a white envelope. Dennison handed it to Erskine, who peeped inside at the cash, and smiled.

"Let me ask you," Erskine began. "How did you know I would say yes to all this?"

"You tell me." Dennison replied.

Erskine looked thoughtful. After some moments he rose to his feet and shook Dennison's hand. "Well, I think I'll be on my way then," he said. "It's been interesting meeting you."

Dennison was insulted by Erskine's use of the word 'interesting'. He'd have preferred if he'd said, 'incredible'.

Erskine turned and started walking. He couldn't believe it. He had the other two thousand after all, even though he hadn't completed the assignment. Dennison allowed him take a few steps before he spoke. "Before you leave, Erskine — tell me something?"

He turned. "What?"

"Did you get what you wanted...out of the experience?"

Erskine hesitated. "I think so," he said. "Why?"

Dennison stared at him for some seconds, as if he was waiting for him to answer his own question. As if there was more to his answer than even Erskine knew.

"Come with me," said Dennison, extending an arm. "There are some people I'd like you to meet."

In the reception room further along the corridor, the three men sat patiently. Hof sat next to Richard, while Rossi sat at a distance, on a chair by himself, staring out of the window. Hof was chewing gum loudly, his mouth producing a squelchy sound, *chglym-chglym-chglym*.

"Eight," he said to Richard.

"No way!"

"Yeah, geezer. Eight minutes. I timed it — from meeting her, to sex. She was an airline stewardess. Virgin. I got talking to her in the street, and then before I knew it she was blowing me in the toilets of a pub. Fucking unbelievable. Un-belie-vable!"

Richard looked impressed. "Respect!" Then he turned to Rossi. "What about you, mate?"

Rossi ignored him. "Doesn't talk much, does he?" said Richard. Rossi looked at him hatefully, as if he wanted to cut his throat.

Hof was distracted. "What do you think that thing is with men?" he asked.

"What thing?"

"Well, it's like, whenever I'm out and I see a fit girl, I instantly feel the urge to fuck her. *Instantly.* I just want to get inside her. Then, when it's over I want to go out and get somebody else and do the same to her. I just love it. What do you think that is? I mean, why are men like that?"

"I don't know."

"I mean, I was on the Tube the other day, and there was this babe sitting opposite me — total fucking babe, wearing this tight, tight, tight, low cut top. She had lovely breasts. Fucking lovely. And when I saw them I just felt the urge to rip the fucking top off her right there and start going at it. I got a hard-on just thinking about it."

As they laughed, the door swung open and Dennison and Erskine entered. Immediately the three men turned to scrutinise the newcomer. They introduced themselves in turn. Rossi was the only one who did not speak as they shook hands.

"Congratulations, gentlemen," Dennison began, pacing the room. "You have all successfully completed part one of the proposition," he said.

Erskine frowned. "What?

"You were all set the same assignment, albeit with different women. To sleep with three in four." Dennison held up the fingers.

"We are the champions of the sex Olympics," said Hof, nodding smugly.

"What is this all about?" asked Erskine.

"You have all been hand-picked by me for the next round."

"The next round of what?" asked Erskine.

"The proposition," said Dennison, holding up a finger. "You men are now a team. I set you assignments to seduce women, you go forth and conquer — you get paid."

"We get laid, we get paid," said Hof, as if the sentence was an advertising slogan or a lyric from a rap song.

"You make it sound so simple," said Richard.

"You think it's complex?" asked Dennison. "It's not. Experimental physics — that's complex."

Rossi looked at Dennison and nodded in agreement.

"Do we get paid the same amount as before?" asked Richard.

"No. A thousand for each of them was, let's say, an introductory offer. From now on you'll get half that."

"So, we're like, secret sex agents," said Hof, warming to his new role. "Superheroes. Like the Fantastic Four."

"Like the X-Men," said Richard.

"Like, Sexmen," proclaimed Hof, striking a pose.

"So you are going to pay the four of us to fuck women?" asked Erskine matter-of-factly. "What is the point of that?"

"Most men are attracted by the prospect of sex with a variety of women, whether there's money to be made or not," said Dennison. "It's primal. Monogamy is a culturally induced habit, not our natural instinct. I'm just putting you all in touch with your true selves, that's all."

"So, you want us to be male prostitutes for you?" asked Erskine. "Is that it?"

Dennison looked offended. "This is not prostitution," he sneered. "To use terms like prostitute or even rent boy is an insult to the creativity of the proposition. There is no category for what I have created. None."

He looked at the gathering of men before him, the group he had created — and he felt a certain contentment — perhaps the same feeling a mother or father might feel at seeing all their children gathered for Christmas Day. Dennison had no family. For now these men were his family. His children.

Erskine surveyed his three new partners. He had not bargained on this. A feeling of insecurity washed over him — they were all good-looking. Better looking than him, he thought. He wondered if they were better at sex too, if their penises were bigger than his, if they could last longer than him without ejaculating. He looked at Hof, all cocksure and confident, and he wondered if he could make a woman orgasm with his mouth, like he could.

He studied Dennison curiously, trying to fathom his rationale. "Can I ask you a question?" he began.

Dennison made a gesture with his hand. "Where are you from? I mean, originally?"

"Let me ask you a question," Dennison countered. "How long can you sustain an erection?"

"Huh?"

"At the age of eighteen a man is at his sexual peak," said Dennison. "According to studies he can sustain an erection for one-hour-and-six-minutes, on average. This ability then declines with age until by the age of sixty-five it's down to just eight minutes."

"Speak for yourself," said Hof. "I'm in my prime right now mate — and totally Viagra free."

Dennison smiled at Hof's arrogance. "In practical terms being good at sex is a matter of simple ergonomics," he continued. "A penis must have a certain depth and girth, coupled with a strong lateral motion in the hips, plus the ability to sustain the action for a certain time span. It's pure mathematics."

Erskine looked him up and down suspiciously. "You batty?"

"Batty?" Dennison replied with veiled surprise. "Such a strange word to describe the homosexual condition, don't you think? Batty also means mad — as if somehow that's what you have to be, to be gay."

Hof looked at Dennison admiringly. "Man, you're as slick as juice," he said.

"But I still don't understand," said Erskine. "Why are you doing this?"

"Sometimes, one should not waste time with the why's of life, Erskine. The great thinkers of our age have pondered such questions throughout time, and it has only led them to one place. Depression."

"Amen!" said Hof.

Dennison's words somehow connected with Erskine. Since the proposition had begun he'd felt a strange energy within him, a craving for more women, something beyond orgasms and money, but he did not know what it was. All he knew was that the opportunity to continue somehow appealed to him.

Erskine looked over at Rossi and asked, "What do you make of all this?"

Rossi shrugged nonchalantly. "No point talking to him," said Hof. "He's the strong silent type."

"The proposition presents a unique opportunity," said Dennison. "The reason it works is because the women *want* the sex. This tells us something — that whatever lives these women lead — whether they're married or with a boyfriend — they are not satisfied. Without doubt, if I was to ask most women currently in relationships if they'd like more sex than they are getting right now, most would say yes."

"So, you're feminist then?" asked Erskine, half jokingly. "You're doing something for the lay-deez."

"These women you're going to choose for us, Dennison," said Richard. "They'd better be fit."

"Why do you always get to choose them, anyway?" asked Erskine.

"No more questions," said Dennison abruptly. "You don't need to ask me anything. All you need to do is what I tell you to do, OK?"

"Yeah but—"

"That is all," said Dennison finally. "We meet tomorrow night for round two."

Dennison escorted them to the door. They filed out of the driveway and onto Addison Road. Hof turned back for another look at Dennison's impressive abode. "This dude's made some serious wedge," he said admiringly. "Check out those cars."

"Not to mention the cut of his suits," said Richard. "What does he do for a living anyway?"

"I asked him that," said Hof. "He wouldn't say."

Erskine was deep in thought. "But why is he paying us to fuck girls?" he said. "It's weird. What's in it for him?"

"I reckon he's just kinky," Hof replied. "He probably goes home at night and wanks into a dirty pair of his grandma's baggies."

"Maybe he's impotent, and he's living vicariously through us," Richard suggested.

"Is that it?" said Erskine. "Just thrills? He's spending all that cash on us — for that?"

16

Dennison Carr was adopted at birth. He'd never met his real parents. He'd never sought them out at any time during his life. He figured that if they didn't want him, then he didn't want them. He did not love his foster parents. He respected them for taking him in and bringing him up, but he did not love them. They were not his real family. He knew this, even before they told him so.

Five years ago, after he had built up his venture capital firm, he was featured in a high profile business magazine. Soon afterwards a man tried to contact him. He ignored the calls to his office. Then the man appeared outside his house one evening when he was out.

Soon afterwards the moment finally came when they would meet. It was six-thirty one evening when Dennison left his office and went down the street to the car park. He'd driven the 1970 olive green Citroen SM on this occasion. As he walked towards it he tilted his head slightly to admire the way the light ricocheted off the curves of its elongated chassis. Much better than the E-type for shape, he thought. He stalled for a second before he put his key in the door, just to check the stretch of its lines, then he got inside and pulled away.

He pressed the button on the CD player and a tune, *Cold Sweat*, by James Brown (1967) kicked in. As he stopped at the car park checkpoint the attendant leaned out of his booth as he heard the music in his car.

"James, huh?"

"Exactly," Dennison replied. His expression suddenly brightened, like an excited child, gratified that he had found an unexpected musical soul mate. "James was a musical genius — but he was also a monstrous egotist," Dennison offered. "If you listen to a masterpiece like *Mother Popcorn* for example, the extended version, you'll hear that even when Maceo takes his solo, James won't keep quiet — he still has to sing underneath the saxophone. He always needed to be centre stage." The attendant narrowed his eyes and nodded slowly and thoughtfully, as if that was the wisest comment he'd ever heard.

As Dennison drove out of the entrance and prepared to pull onto the street, he looked across the road and saw a man on the pavement staring at him. He was tall, elderly, with thick grey hair, wearing a white shirt with beige slacks. They shared the same lean, angular build. The man's eyes were sad and hopeful. Dennison's heart bucked against his rib cage. Instantly he knew.

And where is the accomplice? The bitch that brewed me, then gave me up? I hope she's dead, and I hope you join her soon, you motherfucker, you cunt, you absolute fucking cunt.

Almost involuntarily his left hand came away from the steering wheel, shaking and tensing, and curved into a fist.

The man stepped off the kerb hesitantly and began walking toward the car. Dennison's eyes sparkled coldly, his neck lurched forward like a crow about to strike. As he gripped the steering wheel his arms began to quake slightly with rage. The rage of forty-five years. He punched down hard on the accelerator, a tidal wave of hurt channelling along his leg and through the sole of his foot, and the car roared towards the man, picking up speed. This was the moment he had longed for, that he had dreamt about. Vengeance was finally his. He drew closer and closer to the man's elderly frame, picturing the kill, enjoying it, but then at the final second he swerved the car away and pressed on, driving past the man forever without looking back. For a moment he felt weak for not killing him, but then he thought it better that he stay alive to suffer his guilt.

Sometime later, a letter arrived in the post. It was from him. It was full of the usual apologies and excuses, stretched over two handwritten pages. It concluded with an invitation for them to meet. To start again.

Dennison wrote back. He would not give the man the pleasure of a personal reply scripted in his own handwriting, and so he typed his reply and printed it off in cold black ink on stark white paper.

After forty-five years of silence he only had four words to say to him;

It's too late. Father.

17

Natascha rose early the next morning. Alone. The way she preferred it. Her lovers always left in the night, like satisfied thieves. She slipped her robe over her underwear, and it billowed and rippled gracefully as she walked to the kitchen. After a light breakfast she began rehearsing her set for a gig that evening. First she warmed up by singing along to a compilation jazz CD, *Essential Ella*, by Ella Fitzgerald (2005). As she sang she performed a private dance for herself, swaying and bending her body like a ballerina.

She accidentally kicked the mound of pistachio shells she'd left on the floor. She stooped and picked up a handful, then held them up to her ear and shook them like maracas. Then she threw them onto the floor like dice, just to see where they'd fall.

She stripped off and slipped into a black evening dress she'd bought to wear on stage. It was full-length, sleeveless, sequinned, with a swooping V-neck. She'd purchased it secondhand and had it altered to fit. She checked herself in the mirror, making sure the neckline didn't reveal too much cleavage. She liked to dress up at home. It made her feel detached from the person she was, as if she could only tolerate her true personality for short periods. She drew comfort from her ability to take a brief sabbatical from herself, like a child playing fancy dress.

But for all her tasks and chores about the house, she could not forget him. She replayed the events of their night together, trying to comprehend what had happened. She did not believe in "women's romance" — the fairy tales, the knight in shining armour, mister right, the one, or any such notion that implied that a woman's place was to wait for a man to arrive in order to activate her life. But the facts about Erskine troubled her. And now because of that one night he stood out from all the other men she'd had. Whether she liked it or not this made him special. She hated this, hated being the subject of such a dependency, like some hapless victim from a Mills & Boon novel. She was doomed to want him again.

She tried to busy herself once more, trying not to think of him. She continued rehearsing, only to be interrupted by a knock at the door. It was the postman delivering a large package. She was puzzled, as she was not expecting anything. She put it down on the table and cut it open. Inside was a new bedside lamp with a porcelain base. She froze with disbelief. She took it out of the box, examined it, put it on the table, groped a loose hand inside for a note — but there wasn't one. She stared at the lamp, slowly backed away from it, and then walked toward it again. She picked it up, hoisted it above her head and smashed it down onto the floor.

*

Early that evening Natascha met Megan at a local school for their twice-weekly evening class in still life drawing. It was a mixed group of all ages, but predominantly populated by women. The class were in the middle of a rendering of a male nude, gathered in a semi-circle around him, as he posed semi-reclining on an old grey two-seater sofa, his arm extended along its back. He was young and fit, with a hairy chest and strongly defined facial features. Natascha and Megan were keen students. They sketched with focus and concentration, eager to get the details and proportions right.

"So, who is he?" asked Megan.

Natascha shrugged. "I don't know. Some guy."

"Another guy named some guy," Megan replied with a shake of her head. "Boy, I don't know how you can sleep with them so fast."

"It's better that way."

Megan sighed. "I could never do it."

"What?"

"Just fuck some guy I didn't know," said Megan, her expression washed with slight disgust. "I just couldn't."

She stopped drawing for a moment, studied Natascha's face, then sighed sympathetically. "Darling, aren't you tired of sleeping with these guys?"

"No."

"Oh, come on, Nat. Isn't that what promiscuity is really all about? Finding someone?"

"Not for me. Not after last time. I'm happy on my own."

Megan frowned. "How can anybody be happy alone?"

Natascha thought of her mother, alone and loveless, her husband gone. Megan's face brightened. "So, tell me," she said excitedly.

"What?"

"Come on. What was it like? Did he go down on you for hours? Tie you up? What?"

Natascha looked pensive, despite Megan's childish excitement.

"This one was different," she said.

Megan reached for her coffee. "What do you mean, different?"

Natascha stopped drawing, turned to the window and stared blankly out, as if she was in a trance. "The thing is, when we had sex, it...it was so intense. It was like nothing I've ever experienced before...I don't know Meg...I kind of screamed inside," she said. "I came so hard, it was as if...as if I went mad."

Megan froze — her coffee cup pressed against her bottom lip.

18

For their next assignment the men gathered in a hotel lobby close to Bond Street, in Central London. Rossi was the last to arrive. As he sat down, Erskine turned to Dennison and asked, "Why didn't you tell us Rossi was deaf?"

"He's what?" said Hof. All eyes turned to Rossi.

"Really?" said Richard. "Like Holly Hunter in *The Piano*."

"Very good, Erskine," smirked Dennison. "You are obviously a very bright man."

Erskine couldn't work out if Dennison was being sarcastic. Either way he didn't like being called "bright". He thought it made him sound like a light bulb instead of someone who was intelligent.

"I was wondering why it took you all so long to figure it out," said Dennison. "Rossi and I decided it was more fun to keep it a secret." Rossi nodded and they both laughed.

"I thought he was a bit too quiet," said Richard.

While everyone stared at Rossi, Erskine looked at Dennison, wondering about what else he may have omitted to tell them. Hof was scrutinising Rossi in a new way. "So, how does he get the girls to fuck him, then?" He directed the question at Dennison, as if Rossi didn't understand.

"Why don't you ask him?" Dennison replied. "He understands English."

Hof turned to Rossi and asked him the question, speaking very slowly. Rossi huffed, like an old man huffs at a fool, then indicated that he used pencil and paper.

"He writes his lines down?" asked Richard. "He must be a total poet."

"Why can't we see the women again, after we sleep with them," asked Erskine abruptly. "I mean, if we want to?"

"You cannot carry out the proposition effectively if you become....attached," said Dennison.

The waiter arrived with the drinks and set them down on paper coasters. Dennison frowned with disappointment as he saw the flimsy white squares of paper.

"I'm not filming them again," Erskine insisted. "It's too

perverted."

"You think sex on film is perverted?" Dennison replied. "People dying of famine — that's perverted."

Rossi nodded in agreement. "Filming them will no longer be necessary," said Dennison.

"What will you use as proof then?" asked Richard.

"Nothing. I'll know whether you've slept with them or not."

"How?" asked Erskine.

"I'll see it in your eyes," said Dennison.

Erskine craned his neck. "What?"

"He's going to use Jedi," said Hof with a chuckle.

"There's a technique for telling whether a person is lying or not. You read the signs in the eyes, the tiny inflections in the face," said Dennison, pointing either side of his nose as if no one knew where their eyes were located.

"And you know how to do that?" asked Hof.

"Correct."

"Where did you learn that?" Erskine enquired. "Were you in the Special Forces?"

"That does not concern you," Dennison replied. "Suffice it to say that if any of you fail in your missions, I will know. Believe me."

"But what happens if you make a mistake?" Richard suggested.

"There will be no mistakes," said Dennison categorically. "None."

Erskine looked at Dennison with a mix of confusion and suspicion. "Is Dennison Carr your real name?" he asked.

The question froze the group. Dennison looked at Erskine. "Do you want to continue with the proposition or not?" he asked. They stared at each other until Erskine looked away.

Dennison drove the men to a nightclub in Mayfair. He parked across the street and they walked up to the entrance. As soon as the doorman saw Dennison he immediately unhooked the velvet rope, greeted him politely, then ushered the group inside. The club, finished in mirrored glass, steel, chrome and polished black tiles, was already busy. Dennison had a table reserved adjacent to the dance floor. As they negotiated their way through the crowd a six-foot brunette stepped forward and intercepted Dennison.

"Did you get my message?" she asked.

"Not now," whispered Dennison.

"I need to come see you."

"I said, not now."

He stepped around her and walked on. Erskine looked puzzled.

"Do you know her?" he asked. Dennison kept walking, pretending not to hear.

Behind them, a topless male model with a square jaw and heavy rimmed glasses, brushed by them holding two glasses of champagne. Hof turned to scrutinise his body, checking to see whether it was better than his.

As Rossi made his way through the crowd two women turned and sneaked secret glances. A boyfriend caught his girl staring, and he tapped her on the arm, but she pretended to be looking somewhere else.

The DJ played *Love Like This*, by Faith Evans (1998). A skinny girl with a blonde bob, leather trousers, gold blouse and silver heels, got up and started dancing on one of the tables. Nobody paid any attention, and so after a few minutes she sat down again.

Erskine looked across the dancefloor at the arena of revellers drinking and hunting, and it was at times like these that he missed his Genevieve the most. He remembered the last time he was in a club. It was soon after she was gone. He did not know what drew him there — perhaps the loneliness made him want to be around crowds of happy people. He found himself out on the dance floor by himself amongst the euphoric hordes, searching the eyes of strangers, looking for someone to connect with. He danced by himself to the song, *You're Not Alone*, by Olive (1996), but alone was exactly what he was. As the chorus repeated, the irony of the lyrics, the haunting pathos of the vocal and the sparse, cavernous sound in the room tore open the wound of his grief, engulfing him in loneliness, and he started to cry as he danced and danced and danced.

"Tonight you are all going to perform the classic one-night-stand," Dennison began. "I will select women for each of you in here, and you must have sex with them tonight."

Hof rubbed his hands with glee. "Cool," he said. "Who's mine?"

"Patience," said Dennison, patting down the air with one hand. The men began looking around at random women. Erskine felt ready to participate. He wanted to sleep with the women Dennison would select, as many as he could. He was surprised that he felt this way, as he had never been promiscuous in the past. He did not understand what was driving him to participate in what he saw as a ridiculous, empty challenge — and this worried him because it meant that he did not know himself.

Dennison tapped Rossi gently on the knee. "There's a girl leaning on the bar talking to her friend. Black vest, matching trousers. See her?"

Rossi turned and looked, then turned back, nodding at Dennison. "She's yours."

Dennison scoped the room once again. A few moments later he turned to Richard. "The woman with shoulder-length brown hair, blue top, beige trousers."

"Where?"

"She's about to walk past our table right now."

All the men sneaked a look. Richard nodded. "Got it."

"Good," said Dennison. He looked again into the crowd. "Hof?"

"I'm ready." He spoke like a soldier.

"On the dancefloor. Three women. All in black dresses. Two with brown hair, one blonde."

Hof scanned the dancefloor, his eyes fast and greedy, and saw three well-built women. They were semi-drunk, laughing and dancing wildly. "Which one?" he asked.

"Black sleeveless dress, short blonde hair."

Dennison then turned to Erskine. "Did you notice that woman as we came in?" he asked.

"What woman?"

"Sitting down. Over near the bar."

Erskine looked across the room. "Which woman?"

"You'll know her...She's in a wheelchair."

All the men froze. "What?" said Erskine.

"Oh, shit," whispered Hof.

"Why?" asked Erskine. "Why her?"

"What do you mean, why her?" replied Dennison. "You think only women with legs deserve sex?"

"No, but—"

"But what?"

Erskine fell silent.

"Check your cranium, Erskine," said Dennison, tapping his skull three times.

"Well, you seem to have picked women without any disabilities for the others," said Erskine. "Why do I get the girl in the chair?"

"What makes you think the other women I have chosen don't also have disabilities?" he said. "You think just because you can't see them that they are not there?"

"No, but—"

"The average person loses twenty-three seconds of sight a day through blinking," Dennison interrupted. "Perhaps, Erskine, your blindness lasts a lot longer."

Erskine sighed and looked out into the crowd, wondering what it was that made Dennison select such a target for him, and not the others.

Hof rose to his feet impatiently. "Alright, let's go," he said.

"Wait," said Dennison. "There's one more thing."

Hof made a sucking noise with his teeth, then sat down.

"I want you all to use the same opening line when you approach them."

"What line?" asked Hof.

Dennison smiled cunningly. "I want you all to say..." He leaned in and whispered it to them. Instantly there was an eruption of indignation.

"No, Dennison, I can't go in like that," said Richard, shaking his head sternly. "Too harsh. Too brutal."

"Why do you want us to say that?" asked Erskine.

Dennison smiled. "Because it makes things, let's say, more challenging."

Rossi nodded in agreement.

"I get your vibe now," said Richard. "It's like something I would do in my acting class. A roll play."

"It's a gambler's line," said Dennison. "A Kamikaze approach."

"What's that?" asked Hof.

"I'll tell you," Dennison began. "Women who get approached by men only ever get to hear a certain kind of line. 'Hello, can I buy you a drink?', 'Do you come here often?', whatever. Standard clichés. But whenever a man says a line that is out of the ordinary, it's exciting for a woman because it deviates from the predictable. This is the Kamikaze player's starting point. He plays risk. It means that in that moment he's ready for her to either slap him or kiss him. Fifty-fifty. That's Kamikaze."

"You're as slick as juice Dennison," said Hof, nodding admiringly. "I want to be like you when I grow up."

Dennison could see that Erskine was uncomfortable. "You can still quit, Erskine," he said. "If there's somewhere else you'd rather be."

Erskine sighed, then rubbed his head and checked his palm for sweat. "Let's get on with it," he replied.

"Go." The men dispersed in different directions.

19

Hof had been promiscuous most of his adult life. From the first moment he'd tasted sex. He had too much sexual curiosity about women to restrict himself to just one. Nothing captured his excitement more than sex with different women. He did not believe in masturbation. He preferred not to purge himself on his own skin. He thought it a waste. He wanted to do it inside the pelvis of a woman, where he felt most at home. For him, Dennison's proposition was a dream come true — he got paid for doing what he loved.

He was poised on the edge of the dancefloor, watching the blonde woman in the sleeveless dress. She was dancing and drinking champagne with her friends. As Hof watched her he was not thinking about saying Dennison's line. He had already projected beyond this. He was thinking about the sex. He wondered whether or not she would be silent during sex, or if she would moan with each of his determined strokes. He made a face as his imagination conjured the pictures — a face like a child who'd just seen ice cream. Desire crept into him, pushing against his underwear.

He stepped confidently onto the dancefloor, through the bodies, tapped the woman on the shoulder. She turned, still dancing. He shouted, "I really want to fuck you tonight."

"Eh?"

"I said, I really want to fuck you tonight."

"I can't hear you, love."

"I said, I REALLY WANT TO FUCK YOU TONIGHT."

"Ha-ha-ha-ha-ha-ha-ha!"

Still dancing, she pointed at Hof, two hands shaped like pistols, pointing back and forth at him in time to the beat of the music. "Are you the one, are you, are you the one?"

"Here I am," proclaimed Hof with open arms and a big grin.

"Ha-ha-ha-ha-ha-ha-ha!"

She waved her hands excitedly at her two girlfriends, who huddled in close. "Guess what this lad's just said to me?" she shouted.

"What?"

"He's come up to me, yeah — to me! — and he says, I want to really, really fuck you tonight. Can you believe that?"

"Really?" The women adopted the same look of goggle-eyed surprise.

"Seriously — no word of a lie," she insisted.

"Go for it, girl," said her friend, looking Hof up and down. "He's fit!"

"Ha-ha-ha-ha-ha-ha-ha!"

Hof broke in, trying to dance with them, grinning and sweating. He manoeuvred himself in front of the woman in question, gyrating his hips.

He put his mouth over her ear. "What's your name, babe?" he shouted.

"Danni."

"Hello, Danni, I'm Hof."

"You're off? But you only just got here!"

"No, no, no. My name's Hof. Hof!"

"Alright, love, ha-ha-ha-ha-ha-ha-ha!" She pointed at him, grinning, pistol fingers, shoulders and eyebrows all pumping to the beat of the music.

Her dress had a perforated butterfly motif positioned over her chest, which showed through to her cleavage. Hof's eye went straight to it. "Where you girls from?" he shouted.

"Leeds," said Danni. "This is my hen night."

Hof smiled to himself. He put his hands around Danni's waist and started dancing closer. He felt the weight of her breasts rubbing circles against his chest and he pushed his groin to meet hers. Suddenly she grabbed him around his neck and leapt up around his waist, clamping his midriff between her thighs.

"Ha-ha-ha-ha-ha-ha-ha!"

Hof grunted like a weightlifter, absorbed the weight of her body, then carried on grinning, sweating, dancing. "Let's go in the toilets," he said.

"Ha-ha-ha-ha-ha-ha-ha!"

"Come on," he persisted.

"You're a bit confident, aren't ya?"

"Just like you like it, babe, yeah?"

"Ha-ha-ha-ha-ha-ha-ha!"

"Shall we go, then?"

"Easy tiger — I'm here with me mates."

"I'll do them too if you like."

"Ha-ha-ha-ha-ha-ha-ha!"

"I'll do you, then get them too, like a buy-one-get-one-free kind of offer."

"Ha-ha-ha-ha-ha-ha-ha!"

Danni unravelled herself from around his waist for an emergency conference with her friends. "Come on girls," she said excitedly. "It'll be a laugh. He'll do us all in the lav, one by one, ha-ha-ha-ha-ha!"

"But you're getting married in two days, Danni."

"Yeah, so? Why shouldn't I have some fun before I get married?" she said matter-of-factly. "Mick's probably doing the same bloody thing in Spain right now with his lot. You know how men are. I'm not having that!"

As Hof and Danni made their way to the men's toilets, she stopped suddenly and eyeballed him suspiciously. "You're not into anything kinky are ya?"

"What do you mean?"

"I mean, you're not one of those blokes who likes me to shit in his mouth, then piss over the top of it, are you?"

"What?"

"Because I've had one of those."

"What has that got to do with sex?"

"People get off on the weirdest shit, let me tell you."

On the other side of the club, Rossi was watching his chosen target from a distance, preparing for his approach. Her name was Ida. She was wearing loose-fitting trousers, like she always did, on account of the fact that she hated her short chunky legs.

Rossi's mother was a French prostitute. A poor uneducated woman who had lived a difficult life. "Life is shit, and so you have to be ready for the shit," she'd say to her only child. As a consequence of this belief, she didn't hide her vocation from the young Rossi. They lived in a two-roomed apartment — one room for living, and the other for the business. Many times Rossi saw clients come and go. So many fifteen-minute family men who came and went as quickly as the father he never knew. He often wondered, when he saw them arrive, if any of them could be his real father. He'd look into their faces, searching for anyone whom he thought resembled him. On one occasion he thought he'd found him. As the man stepped into the hallway of their way apartment Rossi came out and said, "Excuse me. Are you my daddy?"

The man smirked with amusement at first, and then slowly shook his head. "I'm afraid not, little man."

"Are you sure?" asked Rossi, stepping closer for a better look.

"You look a bit like me."

"I'm not your father, kid."

"But, you like my mummy, right?"

The man squirmed uncomfortably. "Well, yes, I do."

"So, couldn't you just....be my daddy?"

The man sighed deeply, but didn't answer. He backed away into the next room where Rossi's mother was waiting, and closed the door.

Rossi's mother loved Barbara Streisand. Her favourite track was *Guilty*. Whenever Rossi rang her in Paris he'd play it to her through the speaker of his mobile phone:

> *And we got nothing to be guilty of*
> *Our love will climb any mountain*
> *Near or far we are*
> *And we never let it end*
> *We are devotion*
> *And we got nothing to be sorry for*
> *Our love is one in a million*
> *Eyes can see that we got a highway to the sky*

"Oh, Rossi," she'd whisper.

He would close his eyes and imagine her smiling, swaying her body and singing along. He imagined it just like it was when they lived together in Paris.

*

Rossi positioned himself close enough for Ida to see him. Then he stared at her. He stared until she saw him staring. She smiled. He kept staring. He pulled a card from his pocket and scribbled something on one side. Then he walked over and presented it to her. When she read it her mouth dropped open, her expression softened. He turned the card over and showed her that there was something else written on the other side. She read it and laughed out loud, putting her hands over her face.

One side of the card was printed. It read:

Hello. My name is Rossi. I am deaf.

On the other side was scribbled:

I really want to ~~suck~~ fuck u tonight please.

At the same moment, Hof and Danni were locked in a cubicle in the men's toilets. She stood to the side of the basin, her leg propped on the WC ring, dress hitched to her hips. Hof's trousers were around his ankles, the fabric skimming a shallow urine puddle on the floor. He was moving upwards into her, her earrings swinging back and forth under the impact. Her head was back against the wall, her eyes were closed and her arms were wrapped around his neck. The handle of the toilet flush, mounted on the back wall just above the WC, dug into the flesh of her backside. As her body rode up and down she caught the lever, and suddenly the toilet flushed. They both looked down, startled, as if there was a ghost in the place, then Danni laughed and urged him on.

*

Over by the bar, Richard had his target in sight. He needed a drink before he approached her, to boost his courage. He knocked back two straight vodkas, then began getting into character. He was an out-of-work actor, and so he liked to assume different personalities for each woman he seduced. He reached into his top pocket, produced a pair of spectacles and put them on. They made him look like a nerdy schoolboy. As he worked himself into character he took a moment to reflect. *I'm going to be a famous actor, big in Hollywood. Then I'll show Jane. She'll want me back then — when I am somebody. Someone big.*

The woman's name was Margaret. She was busy talking to a friend. Richard studied her for a few moments. She wore too much make-up and her clothes were too tight — so tight that her panty line showed through her backside. He decided on a certain persona with which to greet her — a meek, apologetic character. He walked up and said the line.

She said, "Fuck off!"

He froze with disbelief, then backed away, bristling with humiliation.

"That'll teach him," said her friend.

"Fucking men," sneered Margaret. "They all think they can just have you. Wankers."

*

Erskine slowly worked his way around to the other side of the club. As he turned a corner he looked low through the bodies of clubbers and saw the girl in the wheelchair. She was black, in her mid-twenties, with a round, puffy face and vine-like dreadlocks cascading down her back. He could see by the length of her lifeless legs that she was tall. Her name was Jeanette. There was an older man sitting by her side.

She was sucking a cocktail through a straw, stooping her head down into it, then peering up from the rim of the glass with curious eyes. As she watched the movement of people, every now and then she'd lean over to her companion to whisper something about someone — a face, an outfit, or the way someone was behaving. In between one of these gestures Erskine saw a sadness wash over her for a few seconds, and instantly he felt himself descending into melancholy, as if his emotions were wired to hers.

A girl walked by her wheelchair. An attractive blue-eyed blonde wearing a shiny half-length dress which showed off her shapely legs. Jeanette narrowed her eyes and shot her an up-and-down look of cold envy. The girl turned as if she'd felt her eyes on her, and for a second they stared at each other, before she turned and walked on.

Erskine positioned himself within Jeanette's eyeline. He waited until she saw him, then he smiled and waved. She balked, looked around to check if he was actually waving at her. He beckoned her over. She put her drink down and whispered something to her companion. He looked Erskine up and down then nodded at her. Erskine watched as she expertly manoeuvred her way through the crowd, turning her chair to avoid bodies, touching their backs to let them know she was there.

Erskine crashed in with the line. "I really want to fuck you tonight."

"Whoah, that's an ice-breaker," she said, her eyes bulging with surprise. They introduced themselves. "So, who sent you over?" Jeanette asked.

"What?"

"Well, y'know — play the joke on the wheelchair girl, ho-ho-ho. Good laugh, right?"

"It's not a joke," said Erskine with a shake of his head. "I do want to sleep with you."

"You want to sleep with me?" she asked, pointing to him and then to herself, as if that was the craziest notion she'd ever heard.

"Yes."

"Sure," she said, curling her lip into a sarcastic sneer. "Haven't you noticed something about me?"

"What? You mean you got a new hairdo?"

She laughed. "Look at all the sexy honeys in here," she said, pointing everywhere. "Sexy honeys who can walk. Who can dance.

Why the hell would you want to have sex with me, cowboy?"

"Why not?"

"Well, because I'm black, I'm ugly, and I live in a chair, for starters." She glared at him, curious to see how he'd handle that statement.

He nodded thoughtfully. "It's true, you are black and you are in a chair, but you're not the ugliest girl I've ever seen. You're not the prettiest, but you're not the ugliest, either. But you are, without doubt, the most distinctive-looking woman in here."

Her face lit up. "Honesty!" she cried, as if it were a radical new concept. Erskine wondered how her face would change if she knew what a deceitful liar he was.

*

Back from the toilets, Danni and one of her friends were talking feverishly about what had just happened, while Hof returned to the men's room with one of her other friends.

"What was it like?" she asked excitedly.

"Fantastic," said Danni with drunken excitement. "I was shaking, you know, like this—" She did a demonstration, like someone experiencing electric shock. "Ha-ha-ha-ha-ha-ha-ha!"

*

Back at the bar, Richard had recomposed himself with the help of two more straight vodkas. He took a deep breath and approached Margaret once more.

"You again," she said with exasperation. "What do you want now?"

"I'd just like to apologise for my behaviour earlier."

"So you should. Why can't you just talk normally, instead of all that shit?"

"Yes, I'm sorry, but what I was about to explain to you was that I work for a new escort agency here in London, and we're conducting a survey to try and evaluate what kind of chat-up lines work on today's generation of single women."

"Are you serious?"

"Yes. That's why I came up to you like that. It's one of a series of lines we were given to test women's reactions."

"Well, that one's a bit stupid, isn't it?"

"Absolutely, and I'll make a note of that when I report back to my boss. But perhaps you can tell me then, the sort of line that would work for you?"

She paused to think. "Well, I like funny guys," she said. "If a man can make me laugh, that's it."

Immediately he took off his glasses and became animated. "You want funny? I got funny. Let me just ask you. Are you a healthy eater?"

"I try to, yeah."

"I am. In fact, I eat so healthy now that my piss has changed colour. Now it's like, this lovely light gold colour."

Margaret chuckled.

"Yes indeed, my piss is full of nutrients, I tell you. One time, when I was out in the forest, I pissed in a clearing — then when I came back a few weeks later there was a big tree growing there."

Margaret laughed harder.

"That's right. My pee is useful. You meet a young guy, he can't grow a beard, right? I piss on his face, next thing you know he's got a forest of hair growing there."

*

Still seated at his table, Dennison Carr watched the men in action. As he amused himself with their efforts, he reached into his pocket and pulled out a silver Zippo lighter. Dennison didn't smoke but he liked to carry it around because it was a beautiful object. He glanced down at its brushed silver finish, caressing its weighty chassis like a beachcomber fondling a pebble. He flicked the lid — open, closed, open closed — checking the sound it made. He held it to his ear, like a gunslinger listening to the sound of his spinning barrel.

As he sat there alone with the lighter between his fingers, he recalled a memory — an incident as a child, when he sitting at dinner in a restaurant with his foster parents. There was a bowl of warm soup in front of him. He became so bored with the whole scene before him — his foster parents lost in their own world, chattering endlessly about their concerns and issues — that he leaned forward slowly and sank his face into the soup. He left it there, holding his breath, counting the seconds before they noticed.

*

Rossi was dancing with Ida. She was holding his hand, smiling at him while he concentrated on copying her moves, trying to keep time to a beat he could not hear.

Hof walked by with Danni's friend in tow, on their way back from the toilets. He winked at Rossi, who ignored him.

Richard was busy entertaining Margaret, acting out the character of the stand-up comedian. He shuffled on his feet, made gestures with his hands as if he was working a stage. Whenever he cracked a joke he'd keep a straight face while she laughed. "Do you remember back in the Eighties when people used to have love bites?" he began.

"Yes, yes," she laughed.

"Disgusting things, right? Disgusting. People walking around with a black wound on the side of their necks, looking like they'd just been attacked by a sabre-toothed tiger."

Margaret put her hand over her mouth and cracked up.

"I don't know why they call them love bites, right?" he continued. "Where's the love in that? How can biting a chunk out of someone's neck be considered a sign of affection? I don't know. I think they should call it an I-don't-love-you-very-much-bite."

Ten minutes later, on the dancefloor, Rossi left his partner momentarily to go to the toilet. As he walked in, Hof was hustling the second of Danni's hen night pals out of the door. Rossi moved to the side to let them pass. Hof winked at him and gave him a discreet thumbs up.

Out near the bar, Ida was conferring with her friend. "He's so sweet."

"He's bloody gorgeous, is what he is," said her friend.

"He asked me to sleep with him tonight."

"No way."

"Yeah, way. He's *so* sweet!"

"Are you going to use him for the special project?"

"I don't know. Shut up, here he comes."

For Danni and her posse it was the end of a wild and memorable evening. The girls clinked their glasses one last time, downed the last of their champagne, winced as if it was medicine, and then it was time to go.

"See ya, lover boy," said Danni, pointing at him with the pistol fingers. "We'll call you...NOT! Ha-ha-ha-ha-ha-ha-ha!" The three of them wheeled away in a chorus of drunken laughter. As Hof watched them leave he felt a deep sense of satisfaction. He had managed the impossible — sex with three friends in a nightclub. He had gone beyond the brief. This was a memory he would cherish for all time — one he would tell his buddies well into old age.

On the other side of the club, Erskine and Jeanette were still talking. "You know the most annoying thing about being in a wheelchair in a nightclub?" she said.

"The stairs?"

"Nope."

"Not being able to see how your arse looks in new jeans?"

"That's funny, but nope."

"What then?"

"It's motherfuckers bumping into you and spilling their drinks on your head. I'm seriously thinking about getting a rain hat."

Erskine laughed. She smiled, pleased with her ability to engage him. She beckoned him closer. He leaned down and she whispered. "Shall we go to my place?" Her voice in his ears sounded like the seashore, and her breath was warm.

"Er...if you like...cool."

Her mouth expanded into a wide grin, proud of the fact that she'd pulled such a man. She looked around discreetly for the golden blonde she'd seen earlier, as if to let her know, but she didn't see her. "Come on," she said. "My dad'll give us a lift."

"Your dad?"

"Yeah. He's sitting over there."

Erskine looked over and saw the man who had been sitting next to her. He was fifty-five, slim, pot-bellied and wearing thick black spectacles.

"That's your dad?"

"Yeah. It was his idea to come here in the bloody first place," she said. "He thought I should get out and meet people. Ones that aren't in wheelchairs."

Erskine looked worried. "Relax, he's cool," she said. "Come and meet him."

"No, I don't think—" Before he could say it, she grabbed his hand and wheeled herself back towards her father.

"Hey, pops, this is Erskine," she said as she pulled up next to him.

"Hello," said her father casually.

"Hi," Erskine replied, rubbing his head, then checking his palm for sweat.

"Guess what, pops?" said Jeanette excitedly.

"What's that, honey?"

"Erskine's going to have sex with me tonight."

Erskine made a face like he'd just been shot.

"Great," said her father with no expression. "I suppose you'll be wanting a lift home then?"

20

Richard and Margaret checked into a hotel in nearby Piccadilly. He kept up the guise of the stand-up comedian all the way from the club. As they sat down on the bed he saw her expression darken, as if suddenly nothing was funny anymore, and so he stopped the jokes.

"You nervous?" he asked.

She looked down at her shoes. "I'm married, you know."

"Are you?"

"Yes."

"So...where is he...your husband...tonight?"

"He works nights. I told him I was out with the girls."

Richard nodded, as if lying was a good thing.

She looked at him, something to say, but she couldn't get the words out. Throughout the eight years of her marriage Margaret had never had an orgasm through penetrative sex. Sex needed to be vigorous and sustained in order to trigger her orgasm, but her husband didn't have the technique. But he was good to her, and so she never complained.

She remembered the night he had the flat of his finger against her clitoris, trying to find her orgasm. But he couldn't get it. He became frustrated and started pressing harder, rubbing faster, and she began to hurt, but she would not say, she just could not. In her mind she half mocked his incompetence, but then she checked herself because at least he was trying to make her happy.

She rubbed her palms against her legs, then folded her arms. Richard scanned around the sparsely decorated room. A bed, a bedside cabinet, a lamp, a dresser, a wardrobe, a TV. He glanced down at the over-tightness of Margaret's trousers. The way the material around her vagina clustered in a grooved V-shape. He remembered how his wife stopped trimming the hairs around her vagina. It was the first sign. She always trimmed her pubic hair, just to make it easier for him when he went down on her, but the fact that she'd stopped indicated to him that she didn't like having sex with him anymore.

Margaret felt the urge to tell Richard about her husband, but she

96

held back. Instead she asked, "You ever been married?"

Richard looked reflective. "Yes. Once."

"What happened?"

"She left me...for somebody else," he said. "Someone better." Margaret touched his hand. He tried to smile, then he leaned across and kissed her.

He remembered a conversation he had with his ex-wife Jane, one day soon after they split and became 'friends'. She rang him to ask a question about men, in relation to her new guy. "If you have sex with a man three or four times in a row, on the third and fourth times, is there still sperm in his penis?" she asked.

"What?...What?"

"It's just that I had sex with Jim, and on the last two times he didn't wear a condom, and I'm worried I could be pregnant."

Her voice faded in Richard's ears as he thought about Jim, his replacement. All he could think about was that he could do it *four times* in a row. That was three times more than he could manage per session. Her words cut into him so deeply that he clamped his teeth together and held the tension there as she spoke. He was no good at fucking, he concluded — nowhere near as good as her new man. He wondered why she had told him this. *Does she not realise how this burns? Fucking selfish bitch.*

As they got undressed and Richard climbed on top of Margaret, he was determined to show her that he was as good at fucking as the best of them. He would show Jim, and his ex-wife. He would show them both.

Margaret grabbed Richard's backside, pulled it toward her and said, Grind me, honey, fucking grind me, come on, harder, fucking harder, that's it, yes, fucking yes — but that was only in her mind, and she knew she'd feel silly saying it, and so she did not.

There was a muffled ring tone from her mobile phone. "Leave it," said Richard.

"No, I have to get it," she whispered. "It might be him."

With Richard still on top of her, she stretched her hand to her bag, found the phone, looked at the caller ID, cleared her throat, then answered. "Hi, honey. You home?"

Richard exhaled, shook his head in disbelief.

"Yes...uh-huh...OK...I left something in the fridge...that's right... just warm it up...yes...Don't leave the vegetables in too long, OK. They'll go soggy. OK? I'll see you later...I love you."

She closed the phone, threw it on the floor. "Come on," she said, pulling him by the neck. "Don't stop."

Richard drove against her hips, and each time she moaned he pushed harder, and as her body inched up the bed he watched her face until he could see her about to orgasm. He quickened the action and she dug her fingers into his back and screamed. The sound twisted in the air, as if she was being released from chronic pain. Richard was taken aback at how loud and prolonged it was, and he thought about covering her mouth to dampen it down, but he stopped himself, as he was enjoying the fact that he was the cause. He thought of his ex-wife, wishing she was there watching him, wishing she could see how good he was now, and how he could make women scream with pleasure.

Afterwards, as they got dressed, he wanted to ask her if she'd enjoyed it. He felt he needed to know, for his own self-assessment — but he could not find the words. They agreed that she would leave first, with Richard following a few minutes later. But no sooner had she walked out the door than Richard was engulfed in loneliness. For her. For Jane. He took out his phone and began to dial her number, but then he changed his mind and put it away.

21

Ida was an artist who lived in a warehouse in Hackney, east London. After the club, she took Rossi home with her. Her studio was one huge white room with high ceilings and large industrial-style windows. The wooden floors were broad and uneven, with knots and cracks. The furniture consisted of deliberately random pieces that didn't match, and the place was strewn with art materials.

She watched Rossi as he surveyed the room. She stood back and assessed the shape of his body and the outline of his backside.

"I really want to fuck you tonight, Rossi," she said as his back was turned. She raised her eyebrows expectantly, like someone waiting for an echo to reverberate from a cave. When nothing happened she laughed to herself. She cupped her hands over her mouth and bellowed, "I REALLY WANT TO FUCK YOU TONIGHT, ROSSI."

At last Rossi turned, saw her smiling suspiciously, and immediately he knew what she'd been doing.

"Do you like my work?" she asked. Rossi made a gesture — half yes, half no.

"I hate all the conventional stuff," she said. "I'm trying to create things that are out of the ordinary. That's what I like about you. You're different. You live in a world without sound."

Rossi smiled. She glanced curiously at his useless ears, all the more intriguing now that they served no more than an aesthetic function. She wondered if one day they might just suddenly start working again, like an old radio.

There was a photograph of her on the wall. She was sitting in a chair, naked, arms on the rests, looking intensely into camera. The shot was taken from the level of her crotch. Rossi studied it curiously, then focused on another of her kissing a girl passionately, then one of two men with erect penises, putting them together like swords crossing.

She waited for him to finish studying everything, then she took him by the hand and they sat down. She moved his hair out of his face and kissed him. Rossi smiled, examined her face, rubbing his fingers in an oval shape around the contours of her mouth.

"Rossi?" she said. "I want to do something special tonight."

He nodded.

"It's something I've asked a couple of my boyfriend's to do in the past, but they just got freaked out...Will you help me?"

Rossi shrugged his shoulders as if to say, whatever. She thought about asking him to masturbate onto a slice of brown bread, which she would then eat like a sandwich, while being filmed, but she changed her mind about that particular idea. She had something else in mind.

She went to the kitchen, came back with a bowl of crisps and placed them on the arm of the sofa next to him. Then she walked over to the television trolley, turned it on, dragged it in front of the sofa and handed Rossi the remote. She proceeded to strip naked. He looked on curiously. She got on top of him and lay flat across his lap, face up. She then took his hand, put it to her clitoris and started moving it in small circles. She lifted his other hand with the remote control in it. "I want you to make me come while you surf channels on the TV," she said. "Eat some crisps as well. When I climax, I want you to carry on watching TV and look completely uninterested, OK?"

Rossi nodded as if this was the most natural request he'd ever heard. After growing up with his mother there were very few things about sex that shocked him. He obeyed her instructions, trying his best to multi-task. When it was done, she put her hand into the back of the sofa, pulled out a camera and handed it to him. Then she unzipped his trousers and took out his penis. She put some saliva on her fingers and rubbed it over the head. "I want you to take some photos of me while I give you a blow job," she said. "It's for an exhibition I'm working on."

She brought Rossi to the brink of orgasm, and then she made him ejaculate into a towel. She walked over to the radiator and placed it on it, face down. Soon, the musty fug of his sperm was radiating around the room.

"I want to put this smell in the air conditioning in the gallery where I have the show," she said.

Rossi pointed both his thumbs upwards.

22

Erskine sat in the back of the car as Jeanette's father drove them toward their house in Muswell Hill, north London. He was uncomfortable about her father's presence — the casual accomplice to his daughter's casual sex. Erskine looked at the back of his head as he sat in the drivers seat, wondering how a father could be this cool about his daughter having sex with a stranger.

"Wait, Jeanette and I'll carry you inside," said her father as they pulled up in front of the house.

"Hang back pops," she replied. "Erskine'll do it. You'll carry me across the threshold, won't you, honey?" she asked with a cheeky smile.

Erskine nodded uncomfortably. In that moment he recalled his own honeymoon, carrying Genevieve over the threshold. He remembered how he laid her on the bed in the hotel room, then left to gather their bags from the end of the corridor where he had left them when he first picked her up. When he returned, the door was slightly ajar, and through it he caught her dancing and twirling around the room, intoxicated with happiness. He stood there watching her in her private joy, unable to enter, mad with love for her.

He hoisted Jeanette out of the car and into the house. She kissed him gently on the cheek, then giggled like a schoolgirl, knowing he couldn't do anything while he was carrying her. They entered the corridor of the house and she directed him upstairs to her bedroom. Her father stood at the bottom, watching them go. "Goodnight then," he said.

"Laters pops," said Jeanette.

Erskine entered the room and lowered her gently onto the bed. She slid back against the headboard and pillows, hands in her lap, dead legs spread out in front of her.

"So you're my birthday present," she said.

"Is it your birthday?"

"No, but it feels like it."

"Why?"

"Because I'm about to have sex. That's special for me. It doesn't happen everyday."

"Nobody has sex everyday."

She laughed. "Knowing you're going to have sex with someone is great," she said. "That's the good thing about a one-night-stand."

"How do you know this is a one-night-stand?"

"It's OK, Erskine," she said with a shrug. "I know you're not going to be my boyfriend or anything. Girls like me don't get guys like you."

Erskine opened his mouth to lie, then changed his mind.

"But we can have one night together, right?" she said.

He nodded, tried to think of something nice to say, but nothing came out.

"I know I'm not attractive, but I've got nice hair, don't you think?"

"Fantastic," said Erskine.

"It's taken me years to grow. Sometimes white people shout— Bob Marley—when they see me. That or Whoopi Goldberg.... Idiots."

Erskine stroked her vine-like locks, brought them round to the front of her shoulders.

"It's not that easy to get somebody to love you when you live in a chair," she said with a feint smile. "Your field of choice is pretty narrow."

"So, you don't go on many blind dates, then?" said Erskine, trying to lighten things.

"I wish the people on blind dates actually were blind," she said. "Then we wouldn't have any of this beauty crap. You'd have to judge on personality."

Erskine nodded. "Good idea."

"That's what love should be about. Character, not the way you look. I thought about cutting off my dreads and getting straight hair, like all the black girls do," she said. "But in the end I just said fuck it. Fuck all that beauty shit. Anyway, no amount of make-up or stick-on hair is going to get me out of the chair. When Clinique invent something for that, they can call me."

Erskine saw the sadness in her eyes again. He wanted to hold her. He opened his fingers, then closed them again.

"Black Americans make me sick," she continued. "They're so fucked up about race and not falling in love with someone white. They're fucking hypocrites. They go on about blackness and all that, and then the men go out with the whitest looking black chicks they can find, and with the straightest hair. You'd never catch them going out with someone that looked like me. Even if I could walk."

Erskine didn't know what to say. He looked up at the light in the ceiling, then rubbed his head.

"I haven't had sex much," she said, staring blankly at the pattern on her duvet. "I don't know....I don't know how much feeling I have...."

He leaned over to kiss her. Before he could connect, there was a quiet knock at the door, followed by her father's voice. "Everything OK in there?"

"Go away pops!" she shouted angrily.

"You need any drinks, or anything? Some crackers?"

"Hello? I said, GO AWAY!" She listened for his departure, then winced at Erskine.

Time seemed to freeze as they stared at each other, then Erskine angled his head and kissed her. She quivered slightly, gulping saliva.

He stroked her face, her hair, and caressed her body. Minutes later, as he entered her, her eyeballs pin-balled around in their sockets, feeling out her body with her eyes.

Erskine lay on top of her, pressing his chest to her breasts, and she gripped him around his neck and back, sliding against his skin with eager fingers, as if this was the last time she would ever hold someone, and then Erskine detected her orgasm, a shivering in her breath, and in the midst of it he realised she was crying. He stopped and held her in the silence.

After a while she looked up at him. "Erskine?"

"Yes."

"Do you believe in God?"

The question startled him. He took his time to answer. "Yes."

"Me too," she replied. "I sometimes wonder what God intended by me being in a wheelchair. What he wants me to learn from it, or what he wants other people to learn." She wiped tears from her face. "Why do these things happen to people like me, Erskine?"

He turned his head slightly and looked out of the window, up into the black sky. "I don't know."

He'd asked himself the same question many times. Why did certain people have to be injured, crippled, or die? He remembered reading a newspaper article about a child in Sweden, twelve-years-old, who was walking along a street one winter when a large clump of icy snow slid from a rooftop and landed on his head, killing him instantly. *Why did he have to die?* Erskine thought. *Where is God at times like these?*

"Will you sing to me?" Jeanette asked. She was gripping him tightly, like a frightened girl.

"What?"

"Will you sing me a song."

"A song?"

"Yes."

"I don't know—"

"Please."

"What do you want me to sing?"

"Anything."

Erskine paused to think. As she hunched down into his chest, he sang *Stormy Weather*, by Lena Horne. Slower than usual, out of tune, and with gaps, as he didn't know all the words.

When she fell asleep he laid her under the covers and put her head on the pillow. He arranged her dreadlocks into a pattern of neat coils either side of her head, like huge earrings. He kissed her on the forehead, then crept toward the door, hunched and cautious like an escaping prisoner. But as he wrapped his palm around the door handle he heard a soft voice.

"Goodnight, Erskine...It was nice to meet you."

He froze, didn't turn around. "Goodnight, Jeanette."

As he walked out Jeanette heard a voice in her head calling out to him. *Please don't go, Erskine. No one else is going to go out with me. No one else is going to love me.*

Her father was downstairs pretending to watch television. When Erskine came down he sprang up, trying his best to look casual, and intercepted him in the corridor.

"How'd it go?" he asked.

Erskine shifted uncomfortably. "Fine....it was fine."

"Good. I'm pleased."

Empty seconds passed.

"Well...nice to meet you," said her father.

"Bye." Erskine walked to the door.

Jeanette's father called after him. "Thanks for being here," he said.

"What?"

"You know, you can come round and see her sometime...If you like...Even though I know you won't."

Erskine rubbed his head, checked his palm for sweat.

"I love my daughter, Erskine," he said. "I'll do anything for her. But I can't...I can't provide that thing. Y'know....Such a silly thing...But I want her to have it. She deserves it, just like anybody else. She deserves a man, or whatever. Or even a woman. I wouldn't even mind that."

104

Erskine stared, blinked, nodded his head.

"Secretly I've thought about it, y'know," said her father. "The sex. About stepping over a father's line...Not for my pleasure, but out of love for my child...you understand?"

"Yes."

"But I couldn't," he said. "I couldn't."

"I've got to go."

23

Dennison was careering along an open country road astride a black Ducati Monster 696. He was wearing a bomber jacket, trousers and gloves in black leather, with a matching helmet. He zoomed up behind an articulated lorry and then swerved out impatiently into the opposing lane to overtake, moving straight into the path of an oncoming car. Instead of moving swiftly back into lane, something inside him compelled him to go head-to-head with the vehicle, as if he was intent on a head-on collision. The oncoming car flashed its headlights, once, twice, and then continuously. Dennison pressed on, his eyes narrowing, his heart bucking against his chest, feeling the exhilaration of the bike rumbling beneath him, until finally, at the last moment, he swerved back into the lane in front of the lorry.

Some time later he pulled up outside an elegant white beach house that cantilevered gracefully toward the ocean. Waiting for him outside, leaning impatiently against her car — a white, 1984 Mercedes 280SL — was an ex-model named Carla. To those who asked, Dennison always referred to her as a 'friend'. She was in her mid-thirties, with a thin, angular face and piercing, curious eyes — a detail that drew Dennison's attention when they first met at Lake Como in Italy some time ago. She wore a pair of black skinny jeans together with a Swarovski crystal and sequinned jacket by Julien Macdonald, plus a pair of gold-coloured sling-backs by Michel Vivien.

Dennison dismounted, removed his helmet and strolled casually toward her. He was late, but he did not think to apologise. Not to her, not to anyone. Not even to Alice when they were together. He regretted that now.

"What took you so long?" asked Carla, holding back her irritation.

"I had a date with destiny."

"I see. So you're two-timing me!"

The house was large and open plan, with a free-standing steel fireplace in the centre, plus a panoramic sea view stretching the entire width of the front of the house. Carla strolled casually about the room, absorbing everything. Dennison studied her clothes and shoes as she walked. He complemented her on her fine taste. At first she looked startled, as if she wasn't used to hearing such things from him. She cocked her head to the side in a satisfied expression, like a cat being stroked.

Dennison put on some music. *It's Alright Now,* by Eddie Harris (1976).

"What is this music?" she asked, frowning intensely and bobbing her head to the beat. "It's funky."

A Fendi clutch bag sat on display on one of the shelves. As she scoped the room it caught her eye. "Whose bag is that?" she asked, pointing with her chin. "One of your other...ones?" She smiled and bounced her eyebrows up and down.

"No questions, remember?" replied Dennison.

She huffed, waving her hand dismissively above her head. "Boring. So boring."

"If you must know, actually the bag is mine."

"Yours?"

"Yes."

"Really? What do you want with a girl's handbag, Dennison? Are you gay?" She chuckled to herself like a schoolgirl. She needed these jokes whenever she was with him. She could not get behind the wall of his emotions, and so this was the only way she could converse with him.

"A bag has no gender other than that placed upon it by society," Dennison replied. "I bought it because it is a beautiful object. A piece of art."

"Why don't you put it to good use and give it to me?" she suggested. "I could use art like that."

"It already has a function - right here on the shelf."

She raised her chin and stared at him curiously. "You're a fascinating old soul, aren't you, Dennison? So stern."

She sauntered over to a framed picture of Alice sitting on a shelf. She picked it up and studied it. "Who's this?"

"No one."

"Liar. Do you normally put pictures of no one on display?"

Dennison's expression suddenly darkened. He took the picture from her and put it back on the shelf, face down. Carla wheeled away, pretending it didn't happen. She turned to him again, glancing up at his hat. "Do you keep that on all the time?" she asked.

"Yes."

"You mean...*all* the time?"

"Yes."

"Fascinating," she replied, raising an eyebrow. She circled him slowly, like a stalking panther, then stood right under him, staring up at him playfully. She tried to kiss him, but he bowed away, then held her by the jaw, gazing at the exquisite shape of her mouth.

"You don't kiss me. I kiss you." He pressed his mouth forcefully to hers.

24

Shepherd's Bush Road. A procession of cheap hotels, fast food stores and grocery shops. On the street, Erskine moved amongst its community of international citizens, listening to its flurry of languages.

A fast wind swirled up, freshened his eyes in its cold wash, and then whistled through his ears like a whispering ghost. His eyes narrowed in concentration, as if he was trying to decipher its language.

As he walked along he noticed a stylish young woman in sunglasses, and immediately it triggered a memory. He recalled the day he bought Genevieve a pair of sunglasses for her birthday. It was early in their relationship and he wasn't sure what style suited her best, so he went to the store armed with a full-sized photocopy of her face and proceeded to try different pairs of glasses against the picture until he found the right ones — a pair of outsized Jackie Onassis-style shades.

He glanced across the street at a sign above a grocery shop. It read, "KWIK STOP". The letters were set in American Typewriter (Bold), uppercase, white on a green background. He saw that the spacing between two of the letters — the 'I' and the last 'K' — was wrong. He was annoyed by the sloppy typography. The urge rose within him to correct that space, but then he realised that he wasn't a graphic designer anymore.

He passed the doorway of the disused shop and saw a young woman, a beggar, sitting cross-legged on a coat strewn beneath her, poised like a sultan on a magic carpet. She had red cheeks and tobacco-stained teeth. Her shoulders were permanently hunched, as if she had no neck. Like the Honey Monster from the cereal box. Beside her were a packet of biscuits and a carton of milk. She asked if he could spare some change, and he stopped and stared at her for some seconds. She stared back, waiting for the money. She scrutinized the look in his eyes, and she asked him if he was OK, and Erskine was startled by the question, by the fact that his feelings seemed so transparent, even to a tramp. Her face exploded with delight when he gave her the twenty pound note he had in his wallet, and he enjoyed seeing her happy for that moment. He smiled, waved goodbye and walked on.

He reached Hammersmith Broadway, took the right turn before the bridge and walked along the riverfront. Minutes later he arrived at Natascha's apartment and rang the bell. In the few seconds before she opened the door he wondered how he should stand. What was the coolest stance? Should he turn his back and then swivel as she opened the door, or should he stand front and centre, looking straight ahead, or perhaps with his head down?

He had no time to try out the moves. The door opened and Natascha appeared. The moment she saw him she felt a sudden involuntary twist in her stomach. She gazed at him with a neutral expression — neither happy nor unhappy to see him. They faced off momentarily, their expressions still, as if they were posing for a photograph. Then she stepped aside and Erskine entered. As he walked past her she instinctively arched her body away from him, then ran a fast eye over his shoulders, his backside, stealing a glance where he could not catch her.

He stood at the window in the lounge, gazing down into the River Thames — into the murky brown water that would never know a spectrum of blue, would never see coral or crab.

He looked up and saw a building on the opposite bank, lit up in the night. There was a flag on its roof, billowing proudly in the stiff breeze. He watched it, mesmerized by its dance, by the natural simplicity of its engine.

His mind drifted, and he thought about being somewhere else, away from the country. He pictured himself selling fresh coconuts on a tropical beach, living under the poultice of a hot, orange sun. But such reflections were far from the reality of the current constructions of his aimless days.

The blackness of the night seemed to press against the windows, and Natascha felt engulfed by it. She said something to him, he didn't hear what, but he turned, reacting to the sound of her. They were nervous again — strangers still.

She wanted to ask him if he'd slept with anybody else since he'd seen her last, but she decided it was none of her business. He was not hers. She felt contempt for herself that she had even harboured the thought. She inhaled sharply, trying to be stronger.

He tried to break the ice. He asked her a question, the first thing that came to him — something about jazz.

"You really want to know?" she asked.

"Absolutely."

She waited for a few seconds, as if she did not believe him. "Well, in terms of its complexity, jazz is an art form," she said finally. "It's as dense as any painting. It was really invented as a reaction against pop music. It was as if the musicians thought pop was too easy, too simple, and they wanted to create something that operated on a much higher level, that didn't appeal to everybody, like a pure definition of avant-garde. I mean, pop music really argues that appealing to everybody was the higher level, but jazz has never worked like that."

As Erskine listened to the passion in her voice he wondered whether she'd ever loved a man with such intensity. She continued, "Anybody can get into pop, but people who like jazz have to learn it, like a language. Like advanced maths. That's what's great about it."

"You really love what you do, don't you?"

"Yes. It's the best thing in my life." Their eyes met. She wanted to ask him about his work, but she was trying not to know him.

"I really liked your gig the other night," said Erskine.

"Really?" she sounded sarcastic. "What did you like about it?"

Erskine paused thoughtfully. "It was sad...and beautiful."

Natascha looked away uncomfortably. Even though they were talking, they were both thinking about that first sex, wondering if their imminent connection would ignite as before. They were together again to confirm it, but they would not confess it, not with words. As she looked at him she felt a mad urge to say, *Fuck me, Erskine, fuck me like that first time, so I can feel the electricity of life.*

She got up to make tea. The way she hoisted her body from the sofa was like a dance or the entré to a performance. Erskine wondered how aware she was of things like this — the details that made men want her.

From the kitchenette she could feel his eyes on her. Unnerved, she took out the coffee instead of the tea, and then she opened the fridge twice, looking for milk in the wrong place from where she normally kept it. Finally she found it, but as she came up from behind the fridge door Erskine was standing there. She dropped the carton to the floor and it splashed as they clashed, their bodies colliding, kissing passionately, the mess at her feet forgotten.

As she felt his body she wondered what rivals he was sharing his mouth with. How generous was he with his soiled lips? She forced the thought from her mind, told herself again that it was none of her business. *He is not mine. He is not mine.*

Impatient with desire, they stumbled into the lounge and subsided to the floor, pulling violently at each other's clothing. She felt a rush of conflict between him and her others – the collection of penises she strung around her like pieces on a necklace. She felt a certain feeling — the meshing of men, the tangle of odours.

Erskine felt the meshing too. Genevieve and Natascha superimposed themselves onto one another in his mind:

genevievenataschanataschagenevieve
natgen aschaevieveascha vieve nat

Natascha grew nervous as she felt a certain passion in the weight and texture of Erskine's touch, as if he was trying to love her. This set off an alarm within her, and she wanted to pull away from him, to cool things, but she could not now.

At the moment of climax it took everything she had to stop herself from screaming. The sensation was so intense that she wanted it to stop. She tensed her fingers, cranked them into a shape, like a crab, and dug them into the bedsheets, waiting for the pleasure to end.

They glared at each other madly, more so than that first time, for now they realised that their connection was no accident. Natascha curled away from under him, frightened of what she was feeling.

In the aftershock of her orgasm she felt a tremor in her legs that would not cease. She could not let him see, could not let him know what he had caused. She lapsed into a calm panic, squeezing both her legs, trying to kill the vibration. She pulled away from him and escaped into the bathroom to compose herself, but she could not, and so she re-emerged like an actress, coated in a fake equanimity. She wondered how long she could pretend at this numbness. How long before she'd be betrayed by unauthorised feelings seeping from her eyes or manifesting in the kinetic language of her hands upon his body.

The two lovers now shared the same unspoken fear — that their connection was somehow beyond their control. They suddenly felt small in the Universe, helpless in the knowledge that the prerogatives they believed were theirs somehow no longer belonged to them, but to some other force.

After a time Erskine turned to her and asked, "Will you play something for me? On the harp?"

She thought about it, not wanting him to stay, not wanting to do anything that might encourage him to like her any more than he did already. She slid to the edge of the sofa and curved her

body upwards with a slow grace. There it was again, he noted—
the beauty in the simple action of standing up. She felt the urge
to take his hand, but instead she simply turned and looked at him,
and he got up too, instinctively. She dragged a low stool up to the
instrument, lowered herself, parted her naked legs, pulled them
between the instrument, tilted it gently back onto her shoulder, just
above her right breast. She started to play. The song was *Kiss Of
Fire*. Erskine sat mesmerised, gazing at her nakedness, her wild
hair cascading down her neck and shoulders, her body's curves in
perfect alignment with the undulations of her instrument, her strong
fingers working bold shapes across the strings.

"That was beautiful," he said when it was over. He looked at her
as if he had something to say. She seemed to anticipate it, stepped
to the window and looked out over the black water. She regretted it
now. Enticing him with her skills. Showboating in the nude.

The silent seconds festered, swelled like a bubble that would not
burst. They'd invested so much energy in not saying, their loyalty
to concealment like knights serving a king.

Erskine waited for her to mention the lamp — to thank him at
least. She did not. He wondered if perhaps she had not received it
yet.

Then she said it, as if she had read his thoughts. "Why did you
buy me the lamp?" She tried her best to sound nonchalant.

"You got it?"

"Yes. Why did you send it?"

"Why?"

"Yes, why?"

"To replace the one I broke, that's why."

She paused, then asked, "Is that the only reason?"

"Yes. What else?"

She searched his eyes for some moments. She was disappointed
with his answer. Disappointed and relieved. She fidgeted, desperate
for some kind of interruption to break the silence that echoed in the
wake of his words.

She recalled the men from her past who had tried to do nice
things for her. She remembered one particular lover — after making
love, he took her into the shower and scrubbed her body from head
to toe with soapy water, as if she was a car. She thought it was the
sexiest, most romantic thing any man had ever done for her. She
broke up with him immediately afterwards.

She looked at Erskine suspiciously. "I don't trust you," she said.

Erskine looked puzzled. "Why not?"

113

Natascha suddenly felt conscious of her nakedness, as if Erskine was an intruder. She went to the bathroom, put on her robe and returned. Erskine got up and joined her at the window. He was drawn to her still, despite her resistance to him. Because of it. He was afraid he was liking her – liking the proud mien of her detachment, the charisma of her sadness – this and the other details. Ten seconds passed, and in that time he changed his mind about wanting her, then changed it back, then changed it back again.

In the same seconds she realised she was liking him too — against her will. She did not understand why. He had said nothing special. His speech was neither poetic nor lyrical — things that would have appealed to her. He had shown her no particular repository of intelligence or notable trait of character. She wanted to deny that the sex alone could be the catalyst. She thought that perhaps it was the sadness she detected in the shape and movement of the skin around his eyes. It pleased her that he was damaged, that there was a submerged pathos to him that she could not fathom, and that mirrored her own sense of melancholy. She liked him in the same way that she liked secondhand clothes. Things that had a hidden history that perhaps would never be revealed.

Erskine was relieved that she did not trust him. Relieved and disappointed. "What have I done to you, for you not to trust me?" he asked.

She shook her head slowly, then buried her hands deep into the pockets of her robe. "I don't just give out trust to random guys who fuck me," she replied coldly.

Random guys. Erskine realised she had other lovers. He bristled at the thought of her carousel of other penises — all of them worming for space to execute their hydraulics at her fleshy aperture. He wondered if they were better at the fucking than him. Where was he in the rankings? He figured he must be high if she was sleeping with him a second time. He concluded that she would not do this unless she was happy with his skills. He felt good about this small success, in a life of so many failures.

"Is that what I am to you?" he asked finally. "A random guy?"

Natascha sighed, as if she'd been asked the question by a child. She fiddled with the cord on her gown, pulled the collar until it covered her neck. "Listen, Erskine — most of the men I've ever known have been unfaithful," she said. "They fuck you — then the next day they fuck somebody else. No big deal." She stared blankly at him, waiting for his counter argument.

It did not come.

25

As he sat at home on that first night after Genevieve died, Erskine's grief and loneliness cut so deeply into him that he cried out and started tugging aggressively at his clothing, desperate to release the maddening energy from within himself. He stumbled into the kitchen, looking for something to release his pain, and in desperation he placed his hand on the hot ring of the cooker. He let out a terrifying wail as he jolted backwards in searing pain, turning to the sink and plunging his hand gratefully under the running tap.

The funeral took place a few days after. Erskine stared at the wooden coffin that housed her lifeless body. He thought about how beautiful a container it was. Perfect shiny wood with bright silver handles and trims. It was wasted in the ground. Something this well crafted should be out on display.

But inside the box, Genevieve's beauty was gone. Her flesh rotting, her eyes withering slowly into the caverns of her skull. He was glad he could not see it.

And then as they finally began lowering the coffin into the ground, he was suddenly overwhelmed. The tears flooded his eyes and his vision became misty, like the view from a cave behind a waterfall. He looked up at the sky, somehow trying to force the tears to drain back into his head, but instead the water blubbed into the channels around his eyes and bled out into his ears, slowly as blood.

As he gazed at the sky, a memory came to him. He recalled one winter's day when he was a boy, and a free-falling snowflake wafted down from the sky and landed in his eye. He flinched on contact as it settled into his lower eyelid, and then he looked up and smiled as if to say, 'Thank you' to God for his present.

The funeral guests were intruding, just by being there. They showed up in their black clothes, staring at him with their sad eyes, each face transmitting grief, reminding him of the tragic reality. Overwhelmed by their collective sadness, he escaped to the toilet and sat in a cubicle for fifteen minutes staring at the back of the door, just to escape their gaze. He did not want their commiserations. He desperately wanted them gone.

When he reappeared he tried to avoid anyone touching him, because he knew the contact would set him off, but then his mother put her arms around him and the tears came again.

She said, "God decided it was her time."

"God?" Erskine replied, almost in shock. "This is not God's work. Jesus is supposed to save, not kill."

This was strange coming from him, as he had never been particularly religious. But with Genevieve's death he now craved God, because then at least he could believe that she was still alive somewhere, waiting for him.

"This is the devil's work," said Erskine finally. "That's what a tumour is. A devil in the brain."

Erskine had imagined the tumour inside his Genevieve's head. Its shape, its aesthetic. He saw a translucent jelly, shaped like a church bell, billowing gently in a light blue fluid.

During subsequent days he tried to compress his grief, to make it smaller somehow. But wherever he went he could not escape the memory of his dead sweetheart. One afternoon he was walking past a bookshop when he heard the haunting strains of the song *Tinseltown In The Rain* (1984) by The Blue Nile, and as the pathos of it cut right through him he was engulfed by sadness. He found himself in tears as he realised again that his Genevieve was dead, and he started running away from the sound, trying to escape the terrible, beautiful tone of its vocals. Then when he was out of range he wiped his face and blinked his eyes clear and carried on walking.

To help him escape his grief he taught himself a positive mental exercise in which he concentrated on his favourite things:

red wine with roast chicken
fresh ring-doughnuts with hazelnut coffee
the soft crunch of fresh snow underfoot
the sheen of a rain-soaked street after midnight
the sound of horse's hooves on cobblestones
the smell of freshly cut grass after the rain
Genevieve laughing from zero to full power

After the funeral his life fell apart. He was not sure when the psychosis started, maybe sometime after he started smoking skunk to help him forget his pain. His intermittent bouts of psychosis no longer terrified him. He did not think to get help. There was nothing for him to be healthy for. In his damaged state he let his freelance graphic design business collapse, and he lost all his clients. His money soon ran out and he began to fall behind with his rent. But he did not care. Over days and nights he wandered the streets aimlessly, mired within his own bleakness. For the first time he questioned the very usefulness of his existence.

For months afterwards he replayed the events of Genevieve's death in his mind. It seemed to happen so quickly. They had only been together for three years. It began when she woke up one morning with a droopy right eyelid. When it did not clear she went to the doctor. They referred her to the hospital for tests. The scan showed a brain tumor. The doctor said she had a few weeks at the most.

Erskine looked confused, as if he did not understand the doctor's prognosis. "But....she can't die," he insisted. "Not now. She just can't. She's...she's too young."

"I'm sorry Erskine," said the consultant.

"I mean...but...so how much money will it take to sort it out?"

"It's not a question of money, Erskine."

He took out his mobile phone. "I can call the bank right now," he insisted.

"The tumour is terminal, Erskine. No amount of money will save her I'm afraid."

Erskine looked scared. "Fuck you, you're wrong!"

When they got home from the hospital he tried to reassure Genevieve. He said, "Don't worry, honey, everything's going to be alright."

Genevieve smashed a cup on the floor. "Don't tell me that," she snapped. "Don't lie to me, Eskimo. I'm going to die!"

"No, you're not."

"I am, and nothing on this planet can save me, not your love, not medicine...not even one of those....those Tibetan-mountain-voodoo-remedy bloody things!"

"Genevieve!"

"STOP IT, STOP PATRONISING ME, I'M GOING TO DIE!"

"But—"

"I'm afraid, Eskimo," she whispered.

"Honey—"

"I don't want to die."

That night they lay silently in bed, embracing in the dark. Erskine was still thinking that there might be something he could do to save her. He thought that perhaps the doctor had her test results mixed up with someone else's. He looked at Genevieve, wanting to suggest it.

She was frightened but was trying to hide it. She looked at him apprehensively. "Eskimo?"

"Yes."

"What will happen to me when I die? Where will I go?" Erskine looked at her painfully. "Will there just be blackness?"

Later that night Erskine awoke from a troubled sleep and saw that Genevieve was gone. He got up to look for her, stepping quietly into the corridor. He stopped at the lounge doorway as he heard whispering. The door was slightly ajar, and so he slowly peered inside. There was Genevieve in the dim light, on her knees, praying to God for more life, pleading that she wasn't ready to die yet and why did she have to go, and why did she have to leave everybody she loved, as she had done no wrong in this world. Erskine listened in the darkness to her desperate pleas, and his face creased in torment. He backed away into the darkness, wiping his face, then went back to bed.

He was surprised he slept. He was ashamed that he had not been up all night, crying or gazing out of the window in despair. In the morning Genevieve woke up excited and full of energy. She made a list of things she wanted to do with the life she had left. Amongst them was a night dancing at a ball. She saw an advert for a weekly event at the local community hall. She went along with Erskine, only to be confronted with a room full of elderly couples in monotone tuxedos and dresses. They moved as best they could with their old bones, but it was a low energy affair. Genevieve insisted on joining them. They paid at the door and then dashed right into the middle of the room, Genevieve spinning like a comic ballerina. They stuck out amongst the crowd in their colourful jeans and T-shirts, everything about them anomalous to their surroundings. Genevieve moved exaggeratedly as Erskine twirled her around, her chin high, wearing the proud mien of a matador. He put his hand around her waist and lowered her backwards to the floor, pulled her back up again, and they galloped and spun in a circle, smiling and laughing like mad children. Then they broke away from each other and danced as if they were in a club, out of time to the formal music, and Erskine crawled under her legs and bucked like a wild horse, and she smacked her thigh and arced her body like a cowboy, all the while oblivious to what was happening around them.

The following week they drove to Cornwall for a few days by the sea. The afternoon after they arrived they went for a stroll along the beach. It was a bright, sunny day, and they walked arm-in-arm, staring out at the ocean. Genevieve smiled from beneath her floppy hat, her senses heightened by the nature around her.

"I've never seen anything more amazing than the shape of clouds," she said, gazing up at the sky. Maybe the shape of the ocean in a storm."

Erskine squeezed her hand. A flock of seagulls passed overhead, flapping their wings wildly, as if they were in pursuit of something ahead of them. Genevieve reached up with one arm, as if to catch one of them.

"Do you think birds love each other?" she asked, her voice suddenly like a little girl.

Erskine watched the seagulls as they disappeared from sight. "I don't know," he replied. "I've never thought about it."

Suddenly she broke away from him excitedly. "Let's run, come on!"

"No, Fruitcake."

"Oh, come on, old man!"

"No, you run," said Erskine, smiling affectionately. "I want to watch you."

"OK, here I go!" She removed her hat and launched it at him like a Frisbee, and he caught it in one hand. She turned and set off running, prancing in and out of the undulating waves, trying not to get her feet wet. Erskine watched the graceful sway and bend of her body as she ran, and still he wondered why she never became a dancer.

He watched her get further and further away until finally she collapsed onto the sand.

He froze with horror. "Genny?" he whispered.

He dropped her hat and sprinted desperately toward her, splashing through the thin film of tide at his feet, faster and faster, the tears already forming.

He fell to his knees at her feet, aghast at his tragic find, afraid even to touch her for those seconds. He dragged her torso gently to his lap and stared down at her, his tears spilling onto her cooling face.

Back along the beach, the dead woman's hat lay still on the sand where Erskine had dropped it. The tide gently washed in, reaching out to the object, and it surfed gently atop the rush of white froth.

26

Natascha and Megan were attending art class. They had completed the portrait of the male nude from their previous session, and now they were working on a portrait of a voluptuous, pale-skinned female nude, who reclined on the battered grey sofa, her back to the class, her long wavy black hair cascading behind her.

"Was it the same again?" asked Megan as she focused on her sketching. "The same feeling as last time?"

"Yes." Natascha was almost embarrassed to say so.

Megan stopped drawing and opened her mouth in disbelief. "You're kidding," she said. "The same mad, crazy, crazy orgasm?"

Natascha nodded.

"Wow. Can you sprinkle some of this guy's magic dust on my husband's dick? You'd really be helping me out." Megan went cold with envy. Her husband had never been this special. She loved him, but sex with him had never taken her to the edge of sexual madness.

"What do you see in this Erskine guy anyway?" she enquired. "That is, apart from the fact that the sex is bloody unbelievable?"

They both laughed. "That would be enough for a lot of women, let me tell you," said Natascha.

"True enough."

Natascha took a moment to think. "I don't know what it is. There's something in his eyes. Something...Some sadness he is hiding. I don't know."

"What, you mean you like him because he's miserable?" she said with a frown.

"No, silly. It's just...I don't know. There's something in him that just gets me." She thought some more, then said, "His left eye is sad."

"What?"

"His left eye. It's sadder than his right. They're different."

"Are they?"

"Yes," Natascha insisted.

"So, what are you saying? That you like this guy because he's got funny eyes?"

Natascha laughed. "No, silly. Everybody's eyes are slightly

different. No one's are completely identical. Has no one ever told you that?"

"No," said Megan. "It's all poetry to me."

Natasha suddenly looked worried. She stopped sketching. "Meg, do you think it's possible to love somebody, even though you've only slept with them once or twice?"

Megan put down her pencil and sighed. "Darling, I've got to say, this kind of orgasmic madness you feel when you have sex with him - it's not love. It's just a kind of intense adolescent lust, that's all. You can't base a relationship on it. It always fades in the end. You need more than that."

"But do you think it's possible?" Natascha repeated.

"What?"

"To love somebody...even though all you've done is...fuck?"

"That question presupposes that loving someone is about sex. It's not. You have to know someone to love them."

"Do you?"

*

Later, as Megan made her way home, her thoughts were consumed with what Natascha had said about Erskine. She compared her situation with that of her best friend. Sex with her husband Gary had lost its potency since their early courtship, but still, overall, life was good. She had a loving husband, two healthy children, and enough money both for life's essentials and its indulgences. But somehow she felt restless. Natascha's experience had unsettled her in a way she had not anticipated.

The following morning she ventured into the West End while her husband was at work, and purchased some items from a sex shop. That evening, after she'd put the children to sleep, she waited until Gary came to bed, then she slipped into the bathroom and changed.

Minutes later she reappeared in a crotchless nurse's uniform and hat. She presented herself to Gary, standing confidently with her legs astride and her hands on her hips — a pose she had practised in the mirror that afternoon. Any second, she expected his eyes to bulge with surprised desire, before grabbing her and throwing her down forcefully onto the bed.

But the way Gary looked at her was curious rather than lustful. "What the hell are you doing?" he asked with a frown.

"Don't you like it, honey?"

He laughed mockingly. "Is it fancy dress?"

"What? No. I bought it for us...I just thought...I..."

She felt a fool now. Her shoulders sagged forward and she abandoned her bold stance, looking away to the floor. Gary climbed into bed, pulled the sheets over himself and turned his head away from her and onto the pillow. "Take it off and come to bed."

She sighed and rubbed her temple painfully, then looked down at herself — her sexy outfit now transposed into a clown's outfit. She walked over to her side of the bed, slipped her hand under the pillow and took the porn DVD she'd bought earlier, and threw it in the bin. Then she turned and stared at the featureless landscape of the back of her husband's head. Facing away from her. Rejecting her. Dismissing her. She wondered how his lust for her had diminished to this, had crumpled and compressed so dramatically from the first passion of their early courtship; from the days when sex between them was so physical, so hard that she was perpetually exhausted, falling asleep on the train, or at her desk at work.

When she was in school she was considered nothing special — her sharp cheekbones and skullish beauty were too advanced for the boys' tastes, and so she went unnoticed. No one asked her out on dates, or to the school's end of year prom. But once in university she blossomed. With the exception of Jessie Rawson, who was one year above her, she was the hottest girl on campus. The one all the men dreamed of sleeping with. The accolade was shallow, but nonetheless she enjoyed the power that came with it. But that was then.

Now she felt lost as she realised that she did not have the power to replenish the sexual peaks of her past. There would have been no such sense of nostalgia, of loss, if she had been born ugly, she thought. Megan had no choice but to mourn the passing of her heyday, her golden years. Now she would give up trying to reclaim it. This was the last humiliation. She looked down at herself with a new sense of disgust. Her perception of her own beauty fell away from her, stripped like a skin, and she felt empty, and ugly, and angry. She looked again at the rear of Gary's skull and she felt a rage swell within her. She wanted to smash his head with a baseball bat for not even trying to engage with her efforts — for not even being able to look at her. Her bottom lip started to quiver and she began to cry — a slow tear. She wiped it away angrily using her knuckle rather than her finger.

But she was still bloated with desire, despite her rejection. She had waited all day to have sex with Gary. She went into the bathroom and locked the door. She sat on the toilet seat, spread her legs and began masturbating through the crotchless knickers of her failed outfit. She closed her eyes and thought of Gary in his younger days, when his lust for her was at its apex. Then she grew angry that she was thinking about him, after what he'd just done, and so she stopped and hit herself three times on the arm. She got up, gathered herself and stepped calmly back into the bedroom. She took the outfit off and shoved it clumsily out of sight, under a chair. Tomorrow she would return it and get a refund.

She climbed into bed, facing away from her husband, and turned out the light. "Goodnight, Gary."

"Love you, Megan."

27

The following afternoon John Carver came to see Dennison at his office. As he moved across the room to take a seat, he glanced around at the television, hoping there might be a football match on, but this time it was not switched on. He hid his disappointment, sat down and smiled at his client. There was a silence between them as Dennison waited for him to release what information he possessed. He was tired of the way the detective always made him wait — his childish game — but he had no choice but to play along.

"It's cool," he began finally. "They're all playing by your rules."

"Good," Dennison replied.

John waited, timed his next sentence. "Except one."

Dennison's attention locked. "Who?"

John slowly produced a packet of biscuits, Bourbons, from the inside pocket of his jacket. They were the supermarket's own brand, the cheapest. He took one and popped it into his mouth whole, then gently dusted his fingers as he crunched it slowly. Dennison watched him, insulted by his deliberate pause.

"Erskine."

Dennison showed no reaction.

"He's still seeing one of them." John took out a pocket book and consulted his notes. "Er....Natascha. Jazz singer."

Dennison sat back in his chair and clasped his fingers together thoughtfully. John leaned toward him with a large envelope in his hand. "It's all there."

Dennison didn't take it from him. Instead he pointed to the desk, as if John had a contagious disease that he did not want to catch. He huffed, then dropped it in front of Dennison. It pleased him that John was insulted. He leaned forward slowly and fixed him with a cold stare. "And what of....the other matter?" he asked.

John acted as if he did not know what Dennison was talking about, then pretended to remember. "The woman? Still on it." Dennison leaned back slowly in his chair and sighed with exasperation.

*

Nearly two weeks had passed since Dennison's men had embarked on the proposition. They were now making regular money doing Dennison's bidding. They had used their earnings for different purposes. While Rossi saved most of his, Hof splashed out on a secondhand car and new clothes. Erskine continued to pay off his debts and to replenish his supply of skunk. Richard used some of his to pay for his acting classes, putting the rest away for his trip to Hollywood, where he was planning to make it big.

"Mick Jagger's fucked enough babes," said Hof, as he and the others sat in a café in Oxford Circus, waiting for Dennison. "Him and Jack Nicholson. And Warren Beatty. Man, those guys! Between them they've fucked enough members of the female species to populate a small country." Hof shook his head, partly in disbelief, partly in admiration. "Do you remember years ago, that actor Rob Lowe going to counselling because he was addicted to sex? I thought to myself, what's the problem there?"

They all laughed. "I mean, nobody ever died from being addicted to fucking, right? I mean, it's not like being hooked on crack."

Just then Richard glanced out of the window and saw Dennison approaching. "Here comes Cary Grant," he quipped.

"Don't you mean Darth Vader?" said Erskine.

"Dude, don't diss the Dennison," said Hof sarcastically. "This cat is so out there, he's intergalactic. I bet he doesn't even have a star sign."

They turned in unison and watched him move purposefully toward the cafe, enter and take a seat beside them.

Hof continued talking, boasting to his fellow seducers. "I'll basically fuck anything, me. Warm melons with holes in them. Anything. As long as I'm in there, y'know?"

Dennison tuned in with interest. "Why?"

"Why what?"

"Why do you want to fuck everything? Have you ever analysed it? Have you ever considered what has happened in your life to make you want to do that?"

Hof was unprepared for this. He looked at Dennison thoughtfully. "Well, I can't say I have," he replied hesitantly. "I just love it. I don't know. I just do."

Dennison leaned toward him and spoke softly, "Check your cranium, Hof." He tapped his temple three times.

Dennison ordered a pot of Earl Grey tea. It arrived on a tray together with some miniature milk cartons. The label on the top of them read:

Half fat cream

Dennison sneered at the language. He wasn't a "half" anything kind of man. He considered himself to be "full". More than full. In his mind he re-wrote the copy to say:

One-and-a-half fat cream

He returned to the table and began pouring his tea from the small stainless steel pot. But as he tipped the spout the tea leaked onto the tray. He sighed disappointedly at the pot's lack of functionality. He hated this even more than he hated paper napkins. As he mopped up the mess he glanced out of the window and saw a tall woman in a half-length skirt and high-heels striding by. They were open at the front, cream with white trims, by Veronique Branquinho. He squinted and adjusted his head to get a better look.

"The high-heel is a challenging shoe to wear," he pronounced to whoever was listening. "The weight of a woman's entire body supported on an area narrower than a one-pence coin. Now that's what I call risk," he said, holding up his index finger. Dennison watched patiently as the woman disappeared from sight, as if she was a light fading into the distance. He touched the rim of his hat, as if to tip his respect to her.

"You're mad," said Hof.

"You think that's mad?" Dennison replied. "That's not mad. Let me tell you what's mad. I was in a shop the other day, and I saw a child reading a comic book. And in this comic book was a story about a werewolf. And the werewolf was wearing tight trousers and a shirt and walking upright and speaking English, just like a man. Now that's what I call mad."

Everybody laughed except Erskine. For him the comment only deepened the mystery about his new employer. As he examined his profile his eye focused on the peak of his black hat. It began to move, slowly stretching forward as if it was made of gum, until it became a huge cantilever, which penetrated through the glass of the café and out into the street like a giant runway. Then Erskine blinked and everything was back to normal.

"Are you married?" Erskine asked abruptly.

Dennison's eyes widened. "Married? Me?"

"Yes, you."

"Marriage is irrational," he replied.

"Why?" asked Erskine.

"Just take a look at the figures. Today half of all American marriages and over a third of British ones end in divorce," said Dennison. "Check your craniums on those statistics. Marriage vows should be revised from 'I will love you 'til death to do us part', to 'I will love you until I don't love you anymore', or 'I will love you until I change', or 'I will love you until I can't stand you anymore'. In 1976 Audrey Hepburn suggested that men and women should live next door to each other and just visit now and then. That was an interesting statement. In the twenty-first century men and women only seem to be able to stand each other for a few hours at a time. Of course, one of the problems is that men have not adapted to monogamy. Imagine if you will, a scenario in which promiscuity became socially acceptable here in the West. How many men would refuse to take up this option on the grounds of their monogamous, loving commitment to their partners, and how many would opt to sleep with whomever they liked without fear of consequences? I'd like to hear women ask their men this question — if he'd stay faithful under such circumstances. I think she'd hear him lie to her face. I think in the future it will be accepted practice for people to have two relationships, one long term, plus one interchangeable lover — like the French. The definition of adultery will be if someone gets greedy and decides to have three partners instead of two."

The waitress arrived and cleared the table. Dennison looked at his watch. It was time. They left the café and walked over to Oxford Circus. They stood at the intersection, a four-way collision of people and traffic, next to the entrance to the Underground. Hof scanned a group of tourists walking slowly by, looking around randomly at everything. His eye selected the young females within the troupe. "Tourists are the easiest fucks," he said to Richard. "So easy. They're in London on holiday, they got nothing to do, and they're looking for adventures they can go home and tell their friends about."

Rossi was looking at Erskine, detecting something in his face. He took out his note pad and scribbled:

u ok

Erskine smiled unconvincingly and nodded. He looked around at Dennison and his fellow seducers, and he thought about walking away and forgetting about the whole charade. But instead he just stood there, paralysed by something he could not fathom.

wots most beautiful thing u ever seen

Erskine smiled, then thought for a long time. "I remember when I was kid, I used to live near this really old church," he began. "One winter we had a lot of snow, and I remember walking past it, and as I looked up at the building, suddenly I saw this huge block of snow slide off the pitched roof. The thing was, the snow was actually in mid-air as I looked up. It was an amazing thing seeing this pure white slab hanging in the air for a split second, like an avalanche frozen in time. It happened early on a Saturday morning when there was no one else around, and I realised that I was the only person in the whole world that saw that."

Rossi nodded slowly, immersed in the sentiment of his story. Erskine asked him the same question:

my mother

Dennison was busy scoping faces, preparing to select the next four targets. He turned to the men, re-stated the terms of the proposition, and set the completion deadline.

Erskine interrupted. "Why should we carry on with this?"

A ripple of silence filtered amongst them. Everyone stared at Erskine. Dennison smirked, almost as if he'd expected the question. "Excuse me?" he replied.

"Well, why?" he shrugged. "It's stupid. The whole thing."

Dennison angled his body in Erskine's direction. "No one is forcing you to be here," he said.

"I don't know why I ever agreed to do this."

"Why *did* you agree, Erskine?" he asked, leaning towards him. "What is it in you that needs this?"

Hof looked curiously at Dennison. The question seemed to unsettle him. Dennison waited for Erskine's response, but he had no answer. "Back to the matter at hand," he said casually, turning once more to cast his eye out over the mass of faces in the street. "As you are so agitated, Erskine, you can go first," said Dennison.

"How are you choosing these people anyway?" asked Erskine. "I mean, what is your criteria?"

Dennison smirked. Erskine wanted to slap the smirk off his face, to hit him so hard that his mouth would fall open and some words would tumble out, explaining who he really was and why he was playing this pointless game, and any other secrets he was keeping.

Just then a woman appeared with two young children, one in a pram, the other at her side.

"There," said Dennison, pointing with the peak of his black hat.

Richard's mouth fell open in shock, Rossi shook his head in disbelief and Hof let out a huge laugh. Erskine shook his head adamantly. "No fucking way!"

"You can still quit, Erskine" Dennison replied.

"You're not serious," claimed Erskine.

"I am," Dennison replied. "You'd better hurry up. She's getting away."

"I can't do it?" he said. "That's a family."

"So what. Don't you think she'd welcome a bit of time for herself, away from it all — the housework, the screaming kids, the two-minute sex from her too tired husband?"

Erskine shook his head in disbelief and set off reluctantly in pursuit of the woman. She was in her mid-thirties, with a lean elegant figure. As he followed her she turned her head to one side to look at something in a shop window, and Erskine could see that she was beautiful. Her face was scored with prominent cheekbones and deep-set eyes — the kind of face that gathered shadows. He watched her for some minutes as she looked in shop windows at dresses.

She went down into Oxford Circus station. He made a move to help her with the pram, but someone else got there ahead of him and he cussed himself for missing his chance at an introduction.

She got off the Tube at Finchley Road and went into a supermarket. Erskine followed her and waited outside, thinking about his approach. Eventually she came out, weighed down with shopping bags, and as she walked toward him Erskine hid around the corner, then as she approached he pretended not to see her, and deliberately bumped into her. The shopping fell to the pavement.

"I'm so sorry," said Erskine, stooping hurriedly to pick up the bags. "Are you alright?"

"Can't you watch where you're bloody going?" said the woman angrily. The children were looking at Erskine. She grabbed the bags from him.

"I'm sorry. Listen, can I—"

She started walking away. Erskine watched her, thinking what to do next. He rubbed his head, checked it for sweat, then ran after her. "Excuse me!"

She turned. "I'm really, really sorry about that. Please let me help you carry your shopping home? You really look like you could do with a hand — and it would make me feel a lot better about being so clumsy."

She studied his face. The children studied his face. He looked down at the boy holding onto the side of the pram. He was about seven years old, with a pageboy haircut, and a face as round as a dinner plate. Erskine smiled and said hello. The boy inched closer to his mother.

"What's the matter?" Erskine asked. "Don't you like my face?" He pulled his ears and stuck out his tongue. The boy started laughing. His mother relaxed and broke a smile.

"So, can I give you a hand?" asked Erskine, reaching for the bags in anticipation.

"OK, thank you." She handed them to him. He took them and they walked on. The boy studied Erskine, curious about his mother's new friend, waiting to see if he would do anything else funny.

"What's your name then?" Erskine asked the boy. He glared at him, then buried his face in his mother's thigh. She pulled his head away. "The man asked you a question," she said.

"Joe," said the boy.

"Hey Joe." They shook hands. "Is this your little sister?" asked Erskine, pointing into the pram.

He nodded. "Her name's Dawn."

Erskine looked into the buggy and saw a two year old child. "Dawn," he repeated. "Like the birth of a new morning."

"What's your name?" asked Joe.

"Ah, that's a secret," said Erskine playfully. "If you promise to be my friend I'll tell you in a little while, OK?"

As they walked and chatted Erskine divided his focus between the woman and her son. He tried to make Joe laugh by pulling more faces. When they arrived at her house Erskine hesitated. "I should leave you here," he said. "I mean, I don't want to intrude."

"That's OK," she said. "Could you help me bring them inside?"

Joe tugged at Erskine's sleeve, pulling him toward the door. They went inside and into the kitchen. Erskine put the bags down on the table.

"Would you like a cup of tea?" she asked.

Erskine looked startled. "Oh, that would be great," he said. "What about if I make it?"

"That's alright."

"You sure it's not too much trouble."

"Trouble?" she said. "I've seen trouble — tea is not trouble. Tea is tea."

Joe disappeared into his bedroom and returned with a remote control car to show the new guest. It trundled into the kitchen and he drove it against Erskine's feet to get his attention. Erskine complimented him on his fine toy, and Joe put on a display for him, demonstrating all the moves he'd mastered. Erskine acted as if it was the most amazing thing he had ever seen.

"Is your husband at work?" he asked the woman, sipping his tea.

"Yes."

As she said it Erskine was seized with guilt about what he was scheming to do. To intrude into a family — a wife, a husband, two children, a house and the things in it that symbolised their union. It was the kind of life he'd wished he'd had with Genevieve. In that moment he changed his mind about seducing her. He wouldn't get the money, but he did not care. He stared into his teacup, suddenly uncomfortable. "I'd better go." He stood up.

She looked surprised. "But you haven't finished your tea."

There was a brief silence while he looked at her. She felt him scrutinising her features and so she looked away, fiddling with the hair around her ear.

Joe rammed the car into Erskine's foot.

Erskine began making his way to the door. She followed. "Well, thanks for carrying my shopping home," she said. "And for bumping into me. It was nice to have some adult company for a change. You do go mad being around kids all day."

Joe's face appeared between his mother's legs. "Bye bye," he said, flapping both his hands.

"See you, Joe."

Erskine opened the door, stepped out, then turned on the landing. "By the way, I don't even know your name."

"Megan."

"Pleased to meet you, Megan. I'm Erskine."

"What?...What did you say?"

28

It has to be him. How many men can there be in this town with a crazy name like that? Megan composed herself, smiled at Erskine as if nothing was wrong, then asked him to wait while she went to the lavatory. Instead she closed the door and frantically called Natascha on her mobile.

"What does he look like?" she asked, trying her best to sound calm.

"What?"

"Your Erskine guy? What does he look like?"

Megan peered out at Erskine through the spy hole in her door as Natascha described him. Her heart punched against her chest when she realised it was him.

"Why do you want to know anyway?" asked Natascha.

"Oh, I er...I just wanted to ask our art teacher if he could get a model that looks like him for our next term. I thought you might like that. A body double."

Natascha laughed. "Don't do me any favours."

After she hung up Megan stood still for some moments. She could not believe she had just lied to her best friend. It was not her intention when she made the call. She did not recognise herself. She shook off the thought, opened the front door and smiled. "Will you stay for lunch?"

Megan's nanny lived in a flat on the adjoining street. She dropped the children off there for the afternoon, leaving Erskine waiting in her house. He felt like an intruder, walking around her home, seeing her things, her décor, her photos and the life she shared with her husband. When Megan returned a few minutes later he was nervous. "Listen...I know you're married and everything, but..." He moved his hands in a circular motion, as if that was a substitute for the rest of his sentence.

"Don't be silly," said Megan, waving an arm dismissively. "You're my guest."

She offered to take his jacket, and as Erskine peeled it off she reached for it but timed it wrong, and there was a clumsy fumble. She laughed nervously, then put it over the knob at the end of the stair rail.

"Just make yourself at home," she said. "I'll be right back." She dashed upstairs for a fast makeover. She brushed her teeth, re-configured her hair, slipped on some different underwear and selected a pretty top. As she rushed about the room, on fire with anticipation, she caught sight of herself in the mirror and froze. The guilt was already there. But then she thought about the back of Gary's head, about how he had treated her, and that she deserved something nice.

When she came downstairs Erskine noticed the change. "You look very nice," he said approvingly. "Lovely."

"Oh, thank you." She touched the back of her hair and looked embarrassed. Instantly she felt beautiful again, his simple words replenishing her.

Physically he was not what she'd expected. When Natascha talked of him Megan somehow imagined someone more stereotypically handsome. She wondered about the situation she had unexpectedly found herself in. She wasn't sure if Erskine had been trying to seduce her all along, or if he had genuinely only intended to help her home with her shopping. She considered that he might be a playboy who did this to a lot of women, including Natascha, but he did not seem the type to her.

"Have you got a girlfriend?" she asked.

"No." He did not hesitate when he replied.

You bastard. Liar.

She kissed him first. She owned the action, the tentative initial exploration of his mouth — as if she was testing a new food for sweetness, expecting incredible flavours. She was surprised by her own forwardness. She had never kissed a man first, never had to. This was new, an incarnation of herself she did not recognize. She took a step back, almost apologizing for her pre-emptive action. But something inside her was triggered now. She peeled off her top and stared at him, her breath heavy, her eyes encouraging him.

As they began to undress, Erskine was still nervous. "Are you sure you want to do this?" he asked.

"Yes, why?"

"Because...Well, I don't know..."

"It's fine...fine." She was more certain than he, more eager. "Listen, Erskine, I've been a good wife and mother. I've put up with a lot. This is about me. I deserve this. I deserve to feel good." Something in the way she spoke drew Erskine to her. She kissed him again, harder this time, gripping the muscles on his arms and shoulders. Erskine thought again about taking a woman with a husband and family, a woman with so much to lose, but she seemed so sure of what she wanted.

If what Megan was doing was wrong, it did not feel so to her in this moment. A latent lust swelled within her. She felt re-fuelled, gorged with life after feeling so disconnected from herself for so long. She could not resist him now, not after what Natascha had told her. She thought about the fact that Erskine was cheating on her best friend, but then so was she. They were equal partners, unknown accomplices to the same indiscretion.

Erskine placed his hand on her face and began tracing the contours of her cheekbones. He liked the way the shadows settled in the caverns of her deep-set eyes. Megan placed her hand over his — grateful that he was drawn to the features that were once such a tenet of her allure.

They were on the sofa, not the bed. She would not take him up there. Not where she and Gary slept. They stripped naked. He was surprised at how fit she was, considering she'd had two children. Her stomach was flat, her body lean and taut. She condensed the foreplay — eager as she was to sample him. Under normal circumstances she'd want more if it, but this was not the occasion for any lingering preamble.

Lunch got lost in the lust. It was never made, never initiated beyond the invitation.

The sex was adequate, and no more. When it was over she turned from him, startled with disappointment, shocked to the point where her eyes widened, as if she'd just choked on some food. She wondered if he was holding back, saving the best for Natascha, now her rival. *How dare you be that selfish.* She waited a while, and then took him again to be sure, hoping the second time would deliver her to the edge of sexual madness, like it did for Natascha. It did not.

Remorse came upon her like a black cloud. She had betrayed them both — husband and best friend — for the jolt of an ordinary orgasm. Erskine's magic had not worked on her. She felt pathetic for thinking it would. She felt like one of the ugly sister's to Natascha's Cinderella.

She posed a question to herself. Would she have felt this remorse if she had succeeded in feeling what Natascha had felt?

She lay quietly next to the stranger, feeling dirty and ashamed. She desperately wanted a shower. She felt herself starting to cry, felt it rising, and she made sure he did not see, made sure there was no sound, and that the tears were brief. She made a decision to hide her disgrace, not to tell Natascha. But then she realised this would not work, as she would surely meet Erskine one day when Natascha introduced them. She could think of only one solution:

"Promise me something, Erskine," she asked tentatively.

"What?"

"That you won't tell anyone about this?"

"OK."

"No, I mean really, you can't," she pleaded, sitting up suddenly. "If you ever see me again, in any circumstance, with anybody, you can never tell, OK? Never. This has to be our secret."

"Well, it's unlikely I'll ever bump into you—"

"Just promise me. Please?"

Erskine did not understand the fear in her eyes. "Alright," he said.

"Thank you." She breathed a heavy sigh. "I have to go now. I have to pick up the kids."

29

That night Erskine waited for Natascha on the Embankment, beside the passenger cruiser on which she sang. Soon he spied her walking briskly up the gantry toward him. He knew her now from distance, from the shape of her hair and the way she moved — with a certain up-down eddy, like a seahorse. When she spotted him she felt a breach of something in her chest – an energy she could not name. She stopped in her tracks and looked at him coldly. "What are you doing here?"

Erskine had no words. He just stared at her. They both had things to say — identical confessions — but truth got choked in the moment. She spoke first, abruptly. "I can't see you tonight."

I didn't ask you.

The sound of an impatient car horn pierced the night. Natascha looked across the street and waved to a man in a parked car. "Who's that?" asked Erskine.

"What do you care?" she replied defiantly.

"I don't."

"That's OK then." She walked across the street and got in. The man looked over at Erskine briefly, sizing him up, then drove away. She hardly spoke during the journey, but he was chatty, pleased to see her, eager to have sex with her again. "How come you never invite me to any of your gigs?" the man asked playfully.

"I never invite people to my gigs." Her tone was harsh.

"Why not?"

She was irritated at his desire for an explanation, that he had not deduced the answer. "Because I'm working, and I don't want to have to look after...people," she replied.

She felt the urge to tell him to stop the car and let her out, but she could not bring herself to do it. Not after he'd waited for her. She felt obliged to have sex with him now. She turned and looked out of the side window and into the darkness of the city flashing by. The architecture, reduced to a procession of angular silhouettes, towered almost threateningly, and she felt a kind of childlike fear. She was comforted by the neon lights of the shop fronts and the black shapes of people on the street. Then she felt something on her body and realised that it was his hand on her leg.

When they arrived at his flat they started kissing almost immediately. Her idea. She wanted it over with. The sex was routine. He was on top, sliding back and forth, his head buried in her shoulder. She stared numbly up at the ceiling, hoping it would soon end. She became irritated when it did not. Usually she enjoyed sex with him, basic as it was. But not now.

"Stop....stop!" she said.

He halted, looked at her quizzically. "What's wrong?"

She could not meet his eyes. She slid away from under him and began to dress. She did it with her back to him, like a wall. He sat up and waited for her to say something. "Natascha, what's wrong?" he asked again. "What is it?"

She turned to him and sighed, thinking about an explanation. In the end she simply said, "It's nothing, OK? Nothing."

As she closed the front door behind her she felt shame wash over her. But she got over it fast, rinsed it from her system. As fast as her father would have. In just a few hours time she would think of him no more.

She was daddy's girl after all.

*

The following afternoon Natascha met Megan in a local park. She had the children with her, who ran ahead manically, screaming and play fighting. They sat down on a bench, sipping takeaway coffees. Megan felt different being with her now. Just the sight of her made her think of Erskine. They now had something else in common. She wanted to tell her that she had slept with him too, but she could not bring herself to do it. She felt a strange excitement that she had this secret knowledge, but at the same time the guilt had crystallised within her, seeping out in tiny ways. Usually when they met in the park it was Natascha who bought the coffee, as Megan held onto the kids, but this time Megan insisted on buying for her.

"I thought you guys didn't have each other's numbers?" said Megan.

"We didn't," Natascha replied. "He tracked me down on the boat."

"Wow. That means he likes you. A lot."

The children were shouting more loudly now. Natascha smiled affectionately, while Megan grew irritated. "OK, you guys! Go and play over there where we don't have to hear you. Go! Away, away!"

The children scurried away. "I think he's fucking other women," said Natascha.

Megan's heart leapt with fear. "What...What makes you say that?" she asked tentatively.

"Well, he's a man, isn't he?"

"Here we go again," Megan sighed, rolling her eyes. Natascha looked irritated. "Hasn't he got the right to sleep with whoever he likes?" Megan offered. "I mean...it's not as if you guys are an item or anything."

Natascha fell silent, looked at the ground pensively. Megan tried to read her mood. She shrugged and held up her palms. "What do you care who this guy's seeing anyway? I thought you didn't even want a relationship." Her tone was more aggressive now.

"Well, I don't...I mean...well...it's just...I can't stop thinking about him, Megan. I don't know. I'm really confused. It's like, when we make love, it's so fucking intense, I just want to scream. And then afterwards I hate him....It's so fucked up."

Megan sighed sympathetically. "Oh, Nat. You've really got to be careful, y'know."

"What?....Why?"

"Well, if you shut yourself off from everything....after a while, you forget how to feel."

30

The day seemed to start suddenly, as if it had stolen hours from the night. The weather morphed from sunshine into wind and rain, and then back again, as if prefacing the coming of something. To Erskine the trees seemed to bend in the breeze but then not spring back, as if they were caught in time. He felt outside it all, separate from the elements. He had nowhere special to be, and nothing special to do — except the proposition.

At another café in the heart of the city, the five men sat together like estranged brothers. Dennison was deep in concentration, staring out of the window at people passing. Suddenly, thoughts of Alice broke through — a memory of her during the times they were happy. He was disturbed by the intrusion, that his emotional defences had been breached, for he believed that he had fortified himself against such recollections. He clenched his fist and concentrated, and soon thoughts of her went away.

Hof glanced out of the window and saw a ballet student walk by — tall and skinny, with a long neck and straight posture. "I want to fuck a gymnast next," he said.

"A gymnast?" asked Richard. "Why?"

"Yeah, you know — all that bendy sex. There's something wild about being able to fold a woman in half, and then put your dick inside her."

As Hof and Richard laughed together, Erskine sprang to attention as he thought he could hear the sound of a soprano saxophone — a wailing, improvised spiral of noise. He turned to see if anyone else was hearing it but him, and he became apprehensive when he realized that he was the only one. He imagined that the sound had escaped from his mouth, and that it found physical form as it met the air, shaping into a sculpture of jagged, crystallised smoke. And then laminated inside it he saw a distorted image of Genevieve's face, serene in her lifelessness.

Erskine looked at Dennison, wondering again about who he was. He focused on his black hat. He wondered if this was where his power was located, and if removing it from his head might neutralise his ability, like Samson without his long hair, or Popeye without his spinach.

Erskine's attention wandered. He stared out of the window at the ground. After a time he saw a pointed black shape appear. As he focused on it he heard a noise, like the low rumble of a distant earthquake, and the shadow began to grow and expand across the ground, up the sides of buildings, coating the entire space until it was engulfed in darkness. Within this expanse was a pattern of thousands of twinkling black hats, identical to Dennison's, set uniformly like a giant wallpaper print — but then Erskine blinked and everything evaporated.

"Why are you always wearing that hat?" he asked finally, pointing to it as if nobody knew where it was located. "Have you got a bald patch or something?" He spoke with a sneering tone.

Dennison pointed at Erskine with the edge of his face. "My style is the least of your worries," he replied.

Erskine narrowed his eyes, wondering what he meant, frustrated at his fast mouth that seemed to conjure a retort to everything.

"Man, you can't ask the cat about his hat," said Hof with a slow shake of the head. "That's like asking Superman why he wears a red cape with an 'S' on it."

"Why does he?" asked Richard. "All that flapping material must create a lot of drag when he flies."

Dennison looked at Erskine and tilted his head slightly to one side. "You've been asking a lot of questions lately," he said.

"Yes. And you've not been answering them."

Dennison smirked. "Well, the real question is, what is it in your life that you're not taking care of, that affords you the extra space to be worrying about me?"

Erskine frowned. "What...What's that supposed to mean?"

Dennison stared at him expectantly, as if he was waiting for him to answer his own question. Erskine shook his head with exasperation, then turned away, deep in thought. Once again he felt the urge to quit, but he could not do it. He was frustrated by his own inertia.

Dennison looked out of the window. There was a café across the street. "See that café over there?" he said, looking at Erskine.

"Uh-huh."

"Your next assignment is to seduce the third person to come through that door."

The men all stirred with excitement. Erskine was speechless with surprise.

"Oh, shit, here we go," said Hof. "The funky rules are back."

"Pay attention," said Dennison, holding up a finger.

All eyes focused on the door of the café. "What if it's a man?" said Hof.

"Shut up," said Erskine. He rubbed his head, then checked his palm for sweat.

The door. First person. A young man carrying a box of sandwiches. Moments passed.

Second person. A six-foot model, with long legs, carrying her portfolio. Erskine exhaled, cursed his bad luck.

Twenty seconds passed. In silence they waited. Then a woman emerged. She was five-foot-four, mid-twenties, with Nordic-style face, ethereal features and long hair tied back. She wore a well-cut black tracksuit with a white trim, running shoes and a baseball cap.

"Unlucky mate," said Richard, hitting Erskine on the back.

Erskine rose from his chair. As he set off Dennison called after him. "Be careful." Erskine turned and their eyes locked. Then he turned and stepped out.

Dennison looked again into the street. His eyes narrowed as he saw someone for Rossi. He tapped him on the arm and pointed. Rossi saw a woman walking slowly. An old woman in her seventies. Rossi smiled gently, as if he expected it.

"Shit," chuckled Richard.

"That's radical!" said Hof, suddenly becoming animated. "That is fucking radical. What next? A Muslim in a burka? A nun getting shagged from behind?"

Rossi calmly rose to his feet and stepped out. Dennison looked again. Women came and went, all shapes, sizes and ethnicities — women Hof would have liked to have had sex with, if only the choice were his.

Then Dennison saw her. She bowled into the café where they were sitting, and stepped up to the counter. She was in her mid-thirties, six-foot-two, lean toned limbs, long straight white hair, pale skin, midnight blue gloss lipstick and a black eye-patch over her right eye. Hof felt a strange shiver course through him. A mix of curiosity and fear. "I don't know about her," he said cautiously.

"What's the matter?" asked Dennison.

"I don't know. I..." He couldn't describe what he was feeling, what was making him apprehensive. The woman ordered a double espresso to go, turned and headed for the door. As she walked past she glanced casually at the men, caught them staring at her. Dennison gestured to Hof with his chin. He took a deep breath as if he was about to dive under water, and set off in pursuit.

141

Richard was last. "So, who have you got for me then?" he asked sheepishly, scanning the street. But Dennison was not looking out of the window anymore.

"Richard?" he began.

"Yes?"

"Your assignment is to have sex with Madonna."

He froze. "Madonna...As in, the singer?"

"Correct."

Dennison smirked as he saw a look of total bewilderment etch into Richard's face. "What are you talking about?" He knew by Dennison's expression that he was not joking. "You want me to sleep with Madonna," he repeated, pointing to himself. "You're crazy. How am I going to get to her?"

Dennison broke into a slow smile. "I know a way."

31

Erskine followed the woman as she meandered slowly along Oxford Street, stopping occasionally to window shop. He moved his head sideways, trying to keep sight of her within the high current of the Oxford Street traffic. The crowds began to grate him. The great shuffling hordes made him feel claustrophobic. He felt an urge to push people out of his way. Buses roared by, grinding their engines, and they made him wince as if he'd been pierced by a sharp object. He looked down at the concrete under his feet and wished it was grass.

As he turned along Berners Street he saw a homeless girl squatting below an ATM machine, begging for change. She cut a strange figure, a low, static ball amongst the upright, shifting hordes. He felt the urge to stop and give her some money, but he did not want to lose the girl. She turned onto Rathbone place and entered a camping store. She went directly to the rock climbing section and began scanning the equipment. She picked up a length of climbing rope and tested it. Erskine came up and stood parallel. He glanced across at her, then picked up a flashlight from the rack, examined it, put it back. He moved closer, then rubbed his head, checked his palm for sweat. "Excuse me?" She looked up at him. "Can I just ask you, are you a rock climber?"

"No." She moved away, picked up a climbing belt and put it around her waist.

He followed. "I mean, you're looking at rock climbing equipment. I'm just thinking about starting, and I wanted to ask you about the right equipment to buy."

She looked him up and down cautiously. "Well, it depends how much you've got to spend."

She waited. Erskine's eyes bustled nervously. "Er...well, I..."

She looked him up and down. *What kind of joker?* Erskine stalled, trying to think of something. Eventually he said, "OK, well the truth is, I'm not really interested in rock climbing at all. I was just walking by outside and I saw you come in here, and I thought..."

"You thought what?"

"Well, I thought I could...I could chat you up, and see if you

143

were nice....y'know."

She looked down and smiled to herself. He opened his palms, shrugged his shoulders.

*

Hof tailed the white-haired woman as she strode along Berwick Street, wondering who she was, and how she came to be wearing an eye patch. She wore a full-length coat of natural Russian sable, by Dennis Basso, £100,000. Collar up. Underneath, a silk crepe dress with silver embroidery at the shoulders and décolleté, by Dominique Sirop. On her right hand, a finger dressed with a £200,000 diamond ring.

After tracking her for a short distance he noticed something. She seemed to be following someone else ahead of her. He could tell by the way her head moved and her pace varied. He tried to look ahead to see who it was but he could not make it out. Then she turned down a narrow street and watched as a man went into a sex shop. Hof stood back as she hesitated outside, then followed him in. He thought about waiting for her to come out but curiosity carried his feet to the door.

He paid at the counter and went through a curtain into a peep show. A naked girl was on a tiny stage in the centre of the room, gyrating and fondling herself. In the dim light he scanned for faces amongst the spectators. She wasn't hard to find, with her long white hair, standing at the back. She wasn't watching the show. She was watching someone else watching the show. Hof followed her eyeline, which led to a man. He was in his early fifties, with thin greying hair, narrow eyes and thick wavy lips. He was watching the stripper. His expression was without excitement or any indication of desire. Hof moved closer. In the flickering light he could make out that she was crying. Suddenly she put her hand to her face and stormed out.

She stood in the street with tears falling from her face. Tears falling from one eye. Beneath the patch covering the other eye, unseen sweet-water was collecting, trapped in her private reservoir. She felt its delicate press against her eyelid, bright and warm. She wedged a finger gently under it, prised it ajar like a hatch, and her tears flushed out. She looked down and watched it splash against the concrete at her feet.

Hof stood a few yards behind her, wondering what was making her cry. He had a black silk scarf in his hand. He stepped forward and held it out to her. "I think you left this inside."

She inhaled with surprise that someone was there, and instantly she quelled her tears. She looked him up and down, wiping her face.

"It was on the floor in there, next to where you were standing," said Hof. She reached out, took the scarf, and then held onto his wrist.

The scarf was not hers.

*

Rossi trailed the old woman along Lexington Street. He paused, scribbled something on the back of one of his cards, walked up to her and tapped her on the shoulder. She turned with surprise, with a slight shake, read both sides of the card, then gazed at him warmly, touched his cheek and smiled as if she'd known him for years. "Hello, Rossi," she said. "Where have you been all my life?"

He shrugged and raised his eyebrows.

"You are pretty, aren't you?"

He made a face. *What can I say?*

"You're a sweet boy, aren't you Rossi?"

Gwyneth was seventy-three. Five-foot-seven. Slightly hunched in the upper back. Grey curly hair, round colourless spectacles and a friendly, smiley demeanour.

wood u like 2 dance?

Her face lit up. "Lovely," she beamed. "I haven't danced in years. Not since my husband died."

I know a nice place.

"You are pretty, aren't you?"

Rossi gave her his arm and they strolled away.

*

The woman with the white hair and the eye patch had parked her black Maserati Quattroporte in Golden Square, off Beak Street. She'd left it on a single yellow line in the middle of the day. She parked where she pleased, any time of the day or night. She spent eight hundred pounds a month on penalty fines. They ticketed her, they clamped her, they towed her. She didn't care. "What's your

145

name?" asked Hof as they climbed inside.

"Domino," she said.

Something about the way she said it made Hof shiver. She took the black silk scarf he had given her, wrapped it around her neck, then she turned the ignition and pulled out around Golden Square, into Beak Street, turning right onto Regent Street. She wore black gloves, and her driving style was fast and responsive, like a getaway driver. She banked left, heading towards Hyde Park, then pulled out sharply into the flow of the Park Lane traffic, moving towards Knightsbridge.

Hof was impressed by her moves. He checked out the interior of her car, then the diamond on her finger. "So, what do you do for a living?" he asked.

She made a face, as if that was the lamest question ever. She turned left past Knightsbridge Underground station and along Sloane Street. "Do you ever take the Tube?" she asked.

"Sometimes, yeah."

"I got on a crowded Tube once." She said it as if it was a rare and special thing. "As I squeezed through, my nipples brushed against a man's chest, a stranger, and instantly I was turned on. I didn't even see his face." She removed a hand from the wheel and brushed her fingers lightly across herself in demonstration.

Hof squirmed nervously. "Wow...That must have been, er... amazing."

"I mean, don't get me wrong, I didn't have an orgasm or anything, but I did feel a little something. A little tingle, y'know."

As the car banked around Sloane Square she pulled off one of her gloves, put her hand under her dress, through her panties, and rubbed it twice against her vagina. Hof looked on silently, dumbstruck with surprise. Keeping her eyes on the road she pulled her hand out and put it to his mouth. Automatically his head jolted back slightly. "What are you doing?"

She ignored his question. Again she put her fingers to his mouth, more forcefully, this time between his lips. This time he opened and let them in, as she demanded. She narrowed her eyes and smiled, pleased with his obedience.

*

At that moment Rossi and Gwyneth were sitting in the back of a taxi heading toward a hotel on Park Lane. "Where does your mother live, Rossi?" she asked.

Paris

"Oooh, lovely. I can tell that you love her, Rossi. A lot," she said, pointing her finger and squinting her eyes. "You must miss her terribly."

I do

"You should be there with her then, silly boy. Paris isn't far. Whatever you're doing with your life in London, nothing is more important than your family, being with the ones you love," she said, smiling and patting him on the knee. Rossi paused, gazed at her thoughtfully. Her wisdom connected with him. He nodded his head slowly.

"So is that where you're from then? France?"

He nodded. "Lovely," she said. "French men. Very romantic, very passionate. I find English men a bit slow on the uptake myself," she said, wrinkling her nose in disappointment. "I've been to a lot of functions, many functions, and they ab-so-lu-te-ly will not dance. They're very stuck in their ways. They've got this idea that if they get involved with us we'll start nagging them or something."

She pulled out a handkerchief and coughed up phlegm into it. Rossi gently patted her back. "Ooh, dear," she said. "The engine's breaking down, Rossi."

The taxi dropped them off outside the hotel. "What are we doing here Rossi?" asked Gwyneth. He jiggled his torso to indicate dancing. "Oooh, lovely!"

He took her hand and led her into the hotel. They took the lift up to the bar on the top floor, which had panoramic views across the city. There was a man in one corner playing classics on a baby grand piano. Gwyneth made satisfied noises as she scanned the space. Rossi showed her to a table by the window.

The pianist played *Under A Blanket of Blue* (1933). Two gin and tonics later, Gwyneth was feeling warm and happy. "The thing is, you see, the elderly are not supposed to want it past a certain age," she said. "It's OK for men, like whatshisname?" She waved a hand in his face. "Hefner-Stringfellow and all that, still to be having sex or taking Viagra or whatever, well into old age, but women can't do the same without people raising eyebrows. That's why I love Joan Collins. I ab-so-lu-te-ly love that woman!" She banged the table as she said it. "She's over seventy and she still enjoys a good old romp, and she's not afraid of getting these younger men who still know how to do it without taking that Viagra stuff."

Rossi smiled and nodded in agreement. "The granny who is still at it is a bit of a joke isn't it?" she said. "But I still feel like it. I do. Should I be ashamed of that, Rossi? Just because I'm old?"

He shook his head. She smiled and touched his cheek. "You're a sweet boy, Rossi. So pretty." She rolled her eyes into the top of her head. "I think I'm getting a bit tipsy." Rossi checked her eyes, then squeezed her hand.

"I think that when it comes down to a bit of the old you-know-what, the elderly should be treated better," she lamented. "They should. After all, who knows more about sex than an old woman? Who's got more experience, more wisdom than us? Young girls today don't know anything about lovemaking," she sneered, pushing out her bottom lip and shaking her head. "They're too busy trying to look beautiful. Trying to get suntans and fake boobies, and posting the pictures on Ista-whatever or Bookface."

Rossi took her hand and they strolled over to the piano and started to dance gently. Rossi had an arm around her waist and the other holding her hand. Surprised expressions broke out around the room as people eyed the lone couple.

Gwyneth fizzed with delight. "This is sooooo romantic, Rossi," she said. "The last time I did this was with my ex-husband, God rest his soul."

At that moment a young couple walked in and saw them. The woman smiled and tugged at her partner's arm. "Look at that man dancing with his granny," she said. "Isn't that lovely?"

After two numbers they sat down and took a break. "Have you heard of that woman, Jane Juska?" asked Gwyneth. Rossi shook his head. "She's an elderly American schoolteacher who wrote a book about an ad she put in the newspaper, looking for men to have sex with. She got sixty-three replies. Lucky cow." She put her hand across her mouth and giggled like a mischievous schoolgirl. Rossi imagined what she was like as a little girl. In his mind's eye he saw her skipping down the road in a pink dress and Shirley Temple hair, singing to herself.

The pianist played *April In Paris* (1932). Gwyneth reacted instantly, throwing her hands into the air. "I ab-so-lu-te-ly love this song, Rossi," she said. "Do you know it?"

He shook his head. "Young people today," she huffed. "You've got no music. No real singers. No real love songs." She closed her eyes and listened to it, then she opened them and asked, "Aren't you in love with someone, Rossi?"

He shook his head.

"Why ever not? You're so pretty."

He shrugged his shoulders.

"Such a waste. The problem with people today is that everybody's been hurt, and so that has made them more sensitive, so they become less tolerant of the problems in relationships, you see. The slightest thing becomes a potential break-up situation. People nowadays leave relationships too easily, whereas in my day you used to fight for them."

u wise lady

She laughed. She was encouraged by his endorsement, warmed by the fact that someone cared what an old lady had to say about life. "You see, what a lot of men don't realise these days is that real love is not about sex," she continued. "It's about being a companion to someone, you understand? That means you could actually love someone and be with them, and never sleep with them. But what man would ever dream of doing that?"

The pianist played *Moonlight In Vermont* (1943). They got up and resumed dancing. After a while she looked up at him and asked, "Aren't you going to kiss me, then?" He smiled and ran his hand gently over her hair. She laughed. "You're a good soul, Rossi," she said. "If only I were forty-years younger, we could really do something, me and you. I'd show you a thing or two. I was a real beauty in my day, I can tell you. I had my pick of them."

When he kissed her she had flat lips. His mouth pressed against the bone underneath her skin. He didn't mind. It was the cycle of life. One day it would happen to him. He left her in the bar while he went downstairs to the hotel reception. He booked a room and came back up with the key. She was standing next to the piano singing *The Nearness Of You* (1937). She had a beautiful voice. Rossi stood back and admired her, and for a moment it reminded him of his mother singing Barbara Streisand songs when they lived together in Paris all those years ago.

When it was over he took her by the hand, led her out of the bar and into the lift:

shall we make lovly luv here

She looked away, put her hand over her mouth and giggled, schoolgirl style. "You want to do it here?" she asked, thinking he

149

wanted to do it in the lift. Rossi wiggled a room key in front of her face. "You booked a room? Ooh, how exciting!" she said with wide-eyed surprise. "Are you sure?" He made the OK sign.

As they entered the room and Gwyneth saw the suite she did a little dance. "This is fancy, fancy," she said, twirling in a circle. "Isn't it lovely?"

Rossi held up his arms. *Of course.*

"You're a sweet boy, Rossi."

They sat on the bed and she told him about her dead husband and her years of loneliness, and how difficult it was to find someone as gentle and as fun-loving as he, her jewel, she called him. Rossi didn't usually listen to the stories of the women he slept with because he was always leaving, but Gwyneth was different. He stroked her grey hair and kissed her flat mouth, and caressed her body through her clothing, and then he laid her gently down, just like her husband used to do when they went on picnics in the long grass of the Dorset countryside, and she closed her eyes and submitted to him as he undressed her and then put himself into her, a young frame on a wrinkled body, the meeting of ages.

"You're a very naughty man, Rossi," she said afterwards, pointing at him playfully. "Very naughty. I haven't done anything like that for years. So many years."

They left the room and went down into the lobby. Rossi put his arm around her and squeezed her at the shoulders. She patted his hand and rubbed it. As they walked out of the hotel he remembered something. He dashed back inside and re-appeared a few minutes later with a large bouquet of flowers. When she saw them she put her hand over her mouth and began to cry. Rossi held her as she stood there shaking, then he pulled away, took off her glasses, wiped her face, then cleaned the lenses on his shirt and placed them carefully back in place.

"No one's bought me flowers for years. Years."

no need - u are a flower

He put her in a taxi and waved goodbye.

32

Domino and Hof turned off the King's Road and into a mews in Chelsea. At the end of the short road was a house with a large creeping vine, almost out of control. She parked, and they went inside.

They settled in the lounge. She put on some music. *La Revancha del Tango*, by Gotan Project (2001). "You like this?" she asked.

"Yeah, cool," nodded Hof unconvincingly.

"Let's have some champagne." He followed her into the kitchen. She pulled a bottle of Krug from the fridge, poured two glasses and handed one to him. "Cheers," she said as they clinked.

She paused to study his face. "My ex looked a bit like you, actually," she said.

"Really?"

"Yes. He's the only man who could make me come in the three ways."

Hof choked on his drink. "The three ways?"

"Cock, hands, mouth."

Hof nodded respectfully. "What about in the arse?"

"No. Not there. Anal is for the gay." She downed her champagne and glared at him. He finished his hurriedly, as if it was a competition, and she refilled their glasses. "Why do people call you Hof?" she asked. "Is it short for something."

"Hoffman."

"Hoffman? What a weird thing. What were your parents thinking?"

"My dad was a big Dustin Hoffman fan. He wanted to name me after him, but he thought his first name sounded too gay, so he called me Hoffman instead.

She laughed. "So, Hoffman. Have you got a girl?"

"Nope."

"How come? Attractive man like you...And with a cock like that."

Hof spluttered champagne through a nervous laugh. "How do you...know what my cock is like?"

"It's obvious," she smiled. "Unless you've got a shuttlecock stuffed down there."

He looked down at his groin and laughed nervously. "*Szee-szee-cheee-cheee-chissss.*"

"So, why don't you have a girlfriend?"

"I don't believe in them," he replied.

She widened her single eye, instantly curious. "Really? Why not?"

"I like women too much to limit myself to just one."

She nodded as if that was the most agreeable thing she'd ever heard. She took his hand and lead him back into the lounge, and they sat on the sofa. He tried to sit away from her but she slid up close, putting her hand on his thigh and rubbing circles with her fingers. "Can I just say, I expect cleanliness, and respect for my body," she began.

"What?"

"I don't like people who don't look after themselves, y'know. Is that OK for me to say that?"

"Er...Yes."

"Good. I just want to be upfront."

"Alright."

"Go and brush your teeth, please."

"What?"

"You need to brush your teeth. I need to kiss a clean mouth."

He breathed on the back of his hand, as if he had another nose grafted on there. "Is my breath that bad?"

"Just do it will you? There's a spare toothbrush in the bathroom cabinet somewhere. Go out this door, turn right, then first left."

He sighed, put his champagne down and went to the bathroom. He began looking for a toothbrush. He opened a mirrored cabinet in front of him, and a wall of condoms fell out everywhere, hundreds of them, different makes and colours.

Back in the lounge Domino had taken the handcuffs out of the draw.

In the bathroom Hof was stuffing the condoms back into the cabinet. He grabbed a handful for himself, figuring they might come in useful another time, and put them into his pocket. As he collected the remainder he noticed a business card sticking out amongst the wrappers. He picked it out. It read:

CYNTHIA MOORE
PSYCHOTHERAPIST

He stared at it for some moments, then put it in his pocket.

In the lounge Domino's mobile rang in her bag. She checked it. There was a text message:

STOP FOLLOWING ME ROUND U BITCH

She stared blankly at the words, and then threw the phone casually onto the sofa. By the time Hof had finished brushing his teeth she had moved to the bedroom. She was gazing up at a picture on the wall, housed within a thick silver frame and mounted forward so it appeared to float. It featured an enlarged photo of a man's face. The same man who was at the Soho sex show. He had a stern, authoritative expression. She always sat down on the bed whenever she looked at it for more than a few seconds, so that when she looked, always looked up at it.

She began talking to it. "What did you say, honey?...of course, of course...oh, please don't judge me darling, please...what?... of course...I'm thinking about re-decorating...it feels really stale in here, don't you think?...Could do with a new lick to brighten things up...nothing like the smell of fresh paint...Or perhaps we've just been living here too long...what do you think?...what?...yes, honey, I'm sorry...I'm sorry...of course, of course...but you see, I was depressed...you understand?...Tell me you do...sex was the only thing that made me feel good...But it's no good is it, really. You can't get fucked every minute of the day, can you?...what?...oh, don't worry, honey. Nobody can fuck me as good as you. Nobody."

She turned, remembering there was a guest somewhere in the house, and called out to him. Hof followed her voice, walked in and saw her sitting on the bed below the portrait. He sat next to her and kissed her. "Is that better?" he asked hopefully.

She nodded, then paused and looked up at the ceiling. She put her hand into the air as if she was reaching for a star, and started chanting a phrase, half reciting, half singing, like a robot stuck on repeat: "The fuck you know, the fuck you know, the fuck you know."

Hof twisted his face in confused horror and leaned away from her. "You OK?" She stopped and looked at him as if she'd just woken up from a bad dream. He was freaked out, but he tried not to show it. He thought about leaving, but his ego would not allow it. He didn't want to fail with a mission. He had a sexual reputation to keep up.

"When we fuck I want you to strangle me," she said casually.

"Huh?"

"I want you to strangle me. Until I pass out. But don't kill me. That wouldn't be fun."

"Wha...er...I'm not sure I can do that."

"You better. Or I'll scream rape. Then you'll be fucked."

"Scuse me?"

She pointed to an open window. "My neighbour across there is a retired policeman. All I have to do is scream."

"Listen, I—"

"Do it," she whispered. "Go on. Put your hands around my neck." Slowly, keeping her eyes on him, she raised her chin, exposing the full length of her elegant neck. Hof imagined strangling her and moving in and out of her at the same time. She turned to the window and opened her mouth, ready to scream. Hof put his hands up, speechless, about to plead.

Then she laughed. "Relax," she said. "I'm playing with you. Strangulation doesn't turn me on."

Hof gulped with terrified relief. "Right...I figured...yeah...You alright?"

Domino read the fear in his face. "What's the matter with you?"

Hof pointed to himself. "With me?"

"Yes, you."

"I don't know," he shrugged. "You freak me out."

She smiled as if that was a compliment. She held that look, then changed it as another thought came to her. "Do you realise that the act of sex is very close to shitting?" she began.

"What?"

"Think about it. Is it a coincidence that an arsehole and a pussy are located so close together?"

"I never thought of that."

"Of course you haven't. Why would you?" He blinked nervously.

"Piss and sperm are also close bedfellows," she continued. "They both come out of the same hole. Two fluids — one represents the end of a cycle, the other, the beginning."

Hoff was baffled by her conversation. He didn't know how to respond, so he nodded and laughed instead. "*Szee-szee-cheee-cheee-chissss.*"

"Why don't you take off your clothes Hoffman?" she said casually.

"Eh?"

"You heard me."

Hof's eyebrows did a Mexican wave. He hesitated. Looking.

Blinking.

"DO IT!" she exploded. Then a second later she was calm. Hof began to undress, trying desperately to compose himself, to retrieve his confidence, to overcome his fear of her. When he was naked she glanced down at his erect penis. Playfully she twanged it with her index finger, as if it was a taut string on a weird musical instrument. He leaned over her and began kissing and caressing her, then he unzipped her dress and started negotiating the unfastening of her bra. She watched him impatiently for a few moments, then said, "Don't take off my bra, idiot. Rip it off me!"

He frowned, then put both hands into her cleavage and ripped the bra violently apart. "That's it. The knickers too," she commanded.

He obeyed, destroying both garments. But before he could do anything else he felt something at his wrist, looked down and saw that he was handcuffed to her. "Wha...what are you doing?...Shit!"

"Relax, Hoffman."

"What are you going to do?"

Domino saw the fear in his eyes. She put her finger over his mouth. He gulped saliva. "I don't want you to move," she said. "Don't move your hand, don't move anything." She raised her chained hand, pulling his wrist along with it, and began moving it over her naked body, caressing herself, touching herself. And wherever her hand went, Hof's followed in a graceful tracing movement. He tried to move the fingers of his handcuffed hand, tried to touch her, but she punched him in his side. "I told you not to do anything!"

He apologised. She closed her eye and resumed the action, dragging Hof's limp hand across her face, her neck, her breasts, her stomach, her vagina, her thighs, and he sat helplessly, confused and mesmerised by the strange action. After a while the twinned hands came to rest on her thigh, and she sat with her eye closed in meditative repose. Hof watched her for a moment. "Aren't you going to unlock me?" he asked hopefully. She opened her single eye, annoyed at the interruption. She reached for the champagne bottle with her shackled hand, pursed her lips and poured it clumsily into her mouth. Hof watched as the champagne overflowed down her neck, between her breasts, and settled in a fizzing lake around her vagina.

She put the bottle down and showed Hof the key to the handcuffs in her other hand. Then she opened her legs and slowly inserted it into her vagina. "Come and get it."

"Oh, man!" Hof slowly stretched his hand down to retrieve it.

She cuffed him around the head — a clip, like a bear swiping a small animal. "With your mouth!"

Hof glared at her. *That's twice you've hit me now, you freaky bitch. If I wasn't so afraid of you I'd...well I...*

He knelt below her and sunk his face into her vagina, probing for the key. She could feel the tip of his searching tongue and she clasped her free hand behind his head, rubbing his skull like a basketball.

Suddenly she pushed him away and he fell back, the key clasped triumphantly between his teeth. "What's wrong?" he asked as he took it out of his mouth and wiped it on himself.

"I'm not sure I should let you eat me out like that," she said breathlessly.

"Why not?"

"My husband wouldn't approve."

"Your husband?"

"Yes." She looked up at the picture on the wall.

Hof followed her eye. "Is that him?" She nodded slowly, without taking her eyes off the portrait. "Where is he now?"

"He's here," she said, pointing dreamily at the picture.

"I know that, I mean—"

"The fuck you know, the fuck you know, the fuck you know."

She was looking up at his picture, her face creased as if she were about to cry. Hof unlocked himself with the key and sat back. "What's the matter?" he asked. She stared at him in silence. He got up and went to the bathroom to compose himself. He looked down at his penis and saw that his erection was beginning to wane. He panicked, grabbed it and started trying to revive himself, rolling it between his fingers, whispering repeatedly, "Come on, come on, don't let me down now, baby, come on."

As he came back into the bedroom and looked at Domino he could feel his erection waning again. He cussed his inability to stay hard. He tried to concentrate, tried to think of something sexy. Sensing his difficulty, she walked up to him, her glass in one hand, poured champagne over his penis. "That'll freshen it up," she said. Then she stooped, licked it off, stood up again, wiped her mouth.

She grabbed his penis in her fist. "Come with me, boy," she said, as she pulled it over to the bed. He lay on top of her and nestled between her legs. She poured more champagne along his back. The effervescence fizzled into the groove, and then flowed down into the crease of his backside, lapping under his testicles. She cupped a hand underneath him and put the fluid to her mouth as if she were drinking from a stream.

He slipped on a condom and then he was inside her, focusing on staying hard, trying to think of something sexy, pumping cautiously, fully alert, afraid of what might happen next. She looked along the length of his body, studying the motion of his backside. After a few strokes she extended a leg and hooked the heel of her shoe into the crease of his behind and pushed, urging him on, dictating the motion. Hof's buttocks clenched at the intrusion. He made a weak smile and pushed harder.

As he moved in and out of her she glanced up at the picture on the wall. Her husband's eyes seemed to be watching them. She spoke to him. "Don't worry honey, don't worry. Nobody can fuck me as good as you. Nobody."

Hof swivelled and looked at the portrait, felt the eyes boring into him, felt his erection begin to shrivel once more.

Then her white hair came off. It was a wig. It slid away, revealing an almost baldhead, with isolated patches and tufts of lifeless hair. Hof jolted backwards. "Oh, shit!"

She grabbed the wig, put it back on, realised it was too late, threw it off. "Just keep going," she said, pulling him back down, trying in vain to rinse away her embarrassment. She glanced up at the portrait. "I'm sorry, honey, I'm sorry. Please forgive me!"

As soon as it was over, Hof dressed quickly, eager to escape. She watched him for some moments, then said, "I think I should give you some money Hoffman."

He looked shocked. "I'm not a male prostitute."

"I know. But I still think I should give you some money. I think you'd enjoy that. What it feels like to be paid for sex."

"OK, what, do you mean — like a couple of grand or something?" he smirked cheekily.

She shook her head. "Drop your trousers, big boy."

"What?"

"I'm going to pay you now. So drop your trousers. Your pants too."

Hof looked confused. She waved a stern finger at him. "Come on."

Cautiously he undid his trousers, pulled them to his ankles together with his underpants. She smiled, circled him slowly, then reached for her purse, took out a crisp new ten-pound note, folded it exactly in half, then inserted it carefully between the cheeks of his backside. Then she patted his behind and pulled up his trousers.

"Szee-szee-cheee-cheee-chissss."

On the way out he turned, hesitated, and said, "Do you mind if I ask you a question?"

"Ask away."

He stared at her eye-patch. Er...I was just wondering?"

"Yes."

"Er...What...happened....I mean.....what perfume do you use?"

She broke into a slow smile. "Chanel No. 5."

33

Dennison Carr drove Richard to a small theatre in south London. It was rundown venue, overdue for refurbishment. A small group of people were milling around outside, queueing for a show. "What are we doing here?" asked Richard.

"Madonna is playing here tonight. A special one-off gig.

"What, here? In this grotty little dive?"

"Correct. I've got front row tickets, plus a backstage pass for you."

Richard eyed him suspiciously. "How did you get a backstage pass to a Madonna gig?"

Dennison smirked. "I'm going to come in with you and watch the first few minutes of the show," he said. "Then I'm going to leave you to it."

As they stepped out of the car and crossed the street, Dennison noticed a man passing, holding the hand of his young son. Immediately he felt a hole open up inside him as he contemplated how his own childhood had been deprived of such simple moments. He could not remember ever holding the hands of his foster parents. If it had happened he had erased it from his memory, like so many other things from that era.

He turned to Richard and asked, "You ever been married?"

Richard was startled by the question. Dennison had never asked him or any of the other men about their personal lives. Richard answered in summary, told him he was divorced. He tried to reciprocate by asking Dennison the same question, but he did not answer. Instead Dennison looked straight ahead, as if he was looking at something far, far way. "One thing I've learned in this life is that people sometimes split up for stupid reasons," he said. "Things they could have worked out if they weren't so busy being angry or hurt or proud."

Dennison slowly turned toward Richard, fixing him with a fierce stare. The skin around Richard's eyes tightened as Dennison's words registered within him.

They stepped into the auditorium, taking their seats in the front row. Richard scanned the crowd. A mixed group of teenage girls, some with their mothers, plus groups of gay men, and other older men sitting by themselves. Richard frowned as he saw that the auditorium was only two-thirds full.

"Why isn't it packed out in here?" he asked suspiciously.

Before he could get an answer the lights went down and the intro to *Lucky Star* began to play over the sound system. The gay contingent and a small group of girls in the second row whooped with delight and clapped their hands. The spotlight went up and there she was — Madonna, circa 1983. The post-nuclear, post-punk rebel. Messed up blonde hair tied across the top with a ribbon, rows of clacking bangles, a black sleeveless off-the-shoulder vest, a distressed ra-ra skirt with a chain of crucifixes around the waist, plus cut-off leggings underneath. She pranced like an excited schoolgirl, and then started to sing.

Richard looked hard at Madonna. Something was not right. He leaned forward and squinted. Then his face changed. "Oh shit," he said. "That's not Madonna. It's one of those look-a-likes!"

Dennison was already smirking cunningly when Richard turned to him. "It is Madonna," he insisted. "Just not the one you thought."

Richard shook his head. "You're crazy," he said.

"Crazy For You," replied Dennison. Richard laughed. Satisfied with his evening's work, Dennison reached into his pocket, handed Richard a backstage pass, then departed.

ANNETTE DOWLING
Annette Dowling is one of Britain's premier Madonna-look-a-likes, who is renowned for her incredible resemblance to the Material Girl. An experienced and professional performer who sings and dances live, Annette's Madonna Revue is constantly in demand across the world. This spectacular show moves from the early days of Madonna's 80s pop hits through to her current material, and includes all the accompanying costume changes. Annette has painstakingly recreated Madonna's persona with such startling accuracy that you will think you are witnessing the real thing.

Since 1995 her show has toured worldwide, including Russia, Japan, Australia, Singapore, Israel, the Middle East, Las Vegas and Butlins holiday centres.

Recent TV appearances include CBBC, BBC1, BBC2, GMTV, C4, Pop Idol, and the programme Changing Rooms.

Annette is available for corporate events, openings, private parties, weddings, live performances, "mix and mingle", exhibitions, pop videos, photo-shoots, TV commercials, films, documentaries and promotions.

Annette is represented by Victor V Management and Entertainment Agency Ltd.

*

Just before Annette Dowling had taken to the stage that evening, she'd prepared in her dressing room. She had straight, shoulder-length natural blonde hair which covered one eye, eyebrows plucked to match Madonna's, a fake mole above her top lip, false lashes and black eyeliner. Her lips were slightly thinner than the woman she was imitating, and so she applied lipstick over the rims to make them appear fuller. She'd buffed her body and worked out until her measurements matched. The same backside, same legs, same toned, wiry arms. She'd also had a breast enlargement. The imperfections were few. She was ten years younger, and at five-feet-eight she was four inches taller.

Replica costumes hung neatly around the room, carefully wrapped in protective plastic. The black bodice from the 1987 Who's That Girl Tour, the conical bra set from the 1990 Blonde Ambition Tour, the cowgirl look from the 2000 album, *Music*.

Pinned to the wall next to her dresser was a short list of songs she would perform that night:

Lucky Star
Holiday
Material Girl
Into The Groove
Like A Virgin
Who's That Girl
~~Vogue~~
Erotica
Frozen
Don't Tell Me
American Life

A few minutes into the show and Richard was surprised at her performance. He was expecting the worst Karaoke, but she had a strong voice. He sat up in his chair and began scrutinising her. She'd studied Madonna's moves and facial expressions. He was impressed with her performance. And so were the audience. They were totally enraptured, singing along and clapping their hands.

Several costume changes later and the show was over. Richard made his way backstage. When he got there he hung back as a flurry of fans came and went from her dressing room. When things eventually quietened he knocked politely at her door. He entered sheepishly, adopting the persona of a shy nerd. "Hello? Miss Dowling?"

"Yes." She spoke with a Liverpudlian accent. She was sitting at the dresser taking off her make-up. She didn't turn around as he entered.

"Hi, I'm Richard," he began. "I was out there watching the show tonight, and I thought you were fan—tastic!"

"Thank you," she said.

Richard had a pen and paper ready in his hand. "Do you mind if I get your autograph?"

"Of course not." She turned with a professional smile and signed.

"You know, I'm really in awe of you."

"Excuse me?"

"I said, I'm really in awe of you."

"Really?"

"Yes. I mean...you looked so confident and beautiful out there tonight. I couldn't wait to come and talk to you."

Oh, god, another creep.

He looked at her face without make-up. A faint resemblance to Madonna remained. "You have incredible radiance," he said.

"What?"

"You shine. You really do."

She smiled, trying not to laugh. "Thanks. You shine too."

"Oh, well...Thank you."

"I just want to say that I think you're really amazing," he said, clutching his autograph to his chest like a devoted fan. "Much better than her." She smiled.

"Your voice is not as good as hers, though."

This got her attention. A criticism. From a stranger. She frowned slightly, and then looked at him properly for the first time. "Sorry?"

"No. Your voice is better. Much better, much stronger...And you're prettier too."

She smirked with relief. "What did you say your name was?"

"Richard."

"Hello, Richard."

"Hello...hello." He stood there looking. She chuckled, then began gathering her things.

"So, why did you come to the show tonight, Richard?"

"I heard about you. That you were brilliant. And I'm a sucker for talent."

"I see." She looked at him again. There was something about his boyish face that relaxed her, made her feel comfortable.

Richard shuffled nervously, trying his best to exude geek insecurity. "I would very much like to sleep with you," he said matter-of-factly. "I mean, if that's possible." He made his request sound so innocent that she wasn't offended by its abruptness.

"I make a point of not sleeping with *her* fans," she said.

"But I'm not a fan," he insisted. "In fact, I don't even like her music — apart from *Human Nature* and *Frozen*. What I admire in you is your ability as an actress. You see, I'm an actor myself, and your ability to mimic her is incredible."

She looked vaguely startled. "Thank you," she replied. "I work very hard at it. As hard as she does. In fact I think I work harder, because she only has to concentrate on being herself, whereas I have to concentrate on being her."

"Exactly. You're so right," Richard gushed. "So, so right."

They stood looking at each other until she smiled warmly. "Would you like to ride with me back to my hotel?"

They exited via the stage door. A small group of fans were waiting anxiously outside. Patiently she signed their autographs, then they made their way to a chauffeur-driven car waiting in the street. They climbed into the back and drove away.

As the car barrelled westwards the neon landscapes of south London punctured the night in sporadic bursts and pulsing intervals. Richard's eyes came away from the window, and he turned to her and asked, "Is your method acting gig full-time?"

She liked him more in that moment — the fact that he didn't call her a look-a-like. "Doing the shows takes up all my time," she replied. "What people don't realise is that my livelihood is linked to Madonna's. If tomorrow there was a scandal about her or she became really unpopular, then I could lose everything, along with the other Madonna mimics. My house, my car, everything I own is linked to her popularity."

She detected Richard's desire in the way he gazed at her. She was flattered, but only in a subdued way, as she had seen that look so many times from fans. She turned to the window and looked out at the world rushing by. "I'm not looking for love, Richard," she said. "I work too hard and I travel too much. I'm looking for... company...a little closeness maybe. That's what I need. Just enough to get me through. You understand?" He nodded. She held his hand and leaned her head on his shoulder.

The men she met socially were put off when she told them what she did for a living. They thought it was a silly, pathetic vocation. "They should see how much I earn a year being silly and pathetic," she'd say. Alternatively she'd meet Madonna freaks that wanted her because of their obsession with the real person. She'd had five stalkers in the last three years. One ex-boyfriend wanted her to wear her Madonna stage outfits when they had sex, at which point he'd call out her name.

Richard could feel her sense of loneliness. It was a feeling he knew well. After he first split from his wife, his own loneliness became so intense that he used to visit DVD rental stores on Friday nights looking for single women. He would stake out the independent film section, checking for the more discerning type of female film buff.

The car drove over Albert Bridge, banked left onto Chelsea Embankment and along Cheyne Walk towards Fulham. It turned left onto Lots Road, and left again into Chelsea Wharf, pulling into the drive of the Conrad Hotel.

Richard helped her carry her bags up to her room. As they stood silently in the lift watching the ascending numbers light up like the route to a jackpot, she glanced away to the floor and said, "I ran away from home to become Madonna, you know that? To stop my dad from beating me up, I ran away and I became her. If Madonna didn't exist I might still be there with him. Or dead. It's funny. Even though we've never met, in a way she saved me." She suddenly looked like a little girl as she recalled her past. Her shoulders were hunched slightly, as if she was cold.

They entered the suite and dropped the bags on the floor. She hung her costumes in the cupboard, then they stood for a still, awkward moment, looking at each other. Her face became sombre as she told him that she was flying to Israel in the morning for another round of shows. A distant look etched into his face. She thought it was a reaction to what she'd just said. She asked him what he was thinking, and he smiled and made up a lie.

He wondered if she would like him. He would make her like him, just like he made the others like him. He would perform well enough so she would. He took her hand gently, lead her to the bedroom, and they lay down gently on top of the sheets. She put her hand on his chest and leaned away from him. "Richard, you have to promise me one thing," she said.

"What?"

"That you'll be gone in the morning. Before I wake up."

"Why?

"Because I hate goodbyes," she said. "I don't want to see you when my eyes open. I don't want to see you ever again after tonight. You understand?"

He nodded.

34

The woman Erskine had followed was called Sophie, but she'd shortened it to So. She'd clipped its length for more impact. She was a thrill junkie. Ever since she was a baby she would jump off things — chairs, swings, anything — just to see what would happen. And hurting herself didn't make her learn. She'd cry, and then do it again. She had a slight scar running vertically through her bottom lip, sustained during one such manoeuvre, aged three. Her first extreme sports injury. She screamed when she saw the blood gush, but she was also excited by it. She was proud of the wound, to this day.

She was travelling the world in pursuit of her passion. Hers was a short stay in London, en-route to the next place. She'd rented a room at a cheap hotel on Gower Street, Bloomsbury. She and Erskine walked back there together.

They sat on the bed — the only place to sit — as if the room was designed to force its occupants together. "I haven't even told you my name," Erskine began. "It's-"

"Don't tell me your name, I don't want to know your name," she replied abruptly. "I just want to know how extreme you are."

"What?"

"I'm into extreme sports, you see."

"OK, well, I may not be into that, but I am extreme enough to have come up to you - a stranger - and tried to chat you up," he said hopefully.

"That's true," she nodded. "You did go for it. I like that. A lot of men don't. A lot of them can't handle me. They think I'm a bit too full on."

"Why do they think that?"

She looked away, almost ashamed of the explanation she had not yet even offered. Instead, she pushed herself toward him and began kissing him. Erskine was surprised at her calm confidence. As soon as he reciprocated she grew excited and began to tug at his shirt, lifting it out of his trousers.

"I think sex should be like an extreme sport, don't you?" she said enthusiastically. "It should have risks. Like skydiving."

"What do you mean?"

"We have to go for it. Just do it."

Erskine looked bewildered. "Uh-huh."

She pushed him onto his back, stripped off his clothing, and then hers. She mounted him, staying upright, one hand behind her back, working her hips back and forth against his pelvis. She looked away from him while she concentrated, her face relaxed, her mouth open.

Then casually she said, "If you don't make me come, I'm going to cut your throat."

"What?"

She brought her hand forward from behind her back. There was a large knife in it. She pressed it to Erskine's neck. He froze. "What the fuck are you doing?"

She smiled sweetly, as if nothing was wrong. "Do you know that if I cut the main artery in your neck, you'll bleed to death in seven seconds?"

"What? Please. Put the knife down."

"What's the matter, dear? Having trouble down there now? Allow me."

She climbed off him, with the knife still at his neck. She put his penis into her mouth, working it in and out. Then she came back up, watching his reaction, revelling in her control. She climbed back onto him and re-inserted herself, working her hips again. "Come on, Erskine," she goaded. "You're fucking for your life now."

"Sophie, please, no."

"My name's not fucking Sophie, right. Sophie's dead."

"Sorry, sorry, I—"

"Say my fucking name, my real name."

"So, your name is So, that's right, isn't it?"

"I'm going to count to ten, and if you don't make me come by then I'm going to cut you open."

"OK, OK, just take it easy." Erskine glanced at the blade nestled against a fold in the skin of his neck, ready to cut. He thought about making a grab for it, but then he thought, *seven seconds*. He started working his pelvis vigorously, his face desperate, shining with sweat. She matched his frenetic rhythm, bucking her pelvis harder and harder.

"That's it. That's a good boy," she said. "Feel the adrenaline? Feel me, feel me!"

As Erskine considered his predicament he thought about Genny. He felt ashamed of what he had become. He closed his eyes to escape her, and then So's voice jolted him back.

"Ten seconds...." she said excitedly.

"What? No, wait—"

"Nine, eight, seven six....."

Erskine worked his hips harder, harder, his face contorting.

"I'm not coming yet....Five, four, three...."

She looked manic, crazed, her eyes bulging.

"Come on, So, please."

"Exactly! Come is the word, baby. I won't fake it, no way, no way."

"So!"

"Three....two.....one....zeeeeero!"

"So, wait!"

She stopped dead. "No orgasm. Now you die!"

"NO!"

Suddenly she began to laugh. "Wasn't that great, wasn't that fun?" she gushed. "Wow, what a rush, I can feel my heart pounding!"

Erskine looked confused. She climbed off him, exhausted, dripping in sweat, and collapsed onto her back beside him, smiling breathlessly. She handed him the knife. "OK, now your turn."

Erskine, still shaking, frowned angrily. "My turn?"

"Threaten me with the knife, like I just did. Go on, make my adrenaline pump. See if the sex and fear will make me come."

"What are you talking about?"

"Come on. Hurry up before I lose the vibe!" She shook her body and flapped her arms impatiently.

"You're fucking sick, you know that?"

She sat up. "What?"

"You think this is fucking funny?"

"Oh, come on, don't be so fucking square," she sneered. "It's about adrenaline, man...about getting a charge, a rush, a buzz. Don't be so fucking conventional."

Erskine's expression darkened. He took the knife from her hand and climbed on top of her, rage coursing through him.

"Come on, come on!" she said, vibrating with excitement.

Erskine gripped the blade tightly and raised it above his head. So smiled with delight.

The blade hovered. Erskine was poised to strike. So was in a state of ecstatic surrender. Erskine brought the blade down hard.

Into the bed by the side of her head.

35

Erskine journeyed back through Soho. He was lost in time, dazed by the cars and the people and their endless faces. He wandered into a bar, the tick-tock of his footsteps slow and weary. He looked at the rack of liquor but didn't know what to order. He put his hand to his neck. *If you don't make me come, I'm going to cut your throat.*

He blinked heavily, as if he had blood in his eyes, then he rubbed his hand over his head and checked it. A film of sweat. He ordered something, a double. He sat down at a table and gulped it all in one. Empty minutes passed, voids of time and nothingness. He thought about all the women he'd slept with, and wondered about the things that had shaped their lives. He was glad they were gone, and that he would never see them again. Except Natascha.

He thought he could hear the sound of horse's hooves on cobblestones, but when he turned around and looked there was nothing.

He wandered into different bars, drinking alone as he'd done so many times before. The nights all meshed into one now. A single looping sequence. He looked up into the sky, staring hard into the darkness, as if to fathom the very secrets of the night.

He thought about Natascha and what she was doing. Like a sudden hunger, he craved her. Impulsively, he began making his way to her apartment. He diverted off the main roads and walked wearily through the back streets, through the darkness of the city. His body was tired but his gaze was busy, as if he was looking for hidden shadows cloaked by the night, their patterns merged, black subsumed into black. He was haunted by the sound of emptiness in the dead hours. A silent chime, a single note within his own concocted nightmare of London town.

He eventually reached the River Thames at Hammersmith. Meandering under the cloak of night, the black water flowed with a certain magnetism, as if it possessed the suction to pull the very night into its drag. The stream had reduced the volume of its flow, as if it was resting, replenishing itself for the morning's high water line.

Erskine arrived at Natascha's flat and pressed her buzzer. There was a long pause when she heard his voice. "What are you doing here?" she asked impatiently.

"I need to see you."

Need. She wondered what he meant. She was afraid he was about to tell her. She didn't want to face it. She did, but she didn't.

"You can't just fucking turn up at my place whenever you like," she said angrily. "What are you doing?"

Erskine had no words. There was another pause, longer this time, then he said, "Just let me in...please."

Reluctantly she buzzed him in. In the moments before he arrived at her door she was thinking about something she wanted to tell him. She felt corroded by the words she had not yet spoken. She did not understand why they were so hard to say. She'd said things to men before. She'd told herself she was going to do it now, but when he walked in the door and looked at her, the words escaped her.

When Erskine saw her he felt the urge to embrace her, as if she was his alone, as if he was coming home to her after a day at work. But he changed his mind, and then changed it back again, and in the end he did nothing except stand there looking at her.

The sex was inevitable. They no longer had control over their mutual desire. It seemed to belong to some force remote from themselves. They were slaves to the intoxication of their connection.

The aftermath was awkward again. They avoided eye contact, Natascha closing hers, and Erskine turning his head away from her. They were strangers still, their secret traumas hidden within their dark lives — concealed from one another like roots underground.

Natascha rolled over and gently placed her hand across his waist, feeling his warm skin. Erskine rolled away, out of her reach. She withdrew her hand, stung by his coldness.

Erskine felt guilty. He turned back to her, remorse in his face, and touched her cheek softly. She closed her eyes and turned away from him. He withdrew, muffling his hurt.

"I had a strange dream last night," said Natascha softly. She did not know why she was telling him, but she felt the need to talk about something.

"What was it?"

"I dreamt that it was raining rice in Africa. Then it rained hot water to cook it, and suddenly there was no more famine."

Erskine was startled by her words. It was the kind of thing that Genevieve would have said. He felt a tenderness rise within him, and he did not know what to do. He lay there staring at the ceiling, thinking about the beauty of her statement, wondering how to respond, lost as to what to do. Unable to deal with his feelings he got up and began to get dressed.

Natascha was surprised by this resolution. She grabbed her robe, slipped it over herself and tied it firmly at the waist. She sat on the edge of the bed, watching him expectantly. In the silence she stared at herself. At her own body. She wondered what it was about her that so drew his displeasure now — enough for him to leave. She was resenting him now, hating his silence, despising the fact that he was dressing as if she was not present, with his back to her, just like she had done to her lovers in similar circumstances.

In the cauldron of her mind she cooked her resentment. She was searching for something to fix it to. Any little spark.

"Is there something you want to tell me?" she asked. Her tone was like that of a schoolteacher.

Erskine turned, feintly alarmed. "Like what?"

"I don't know. Something. About you. About who you are."

"There's not much to say."

"Yes there is. Everybody's got a story, right?"

Erskine looked uncomfortable. She stood in front of him, searching his eyes. "What happened to you?"

"What?"

"You're sad about something. It's written all over you."

"That makes two of us."

Natascha sighed and rubbed her eyes. "Look, don't you think we should talk about this?"

"Talk about what?"

"You know what...We both know." They looked at each other, Natascha's gaze more confident, more open than his. Fighting his own compassion Erskine averted his head, as if burned by her stare. Natascha stepped back and gripped the neck of her robe, as if to protect herself from his hostile energy. She looked down at her feet and sighed, and her face softened. "Do you ever think....we could make each other happy?" She looked confused as she asked, as if she could not comprehend her own question, as if the words belonged to someone else.

Erskine was shocked by her statement, but he shrugged as if he did not care. "No. I never think that," he replied. "I never think this is more than it is." Despite his brutal words, his eyes were soft and shiny, gentler than that first night when they knew nothing of each other.

Natascha curled the fingers of her right hand. She wanted to punch him in his mouth, to halt his harsh words, to punish his careless disclosures. She glared at him hatefully. Erskine saw it and his face swelled with reciprocal anger. "Let me ask you something," he began. "How do you feel about me?"

She was startled into silence. "What?"

"Do you love me?"

The words hits Natascha like a punch. For those first seconds she could not speak. "What? Don't be ridiculous!"

"Do you?" Erskine stared, coldly serious.

Natascha relented, finally. "Yes," she whispered. She looked away from his eyes, shamed by her own feelings.

Erskine's hand came up fast and slapped her across the face. She flinched with shock, her eyes bulging, unable to speak. "Do you love me?" he asked again.

"No." She turned back to him slowly as she spoke, her face defiant, seemingly ready to absorb more of his cruelty.

He slapped her again. She staggered backwards, this time in a resigned manner, almost accepting, as if she'd been hit by someone else in the past.

"Do you love me?"

"Yes." The word stuttered from her mouth in broken sections.

He hit her harder, "DO YOU LOVE ME?"

She cried out and spun away to the floor, her hair following her face, coiling after it like thread around a spindle. She spat back, "NO, NO, I HATE YOU, GET OUT, GET OUT!"

At last. She hates me. At last.

Erskine nodded with brutal satisfaction. But then as he looked down at her, curled helplessly on the floor, he was filled with remorse. He suddenly looked terrified at what he had done. He tilted forward as if to embrace her, but he held himself back. Instead he stormed out of the room, heading for the front door, and Natascha heard a voice in her head that horrified her — *Please don't go*. She leapt to her feet, dashed ahead of him and stood in front of the door, blocking his exit. Erskine saw that her eyes were glazed and that she was shaking — tiny vibrations, holding everything in, imploding silently. He tried to move her out of his way, but as soon as he touched her he unleashed her rage, lashing out suddenly, punching his face and body in a flurry of percussion. Erskine absorbed the blows without flinching, disconnected from the hurt she was desperate to inflict. Then she turned on herself, slapping herself around the head like a crazed infant. Erskine watched, curious and confused, until finally her energy expended itself. She came to an abrupt stop and fell back against the door, dizzy with hopelessness.

She slid down to the floor in a resigned heap, her legs sprawled haphazardly beneath her like a rag doll. She hated that she was crying now, in front of him — that she'd given away her strength — that he was seeing her broken. She felt diminished in his presence. Erskine knelt and hoisted her to her feet by her shoulders, and then she broke away from him and he was out the door.

As he made his way out he did not see the broken biscuit lying at the bottom of the stairs.

36

Shortly before Genevieve became ill there were complications in her relationship with Erskine. They were lying in bed one night. She was wearing a long t-shirt, while Erskine was naked. She was facing away from him, looking quietly pensive. She could feel his penis through the fabric of her garment, nestled against the groove of her backside, gorged thickly with blood.

Erskine leaned across and kissed her gently on the neck. She shrivelled into herself, her neck shortening, although not enough for him to have seen her repulsion. She did not reciprocate his kiss. She lay still, unstimulated by his best touch. Humiliated by her stillness, he slowly turned away, burning with hurt, wanting to grab her by the throat. She closed her eyes with relief, and went to sleep. She had escaped him. Again.

The following evening they went out for dinner with friends. Genevieve started drinking early, buoyed by the company and the fine food. Erskine watched as she laughed in that special way he liked, sudden and dramatic, her excellent mouth and teeth shining through her face. He decided to get drunk with her. That much they could do together.

When they arrived home they stumbled into the lounge, drunk and in high spirits. Genevieve sang and twirled around the room like a delirious child, while Erskine watched and laughed, waving his arms like a conductor. He flopped onto the sofa, watching her, and immediately he felt a powerful lust. It was another kind of desire, born not of love, but of the hunger of being starved of her.

He leaned across impulsively as she twirled past him like a ballerina, oblivious to what he was feeling, and he pulled her down onto him. She fell into his lap like a present, laughing with surprise. She was even more theatrical when drunk. He kissed her cautiously, an action like a food taster checking a king's meal for poison. He waited for the rejection, expected it, but this time she surprised him, responding willingly, pulling him to her. Encouraged, he lunged gratefully at her.

She was his wife, but not now. Now she was a rag doll with a smiley face, its head flopping from side to side. She was offensively

174

compliant to his will, and it made him feel like a rapist. His sex was over eager — a dog-like staccato jig. She bounced to his rhythm like a puppet on a string, doped by the alcohol. She had to be drunk to comply, in these days before her deadly diagnosis, to forget that she did not want to any more. He clawed at her flesh as if he were a beast scaling a slippery wall. Everything was rushed, like he had but a few minutes before she changed her mind. Before some kind of bell would ring telling him his time was up. The foreplay was short, he entered her too soon, he came too quickly.

And at the moment of ejaculation he felt lonely, despite the fact that he was next to her, where he wanted to be.

In the morning Genevieve woke first. She saw herself under him, naked on the sofa, and instantly she was confused and shocked and repulsed. *How could this have happened?* She cussed the alcohol that had made her insane. She rubbed her head painfully, then as she looked at Erskine her face contorted as if she had been violated by a monster. Slowly, desperately, she unpicked herself from his embrace, pushed his body away and slid out. She went straight into the shower.

*

Two days later they were in the car on their way to the supermarket. Erskine was driving. Loud rock music was playing on the stereo. Genevieve, never a fan of Erskine's music, winced with displeasure, then turned the sound down. Erskine frowned with irritation. "Will you not fiddle with that, please?" he said abruptly. His tone was coarser than it should have been for such a slight action.

"It's giving me a headache," Genevieve replied. "It wouldn't be so bad if the music was better," she joked.

"What do you know about music anyway?" sneered Erskine. "You're tone deaf."

Genevieve looked at him with shock. "What?"

Erskine ignored her, turned the music back up. Genevieve angrily turned it back down again.

"Didn't I just tell you not to mess around with that?" he said.

"Why are you talking to me like that, Eskimo? What's wrong with you?"

"What's wrong with me?" said Erskine, his expression tightening, his voice growing louder. "What's wrong with *you*, more like?"

"What's that supposed to mean?"

"Well, I'm not the one that's not into sex anymore," said Erskine.

175

"I'm not the one who won't even discuss it. What's wrong with you is the fucking question, isn't it?"

Genevieve was aghast. "You insensitive arsehole!"

"Oh, fuck off, Genny!"

"No, you fuck off, Erskine...You fuck off!"

*

Sandy had always liked Erskine, but always in the safest way. She was a client, and he was her graphic designer, and so there was always a certain formality between them, despite their dormant attraction. Neither of them would ever do anything about their innocent attraction, so long as they each had their respective partners. Partners they were happy with.

He had come to the offices of the publishing company where she worked, to show her some book cover design proofs he had been working on. She was dressed smartly in a fitted navy trouser suit with flat shoes. She wore her black hair loose around her shoulders. He looked at her differently this time. The outline of her body through her clothes. The line of her breasts. She picked up on his curious eyes, guessed about his sexual imaginings, and it pleased her to be the subject of his desire, after all this time. After all the occasions she had wondered about what he would be like to have sex with.

Erskine laid out several sheets of paper on the table containing the design ideas he'd been working on. They huddled in closely to view them, their shoulders lightly touching. He could smell her, her hair or her perfume, he couldn't tell which. She tried to sound businesslike — more so than usual — trying as she was not to think about him taking her.

She told him she had some other visual references she needed to show him, but that she had left them at home. Erskine took the bait and offered to come around and pick them up.

When he was in her bed he felt guilty during the foreplay, but he went through with it regardless. His penis was pregnant with stiffness, gorged with unused fluid. His hardness belonged to her, to Genevieve, but now he would give it away, its value diminished like a sale item in a store. Sandy's flesh was warm and firm, and her movements skilled and graceful. She was better than Genevieve, he thought, or so it seemed amidst the anger he now felt towards her. He justified his adultery by reasoning that Genevieve no longer wanted him anyway, and so he was entitled. He had a right to give away his hardness. It felt good to be wanted by someone. He felt normal again. He conceived that this could be his new life. He wanted to see her again after this introduction, to continue to feel this good with his pelvis between her thighs.

But afterwards the guilt descended. He made his excuses, got dressed and left abruptly. There would be no affair.

*

A week later, Erskine found himself at the hospital with Genevieve, receiving the results of her brain scan. Numb with shock, they stepped slowly out of the consulting room and into the corridor. They held each other tightly and fell against the wall. Genevieve began to shake, crying quietly, digging her nails into Erskine's arms. She spoke quietly. "I'm going to die, Eskimo. I can't believe it. I'm going to die."

The journey home was silent. Nothing was said until they entered the flat. "Shall we make something to eat?" he offered quietly.

"What's the point," said Genevieve, her voice suddenly harsh and bitter.

Erskine clenched his fist and looked away, trying to hide his face. Genevieve saw his reaction and softened. She rubbed her eyes in disbelief at what was happening. She was tormented by the silence in the room as she thought about the life she had lived, and the life she would not.

She spoke in a quiet, cracked voice, not her own, like a frightened child. "Eskimo?"

"Yes."

"I'd understand, y'know."

"You'd understand what, Fruitcake?"

"If...if you wanted to go off...with someone else, I mean. Instead of waiting."

Erskine froze. "What?"

"I mean, life goes on, right?"

Erskine looked at her guiltily. "Stop it, Genevieve," he whispered. "Please."

She tried to smile. "Just make sure she's not prettier than me.... OK, Eskimo?"

Before the end he had planned to tell her what he had done, to ask her forgiveness before she left this world. But he could not bring himself to do it. He was too ashamed, too afraid, and he wanted her to live her last days with only good memories. When she departed he was left to choke on the guilt of his unspoken confession. At the funeral he whispered, "I'm sorry," as they lowered her coffin into the ground. The guests thought he was crying just for her, but they would never know the truth. No one would know. Except him — and Sandy.

37

Rossi's mother Gabriella was waiting anxiously on the platform for the early evening Eurostar from London Kings Cross. She was in her late forties, with attractive, Mediterranean-style features. She was dressed smartly, with her wiry grey and black hair tied back in a neat bun. Usually she wore a flower in it, but on this occasion she did not get to the florists in time.

As Rossi sat on the train speeding toward Paris he thought about Gwyneth and what she had told him about his mother and the importance of family. He probably would never have listened to such advice from anyone other than an old woman, as throughout his childhood he had been taught to respect such people above all others for their knowledge and wisdom.

Soon the train pulled into the station and the passengers began to alight. Gabriella couldn't wait to see her son, and so she walked beyond the barrier, onto the platform, dodging the people, tip-toeing to look higher at the heads coming towards her. Then she saw him. Her face crinkled elegantly, creased as if she was about to cry, but instead she smiled, and when he saw her, his returned smile was a perfect replica of hers. He opened his arms wide and gathered her up and kissed her and lifted her from the ground as if she were a child. She pulled back from him, squeezing both his hands, just to look at him, and then she moved in closer and put both hands on his cheeks as if he was the most precious thing. "Oh, Rossi."

He kissed both her hands and hugged her again. Then he made a sign, *Wait*. He looked around, then pulled a package out of his bag and discreetly showed her the contents. She breathed in with shock and put her hand to her mouth. "Where did you get all this money?" she asked. "You didn't do anything bad did you, my son?" He smiled and shook his head:

no more work 4 u mama

She looked at him, her mouth open, speechless. Rossi smiled, then pulled out a digital music player and put the headphones carefully over her hair, as carefully as if he were placing a tiara on the head of a princess. Then he pressed a button. She smiled as the track filled her ears. Rossi took her hand and they strolled out.

And we got nothing to be guilty of
Our love will climb any mountain
Near or far we are
And we never let it end
We are devotion
And we got nothing to be sorry for
Our love is one in a million
Eyes can see that we got a highway to the sky

*

Richard was lying at home in the bath with a flannel over his face, thinking about his planned trip to Hollywood. He was excited as he thought about the roles he might get — maybe a part in a sitcom to begin with, and then graduating on to movies. In his mind he had already bought himself a red convertible sports car, and he was dating a California blonde with a sunshine smile and an incredible body. He pushed himself down against the back of the bath and submerged himself under the water as he thought about it. But then as he came up he felt an unexpected sensation of despair. At first he did not know why, as his planned trip was the most exciting thing he had to look forward to.

But then, as the feeling took hold he became restless, and began fidgeting in the water until eventually he hoisted himself out of the bath and threw the flannel back into the soapy water. He put a towel around himself, picked up his phone and began dialling a number. Then he stopped without completing it. Instead he washed out the bath and dried himself. Then he busied himself around the flat, trying not to think about what he wanted to do. But he soon succumbed and dialled again.

A voice answered. "Hello?"

"Hello, Jane. It's me."

"Richard?"

They exchanged pleasantries. Jane was wondering why he was calling, and Richard felt he had to get re-accustomed to hearing her voice again before he could say what he really wanted to. "I've been thinking about you, Jane," he began.

There was a silence that encouraged him. She could have cut him off right there, told him to stop, but she did not. "Really?" she replied, her voice suddenly softer.

"I just want to say, that I'm sorry about everything. I've tried to...to move on from you, but I just can't get you out of my mind. I just want you back. I'll do whatever you want me to do. I'll change whatever you want me to change. I just want us to be together again...I suppose what I'm trying to say is that, that I still love you. I still love you, Janey. I want to spend the rest of my life with you. Now...I know that may seem like a long time, but I promise I'll make it worth your while...If you'd just give me a chance."

He kept on talking, kept his monologue flowing, repeating sentences, stuttering and stammering his way through. He didn't want to give her the chance to interrupt and possibly say no to him. He was afraid she would, that she would say, "Listen," always that word before the bad news — "Listen, Richard, I am seeing someone, and it's serious," and if she would say that he would be lost. Somehow he thought that if he kept talking he would turn her around, convince her that he was worthy, so sure was he in his broken self-esteem that she did not want him back. Throughout his plea he avoided asking her about the other men she had seen or slept with since they parted, or whether or not she was in a serious relationship now. He did not care. Whatever these men were to her, they could not be what he was — her husband.

"Richard, Richard, Richard," she said, trying to interrupt.

Richard fell silent, his heart pounding, his hands clammy. "Yes."

"I love you too."

*

Hof was walking along Charing Cross Road when something caught his eye in the window of a bookshop. He stopped for a closer look. It was a picture of a human brain on the cover of a new book about psychology. Instantly he thought of one of Dennison's catchphrases, *Check your cranium*, and he chuckled to himself at the man's humorous originality. Then he remembered something. He reached into his back pocket and pulled out the psychotherapist's business card he had taken from Domino's bathroom cabinet. He looked at it thoughtfully.

Cynthia Moore ran her private practice from the living room of her four-bedroomed terraced house in Wimbledon. Her clients did not like the fact that she was not located in the centre of the city — in order that it be easier for them to get to her — but they came anyway, such was the quality of her service. She never advertised,

181

not for years now. All her clients came by word of mouth. She had enough business to work every single day, if she so desired.

She was medium height, with short black hair, glasses and no make-up. Her clothes, though expensive, were black and austere in design, minimally detailed and loose fitting. To the naked eye, one would not know that she was wearing Issey Miyake and Miu Miu. Her deportment was imbued with a static grace, like that of a ballet teacher watching her students. The lenses in her glasses gleamed with pristine clarity — a detail that seemed to reassure her clients that she would do the same to their minds also. Her whole aesthetic was designed to make it hard for her clients to find her remotely sexual, impossible though this was.

Her plain, featureless armchair was positioned directly opposite Hof's. She had measured what she considered to be the ergonomic distance between the two points, between client and patient. Not close enough to feel too intimate, not far away enough to feel disconnected.

She began with some informal market research, asking Hof how he found out about her. He told her where he got her business card. She nodded when she heard Domino's name, in a way that didn't mean anything or give anything away. He tried to ask more questions about her but Cynthia cut him off, telling him firmly that she did not discuss her other clients.

He told her that he felt stupid being there, that he had never been to a psychotherapist before. She asked him if he was embarrassed, and he lied, then she asked him why he had come, but he could not find an answer. She began probing him with questions. When she addressed him her concentration was absolute, as if the outside world did not exist, as if nothing else mattered but him, and what he had to say.

She asked him, "So, why do you feel the need to sleep with all these different women?"

"Someone asked me that recently," Hof replied, thinking about Dennison.

"And?"

"I don't know...The thing is, I'm never going to be rich," he lamented. "I was crap at school. I'm not good at anything. Fucking is the only thing." He shrugged his shoulders, resigned to his predicament.

Cynthia held back for some moments while Hof considered what he had said. He was uncomfortable with this controlled silence, and the way it drew out his thoughts. "And...what do you feel after you've slept with these women?" she continued.

Hof thought for a long time, then said, "Nothing. Just emptiness. I don't feel anything. I just want to leave."

"OK, but what would happen if you didn't leave?" she replied. "If you stayed?"

Hof looked confused. "What?"

"What would happen if you didn't get up and leave these women straight away?"

He shrugged. "I don't know."

"Perhaps you would get to know that person more — maybe start liking them, or maybe they would start liking you. Maybe you're afraid of that. Maybe that's why you want to leave."

He fell silent with his thoughts. "I don't know...maybe."

She paused, waiting for him to speak. He shifted uncomfortably in his seat. "All I know is, I've never been in love," he said finally. "I've never been in a monogamous relationship. Sometimes I wonder if there's a piece missing inside me. What do you think?"

"Well, one viewpoint is that promiscuous people are really only looking for love. That's why they sleep with so many people. It's a quest within their sub-conscious to find the one who will love them...Perhaps to compensate for not feeling loved as a child."

"I never thought of it like that."

"I am not necessarily saying it is like that, Hof, but it's one point of view. In your case, I would say, keep going with your promiscuity if that's what you really want — there are plenty of women out there who want no strings sex — but I would be upfront with them — it's best not to lie about your intentions."

Hof looked confused. "But aren't you supposed to tell me to stop being promiscuous, doc? Aren't you supposed to cure me into monogamy, or something?"

"Is that what you want?"

38

Natasha was sitting at the front of the top deck of a bus, on her way to see her masseur. She stared out of the window at the scurry of shoppers. She eyed a group of workmen, looking like Lego men in their yellow plastic vests, white hard hats and oversized boots. They were on their break, perched like budgies on a line of railway sleepers, legs out, ogling every woman who walked by, saying the things that men say when they congregate in herds. She imagined she had a hosepipe and that she washed them all away, down the street on their backsides.

As the bus idled in traffic she closed her eyes and pressed her head gently against the glass, feeling the epileptic shudder of the engine reverberating through the superstructure. Then she straightened up as she thought of Erskine, and a sudden sadness washed over her. She lay her head down on the seat next to her, using her palms as a pillow, and from the back of the bus, with her body out of sight, it looked as if no one was sitting there, and then someone came to occupy the seat, but stopped and backed away as they saw her lying there like a secret baby.

As she arrived at the health club she felt disoriented. In the waiting room they had to call her name twice before she heard, and then she reacted slowly, as if she'd been drugged. She rose to her feet and followed the masseur into the treatment room. He knew her well, as she'd been to him many times before. She'd tried the female staff, but she found that the men had stronger hands, and she liked a heavy touch. He made small talk in the build up, like he always did, and Natascha did her best to pretend she was fine when he asked how she was, even though she wanted to tell him to just get on with it. She stripped to her underwear and climbed gently onto the massage table, lying on her front, her face nestled in the aperture. Whenever she did this it always reminded her of being at the seaside as a child, putting her head through the cut-outs of fat men and curvaceous women painted on wooden boards along the promenade.

The masseur rubbed some oil on his hands and then began working Natascha's back and shoulders — kneading her with a forceful, probing action. The pain seemed sharper than usual on this day, and as her flesh began to release its pent up energy it wasn't long before the pain seemed intolerable. Gradually she began to cry. The masseur stopped working and held up his hands as if he'd just broken something. "Are you alright?"

"No."

She cut the session short, got dressed and left. As she stepped out into the street, still wiping her eyes, her phone rang. It was her mother, sounding tearful. "Mummy, what's wrong?" she asked.

"I...I don't know, Natascha."

"What do you mean, you don't know?"

"I woke up this morning and I just..."

"What, mummy?"

"I...I just felt this wave of sadness. It just hit me, and I haven't been able to stop crying."

"Oh, mummy."

"I don't want to be alone tonight...Can you come, Natascha? Please."

"I can't tonight, mummy. I—" Natascha heard the sound of crying. She held the phone away from her and sighed with quiet exasperation. *STOP FUCKING CRYING AND GET YOURSELF TOGETHER, YOU WEAK BITCH!*

She'd heard her mother like this on so many occasions, and countless times she'd dashed over to the house to comfort her, only to be called again a few days later. She was tired of it, and her emotional responses were blunted. "Did you forget to take your tablets again, mummy?" she asked, trying not to sound angry. "You have to take them every day. Did you?"

"I don't know."

Natascha swore under her breath. "Just take one, mummy, OK? Take one, please."

"But—"

"Just take a tablet, mummy, OK, and I'll call you tomorrow morning. Alright?"

Natascha hung up, feeling as though her head was about to explode. She walked along the street aimlessly, unable to escape thinking about her mother, or Erskine. She called Megan. When she saw Natascha's number come up on her mobile she did not want to answer it. She ignored it for the first few rings, then reluctantly she cleared her throat and answered. She had never heard Natascha this upset. She explained what had happened with Erskine, about the final bust up.

"You have to stop the deceit," said Megan resolutely. "You have to tell him how you feel. If he really loves you, he'll welcome your honesty. And if he doesn't, at least you will have told him, then you can rest easy, and move on."

"You think?"

"Absolutely."

"I...I don't think I can," said Natascha hesitantly. She thought of her mother, damaged and alone, crying by herself right now.

"Yes you can, Nat, you can," Megan insisted. "This is no time to be proud or hurt or afraid...Y'know, in life, true love is so hard to find, if you think this guy is it, you have to go for it. You have to."

Natascha thought for some seconds, then concluded, "You're right. You're such a good friend to me, Megan. You really are."

The line went silent.

Then Natascha asked, "Do you want to meet up later?"

Megan hesitated. "No. I can't. I mean, I'm not feeling too good today. I think my period's coming...I'm in pain."

"OK. I'll call you later."

"Goodbye, Natascha." She hung up. "Goodbye."

*

Shepherd's Bush Green. The fresh sheen of rain over everything. A varnish black and silver, lustrous as a shoe shine. The splash, indiscriminate in its reach, had purged the after-light loafers, the street leeches, the troublemakers, the drunks. The neighbourhood was serene and beautiful. Until morning.

Erskine walked the stretch of Uxbridge Road overlooking the Green, at one with the gloss of the street, one of his favourite sights. He wanted to roll himself in it. To coat himself in the silvery juice like a new kind of sweat. The grass on the Green was freshly cut, the rain lifting the odour into the air, and his head rose slightly as the fumes caressed his nostrils. He crossed the road onto the Green and lay down and placed his face upon the wet grass. The neon from the parade of shops along the street filmed across the blades and clipped the tips, dusting them with light.

He thought of Genevieve. He hated himself for what he did to her before she died. And now he had replenished the offence with Natascha. He had reaffirmed his inclination to hurt. He closed his eyes, ashamed of the violence, the coldness, the cruelty he had inflicted upon her. Slowly he hauled his body off the turf, dizzy with remorse, his whole frame feeling twice its weight.

That night he dreamt that he was sitting on a beach amongst a bank of rocks, when a silver body bag washed ashore and lodged itself there. He went to it, unzipped it and there inside was Genevieve — ashen white, lips of blue. He fell backwards, crying into the sky with shock and despair, his eyes bulging, his mouth wide, and in that moment he saw a white eagle hovering gracefully above him, looking down on the scene. As he looked back at her body he noticed that tucked inside the flap of the body bag was a black and white photo of him and Genevieve smiling together, taken on holiday in Thailand four-years earlier. He pulled the picture out and put it into his pocket. Then he kissed her goodbye, zipped up the bag and cast her back out to sea forever.

Morning came, with skies like paintings. Colour pulped against the canvas in the high air. Clouds like candyfloss wafting in stasis. On the street, the rain had evaporated, leaving the residue of dry concrete, grim and tough as always. The winos had resumed position on the benches, while the cars, as usual, circled the Green in an angry chug, spewing forth their fumes.

Erskine turned and looked around him at the mess in his flat, as if he was seeing it for the first time. Immediately he set about clearing up. Feverishly he filled several bin liners with rubbish — newspapers, bottles, cans, cardboard food containers — everything that had been lying around for months. He washed the dishes, vacuumed the carpet and cleaned the surfaces. When he was finished the place was cleaner than when he'd moved in. Then he took the remainder of his stash of skunk, took a last look at it, and flushed it down the lavatory. Finally, he gathered up Genevieve's things, the belongings he had saved — a black trouser suit, a pair of her shoes, and her floppy felt hat. He lingered with the hat in his hand, remembering the times she wore it. He recalled one Sunday morning. He woke up late and caught her in the kitchen, naked except for her trademark item, eating last night's cold pizza while dancing to music on the radio. He admired her gyrating body from behind until she turned and saw him, but she simply carried on as if he was not there.

Erskine smiled slightly at the recollection, then he put the hat and all her other things in a bag and took them to a charity shop on the Uxbridge Road.

39

Dennison was in his office with Trevor, his managing director, who was frowning worriedly. His boss was looking intensely at the base of an upturned Charles Eames leather chair. "It's a design classic," said Dennison enthusiastically. "Every inch of its construction is beautifully thought out. Even the underside, where no one is supposed to look. Can you see?"

Trevor sighed impatiently and looked at the object, trying his best to appear interested. "Yes, it's...very nice, Dennison," he nodded.

Dennison flipped the chair and sat down on it. Trevor sat down opposite him. "Listen, Dennison, that idea you had recently — to pick the most exciting business ideas that need nurturing, then take a bigger cut...I think it's risky," he said with a cautious shake of his head. "I didn't want to get into it at the meeting, with everybody there, but I've looked into it now, and aside from the extra resources it'll take from our side, we could end up getting stung and not making any money at all.....This strategy is simply not intelligent, Dennison."

Dennison sighed impatiently. "Intelligent, you say?....There are six thousand languages in the world, Trevor, and yet you only speak one of them. Is that what you call intelligence?"

"What?"

"Trevor. Why are we in business?" asked Dennison.

"To make money, of course."

"Correct. But business also presents an opportunity to explore the soul."

Trevor slowly shook his head in resignation. This wasn't what they taught him at Harvard business school. Dennison stood up and took off his jacket. The friction of the fabric sliding against his shirt made a certain sound, like wind blowing through dry leaves.

He hung it up, looked at Trevor and rubbed his fingers together. "Do you know what Soul Power is, Trevor?"

"Excuse me?"

"Soul Power? Do you know what it is?"

"What are you talking about?"

"I'm talking about Soul Power, Trevor." Dennison tapped his

skull three times. "Check your cranium." Trevor grew irritated. He took off his glasses and pinched the bridge of his nose. "Soul Power," said Dennison, as if it was obvious. "By James."

"Who?"

"James...As in Brown, Trevor."

Trevor was at his wits end. He hated the games Dennison played with language. "OK, so what about it?"

"You need to listen to that track. You need to feel the bassline and the vocal...then you'll know."

Trevor glared at his boss. *What the fuck?*

"You know, many rich people — for all their smartness in knowing how to make money — are essentially stupid," said Dennison. "They never know how much money is enough. The only language they understand is the language of blind accumulation. Bill Gates has finally woken up to this, which is a good thing."

There was a knock at the door. John Carver entered without waiting for the invitation. Trevor was glad at the interruption. On the way out he passed him at the doorway and the two of them eyeballed each other suspiciously. John shut the door, then waved a large envelope above his head. He dropped it on Dennison's desk. He stared apprehensively at it.

John reached into his pocket for a biscuit. There was an awkward silence as he waited for Dennison to react. Eventually he asked, "Do you like biscuits, mister Carr?" Dennison stayed silent, lost in thought, his eyes still on the envelope.

"I love them," John continued. "Always have. Ever since school. We used to eat packets of them, everyday, like crisps we did. We used to eat them instead of school dinners — that's how much we loved them. I know they are full of stuff that's not healthy, but they taste so damn good. If you were poor at my school you ate Custard Creams — my personal favourites — or Rich Tea, Morning Coffee, Jammie Dodgers or Nice biscuits. The trick with Custard Creams is to get them in those little compact packets, so they fit nicely into the pocket of your school blazer. Really handy that, although I wouldn't advise it for you, mister Carr. That would really spoil the line of your fine tailoring....I remember some of the kids actually had chocolate digestives. Can you believe that? They were the ones who's parents had money...yeah, those were the days."

John put another biscuit in his mouth and crunched loudly. Dennison finally picked up the envelope, opened it and pulled out the first photograph. He took a glance, and then slowly slid it back into the envelope. He turned his back and looked sternly out of the window.

"She's in Valencia," said John. "She's got this guy out there. Name's—"

"Enough!"

A tremor coursed through Dennison — a breach in his emotional armour. The fingers of his right hand came together in the shape of a beak, his hand trembling with coiled tension. John, looking slightly amused, leaned to one side, trying to catch Dennison's face to see how the news had rattled him. He popped another biscuit, crunched it smugly. Dennison turned as he heard the loud crunching, insulted by John's casual disrespect. Dennison opened a draw, removed an envelope and threw it at him, harder than he did normally. John caught it with one hand. "Thanks...Er....do you—"

"That's all."

*

On the way home that evening Dennison stopped off at Notting Hill Gate to buy a newspaper. As he came out of the shop and walked back toward his car, a fast wind suddenly gusted up, buffeting the flaps of his jacket, exposing its coloured lining — a movement like someone turning the page of a book then changing their mind. As the fabric danced with the breeze his hat suddenly blew off his head, swirling up and away. He watched it calmly as the force of the wind carried it over the roof of a building. There was a feint look of resignation on his face, as if he was saying a final goodbye to an old friend.

Alice was gone. Forever. And for the first time in years, Dennison was frightened. And there was no one in his life that he could even begin to talk to about his vulnerability, as everyone who knew him considered him never to be vulnerable.

As he stood there in the street he looked strangely incomplete without his trademark black hat. Like a house without a roof. Like an aeroplane without wings. He ran his hands through his hair as if he'd forgotten he had any. He was still looking up at the point where his hat had disappeared over the building, as if somehow he thought it might come hurtling back like a boomerang. He wondered what had become of it. He imagined that it had sailed right over the top and landed on someone else's head on the other side, catching them mid-stride, and they simply adjusted it to fit, then carried on walking.

As he climbed back inside the car he opened the glove

compartment. Inside was a neat row of identical black hats, stacked like CDs. He selected one, placed it carefully on his head, adjusted the angle in the rear-view mirror, smiled to himself and then drove home.

*

Two miles away Erskine arrived at Natascha's flat, ready with words packaged in his mind — the apology first, for the violence, for his coldness — then a confession about his promiscuity via Dennison's game — then the suggestion, the desire, that they be together, the admission of his feelings for her — of his love for her.

He rang the bell several times, but there was no answer. He called her phone but it went straight to voicemail, and he did not want to leave a message for what he had to say. He hung up, wondering whether she was deliberately avoiding him, thinking that maybe he had blown his chance. He would not blame her if he had. He decided to try again later that evening.

40

There was black coffee in the cup. The cup was white porcelain, the whitest finish money could buy — just so Dennison could enjoy the contrast between the cup and the coffee. The black lake of rich fluid was perfectly encapsulated within a perfect white seal. He was more interested in the aesthetic of the composition than in actually consuming its content.

There was a low sound in the room: *Piano Sonata, Op. 1*, by Glen Gould (1958). On his desk next to the coffee was a framed picture of Dennison together with Alice, taken in the Maldives in 2010. Adjacent to that was the envelope of photographs that John Carver had given to him earlier. Dennison had not looked at them, except for a single glance back at his office. He did not need to see any more. He turned and stared out of the window, lost within himself, brooding deeply.

He recalled a certain incident toward the end. A final row with Alice. She was tearful, with demeanour of a frightened child. Her lean frame quivered with vulnerability, and her voice fell lower than its usual pitch. She was pleading with him to stop being angry, to be more loving instead. Eventually Dennison walked out and left her there sobbing. To leave was all he could do. That was easier for him than granting her what she'd asked for.

As he contemplated this he suddenly found himself laughing. And the shock of this realization made him laugh even more, until he was almost hysterical, laughing louder and louder, more and more manically, until his whole body was vibrating.

He was interrupted by the sound of the doorbell. He cut his laughter dead, looked about him with bewilderment, then went to answer it. It was Erskine. Dennison had been expecting him. Nevertheless, when he opened the door he stared at him for a fraction longer than normal, as if it was the first time they had met. Erskine stepped inside and motioned toward the lounge, but Dennison intercepted and steered him away to his study near the rear of the house.

He settled at his desk with Erskine across from him. He sat still, with his hands clasped symmetrically in front of him. Erskine became uncomfortable and looked away, scanning the room. "I must say, you got great taste in stuff, Dennison," he said.

Dennison stared at him without responding. As Erskine looked around, something caught his eye — an elegant pair of women's shoes positioned neatly on a shelf. "Whose shoes are they?" he enquired. "Your wife's?"

Dennison looked mildly insulted. "No. They are there because they are beautiful objects."

"But they're not beautiful if there's no one in them," replied Erskine. "They're just empty things....Don't you think?"

Dennison smirked as if the comment meant nothing. And within that smirk there were secrets that Erskine would never know. Amongst them was the fact that he and the other men were not the first players to participate in the proposition. There had been others before them, and there would be others after them. Dennison was always recruiting new talent for subsequent rounds. Players of both sexes.

"So you're here to tell me you want to quit?" Dennison began.

"How did you know?"

"Everybody quits. In the end," said Dennison matter-of-factly. "The question is, why?"

"I've made enough money, Erskine replied. "I've had my fun. Now it's time to get out."

Dennison searched his face. "Is that why you joined my game? To get money and fun?"

"Sure. Why else?"

Dennison looked unconvinced. He shook his head, then tapped his temple three times. "Check your cranium, Erskine."

Erskine frowned curiously. "What do you mean?"

Dennison stared at Erskine. "The lower the self-esteem, the greater the need," he said.

Erskine looked perplexed. He rubbed the top of his head in a circular motion, then checked his palm for sweat.

"Psychological dysfunction of the love response," said Dennison. "That's what you all have in common. That's why it works."

"What are you on about?"

"You really don't know, do you?"

"Know what?"

"Why I chose you for the proposition."

"Why did you?"

Dennison readjusted his torso, pointed at Erskine with the side of his angular face, his glassy eyes sparkling. He gestured as if he was about to tell him something, but instead he paused, got up and gazed out of the window, his back to him. "History is a fascinating thing, don't you think? I mean, without it, how could we make sense of the present?"

Dennison turned and faced him. "The question is, what's your history, Erskine?"

"That's none of your business."

"True. But it's someone's business, isn't it?"

Erskine thought for a moment, then said, "No."

"Yes."

"No."

"Yes," said Dennison finally, pointing his finger at Erskine three times. He took that same finger and used it to caress the rim of his hat. "It was Jung that said, the desire to reveal is greater than the desire to conceal."

"What?"

Dennison waited. He waited for Erskine to comprehend what he was saying. But he did not. The silence in the room lay fallow of realization, and so the opportunity lapsed, perhaps for good.

He was disappointed that Erskine and the other men presented no intellectual challenge to him. He rarely met anyone who did, a reality that continued to frustrate him. He felt like a chess master who struggled to find worthy opponents. He sighed with resignation. "Come with me," he said. They went out of the room and entered the lounge. As Erskine came through the door he realised there was somebody already there, and then he saw Natascha sitting on a chair.

When she saw him she rose abruptly to her feet and backed away to the window, as if she wanted to jump out of it. Instantly she felt a knot in her stomach, as if someone had plunged a fist through her belly button. She stared blankly at him, paralysed with surprise. "What are you doing here?" she asked.

Erskine's face tightened as he tried to figure. "What are you doing here?" he volleyed back. "How do you know him?" he asked, pointing at Dennison. *Are you fucking him too?* He felt his hands curl into fists.

They both looked at Dennison with shock and bewilderment. He smiled like an ace gambler who'd just showed a winning hand.

"What is all this?" asked Erskine angrily.

Dennison made Erskine wait before he answered.

Then Natascha asked, "Dennison, what's going on?"

"You tell me," Dennison replied. "You hired me to get Erskine to seduce you."

Erskine frowned. "What?"

"Ask her, Erskine. Ask her if it's true," urged Dennison.

Natascha looked away shamefully. "I...I need to go," she said. She did not move.

Erskine asked her softly, "Are you part of this? This game?"

Natascha looked at Dennison guiltily. "She is a client, Erskine," said Dennison. "All the women are clients."

Seconds passed as Erskine processed the words. He looked at Natascha. "You paid him?"

"Actually, the arrangement was for one night only," said Dennison. "That's the service. But then, something happened.... didn't it?"

Dennison waited for either of them to reply, but they could not. Out of the stillness their eyes met fleetingly in a look of mutual shame. They were caught in each other's lies, like two spiders in the same web.

"Don't you have something you want to say to each other?" he asked them both.

"What do you mean?" Natascha replied.

"About the way you both feel."

"That's none of your business," said Erskine defensively.

"No, but it is hers," said Dennison, pointing at Natascha.

He turned to her. "Natascha, why don't you tell Erskine how you feel about him?"

Natascha felt the skin on her cheek twitch. "I don't have to say it for you," she said defiantly.

"Then say it for him."

Silence filled the room, gorged with expectation. Dennison frowned curiously. "I think I should leave you both alone to discuss exactly what—"

"Don't!" Natascha whispered loudly. She was trembling slightly now. She looked at Erskine, calling him with her eyes, her hardness evaporating. She was more disarmed now than ever.

Erskine opened his mouth to speak, to finally say what she wanted him to, but there were no words in him, as if they had been stolen from his mouth.

Eventually Dennison smirked to himself, then stepped toward the door and opened it. He turned and gave them both a final, hopeful look. "Good luck." He walked out and closed the door.

Erskine and Natascha stood trapped in silence, staring at each other.

Made in the USA
Charleston, SC
21 July 2016